THE SONG OF THE SISTERS

JESSICA GOLLUB

First Printing, 2014

ISBN: 978-0-9936388-7-9

To my Mom, because she said I had to, and because I also kind of wanted to.

ONE

I COULDN'T SEE ANYTHING through the window but white.

The steady whirr of the rotors was the only sound I could hear. Some of the people on the helicopter wore headphones so they could hear each other, but we weren't given any. We sat, buckled into this giant metal hummingbird, unable to see or hear anything that might give us a clue as to where we were headed. What would meet us on the other end of this trip was a mystery to me. We flew into a blank sky, over blank terrain to a blank future. Though, I suspected someone else had mapped it out for us.

There were eight of us.

We were not allowed to speak, even if we could make ourselves heard over the steady beat of the helicopter blades.

I watched them, as they did me, looking for a hint, some understanding of our purpose, but there was none. One of them, a girl with pale eyes and black hair, wept silently under a swollen, bleeding lip and a puffy eye that threatened to blacken. She had cried and screamed as they had loaded us into the helicopter and was rewarded with the butt end of a rifle. No one spoke after that. Not even silently. They always knew. Even though I could see that no one was looking in our direction, it wasn't worth the risk.

We were all dressed identically. They had given us the clothing this morning. Red parkas with fur-lined hoods, matching ski pants, neck warmers, mittens, boots. It was all the highest quality. We had pulled it over the filthy clothes we wore. I hadn't showered or had a change of clothes in almost a week. At least that's how long I thought it had been since they brought me to the warehouse.

My throat tightened at the thought. So much had changed.

I would not think about before—I couldn't. It was too painful.

They had given us goggles too, but none of us had them pulled over our eyes. It seemed odd to look through their distorted lenses while we sat confined in the helicopter. They must be planning on taking us out there, I had thought, out into the snow, the cold. It was July. It wasn't supposed to snow in July—but that was far from the most important thing on my mind. Any foolish childish hopes I had held were fading with every minute we were in the air. No one would find me. I was gone, disappeared into the swirling blizzard. Nothing more than a memory to those I had left behind.

SOMETHING WAS WRONG. I didn't know what it was, and I couldn't hear the words that were coming from the panicked faces around us. The helicopter dropped suddenly with a lurch and I floundered for something to hold onto. There was nothing--no handles, no bars or handholds. Everything in here was smooth and clean. Even our seats were molded out of the same plastic that formed the walls. We had seatbelts, but other than those rigid straps around our hips we were tossed like ragdolls, unable to control our flailing arms and legs. My seatbelt wasn't tight enough, so as the helicopter dropped I lifted off the seat. The aircraft stabilized and I hit my seat again with a bang as we started to climb. Eight sets of eyes watched each other, the same fear and panic mirrored in each one.

The pale-eyed girl closed her eyes, shut herself off from the rest of us and started moving her lips silently. We were seated in two rows, facing each other—four on each side, facing the middle—close enough that our knees touched. There were three others with us, two men and one woman—who could easily be mistaken for a man—who sat in the front of the helicopter. She was the one who had hit Pale-eyes with her rifle. There was nothing at all feminine about her. She was the only one familiar to me—she had been in the warehouse. I could hear her voice in my head, raspy and sharp, unforgettable. The other men were in the helicopter when we had arrived. I couldn't remember seeing any of them before, but that didn't mean they hadn't been around. There were a lot of people in the warehouse, exactly how many I couldn't be sure, but voices had murmured around me day and night. At the beginning there was maybe one or two, but as the temperature dropped more voices had joined them. I had been blindfolded, and wasn't even aware there were other girls with me until they brought us the heavy outdoor clothing and told us to get dressed.

I had seen them then, my silent partners, all of them close to my own age—perhaps fourteen or fifteen. Pale-eyes looked like she might have been somewhat younger, but perhaps her petite childish frame just skewed my assumptions.

The helicopter lurched again and began to list to one side. I felt myself falling forward, off my seat, the seatbelt straining against my hips. My hands flailed once more, looking for something to hold onto and finding nothing but air. Only gravity gave any clue as to which way was up as the machine bucked and rolled back and forth. A loud beeping noise cut through the sound of the motor, screeching through the other noises until it was all I could hear. Something grabbed my hand. The girl beside me—she was reaching across the centre to the girl across from her too. I clenched my hand around hers and fumbled for the hand of the girl on the other side. One by one we grasped hands, until all eight of us were linked together. The helicopter began to spin, pressing us back against our seats, and I felt weightless for a moment as it began a descent that was fast—too fast.

I braced for impact, though I couldn't be sure when it would happen, since nothing was visible beyond the blowing white snow. A tear slid from my eye, tumbled down my cheek and soaked itself into the fleece neck warmer I had pulled up over my nose. I squeezed my eyes shut as we landed with a bone-jarring blow. The shrill howl of metal on metal made me clench my teeth and sent a jolt of electricity from my jaw to my hip. I felt my shoulder crack against the molded plastic seat, hard, and I could feel something pop as my arm went numb. My head bounced off the hard plastic wall of the helicopter, cushioned only by the fur-lined hood I wore. Pain ripped through my head and neck as I waited for the aircraft to stop moving, but it didn't. Now that we were on the ground the whole thing began to roll. We all screamed as we were flipped head over heels, over and over again like a barrel rolling down a hill. Nothing held us in but the seatbelts, and the whole space was a tangle of legs and arms, some of us still holding tightly to the hands of those around us.

When we finally stopped, there was silence. No engine, no screaming, no crash of trees and metal, nothing. It was as if the world had stopped to breathe, just for a moment. And then the panic started.

"Fuel!" someone shouted, and I could smell it too. I didn't know if there were any sparks to ignite it, but I wasn't planning on sticking around long enough to tell. Only one person moved in the front of the helicopter, one of the pilots. The woman with the gun was unconscious and so was the other pilot. The front windows had shattered and glass shards impaled their faces. I could see the pilot unbuckle his belt and pull himself through the front window.

So much for chivalry.

I was lying on my back against the wall, my feet suspended above me comically. The girls across from me dangled from their seatbelts, screaming. I clicked the buckle of my own seatbelt and slid backwards off my seat onto the wall above me. I winced as I rolled over and pushed myself up. There was a door above me; the one on the other side was buried in a snow bank. I reached for the handle with my left arm and yanked it enough to slide it to the open position. The metal of the door was bent and I couldn't get enough leverage with one hand to push it far enough that it would slide open. I felt someone beside me, throwing her weight against the door as I cranked the handle. It didn't move much, but it moved.

"Again," I said.

We pushed against it again, this time moving it enough that snow could find its way through the cracks. Behind us the other girls that had been lying on their backs had freed themselves from their seats and had stood up to help the ones dangling upside down. I heard them fall with shrieks and grunts and bangs against the wall of the helicopter.

"One more time," I said to the girl beside me as another joined us. I cranked the handle and pushed with my one good arm while they heaved and swore. The door slid open, blinding us with a flurry of wind and snow.

"Everyone, put your goggles on!" someone shouted.

Obediently my hand went to my forehead where miraculously the goggles were still sitting snug against the fur of my hood. I pulled them down over my eyes as one by one the girls climbed through the open door, jumping down into knee-deep snow.

"Is there something wrong with your arm?" asked the girl who helped me get the door open. She shouted over the sound of the wind.

I nodded. "I think something's broken."

"Let me help you out."

I grasped the side of the door opening with my good hand and she boosted me from behind until I could fold my waist over the edge. I lifted my feet behind me and slid out head first into the snow. I landed with a silent thud, thankful for the snow that cushioned my fall but cursing at the pain that radiated down my arm. The other girl landed beside me, helping me to my feet.

"We need to get away from this thing," she shouted. "It's leaking fuel everywhere!"

I nodded and together we followed the others away from the wreckage, plodding through the snow toward the other red parkas, hoping we would make it far enough away in time.

I didn't hear the blast as much as I felt it, pushing me forward and down into the drifting snow banks. I could feel the warmth on my back, even through the heavy parka, and the blowing snow around us melted into rain in mid-air, pelting me with icy raindrops.

I didn't move from my facedown position in the snow for a minute, taking stock of any new pains, but there were none. Breathing a sigh of relief I used my good arm to push myself up as the others were doing. We sat in the snow, watching the flames lick at the sky from the burning helicopter. I was familiar with cold and snow, but this was different. It was colder than any winter I had ever known and based on my count, it was still July. Something was wrong—no, everything was wrong. I had no idea where we were, or where we were going, and I had a hunch all of the other girls with me were in the same boat.

"The pilot!" I blurted.

"What?" asked someone beside me.

"One of the pilots got out of the helicopter before we did, through the broken windshield. He must know where we were going."

One of the girls heard me and shouted to the others.

"Split up in pairs," she said, "See if there's anyone around here. Stay where you can see the fire so you can make it back."

"There are eight of us," someone else shouted. "Remember so we don't leave someone."

"No," shouted the first girl. "There are only seven."

"There were eight of us on the helicopter."

"Only seven people came through the door."

I was one of the last people out of the helicopter, and I didn't remember anyone else in there, but I couldn't remember looking.

"I saw her," shouted someone else. "She was unconscious from the crash, didn't anyone pull her out?"

"What good would it have done? She'd be as good as dead out here."

We all looked back at the fire. There were three souls in there, and as I looked around at the wall of white that surrounded us, I couldn't be sure which of us were the lucky ones.

"OVER HERE!" I HEARD the shouts and a shrill whistle, the sort my mother used to make to call me in for dinner, the kind where you put your fingers in your mouth. I had always tried to do that, but had never quite mastered it. I turned toward the sound, reaching out to the girl with me—the one who had helped me get out of the wreckage. She was looking too. We both began slogging through the snow in the direction of the sound, tripping over snow banks that seemed to be growing around us as we walked. We held onto each other for balance. The fire was still bright, but I could see that it was less violent than it had been originally. The constant snow was dampening it, and as the fuel began to burn away, the raging fire had begun to fizzle.

We were the last to arrive to the identically clad gathering. We stood in a circle around the body of a man.

"It's the pilot."

"He didn't make it far."

"Do you blame him? Look at that gash."

Even with his heavy parka on, I could see where the glass from the windshield had cut him from his shoulder to the opposite hip. It was a miracle he had survived long enough to even get out of the helicopter.

We watched him, unmoving, eyes open but unseeing. I could feel the dread start to seep through me, from my feet to the tips of my fingers. It moved like the cold, insidious and treacherous—creeping into my mind.

One of the girls dropped to her knees and began to dig. His arms and legs were already buried with snow.

"What are you doing? He's dead, there's no hope for him."

The digging girl didn't answer, but kept digging. The rest of us just stood there in silence, watching her.

Finally she shouted and laughed, pulling his arm from the snow. In his hand was a small black device, and even in the gathering darkness and blizzard conditions I could see the faint blinking lights of a digital display.

"What is it?"

"A GPS locator," I said quietly to myself, smiling as the realization hit me.

The mood lifted as the girl shouted an explanation to the others, showing them that the pilot had set coordinates to where he was going, and this device would show us the way there. It was funny to be relieved. We still had no idea what awaited us at that blinking red dot, but we knew how to get there, and for now, that was enough. It gave us something to work toward, a purpose. We would survive, and survival was more than we could have hoped for.

MY ENTIRE BODY THROBBED as I walked, stumbled, and even crawled through the snow. I held back tears as pain plagued my shoulder and useless arm. We walked together, sometimes holding each other, never letting the others out of our sight. If we did we would be lost for sure. We took turns holding the GPS, watching as slowly—so very slowly—the green dot that marked our location moved toward the red dot we presumed was our destination. I walked with a mix of hope and dread, trying not to guess at what awaited us at that red dot, but focusing instead on putting one foot in front of the other. We could make it, we must.

It had been hours of walking, mostly uphill through ever-deepening snow. My hands were numb and my lips felt funny and slow under the fleece neck warmer. I had pulled it up on my face so it covered everything the goggles didn't, and a fleece hat covered my forehead. Thankfully the wind mostly came at our back, allowing our downy fur-lined hoods to shelter us from the worst of the weather.

I slammed into the back of the girl in front of me as she stopped suddenly. They were talking, shouting.

"What is it?" I asked the girl nearest to me.

"They could hear something. Motors."

We stood silently and I strained to hear anything above the shrieking wind. It seemed pointless until a burst of hope caught my breath. It was there. It was hard to hear, but it was there. Everyone started shouting at once, waving their arms and jumping up and down, anything that might get the attention of whoever was driving those machines.

They seemed to be getting closer and soon I could see headlights bouncing over the snowdrifts. There was more than one, at least four, maybe even five. The blowing snowflakes caught the light and danced around us as the lights circled our group, closing in on our exhaused party. They came closer and then the lights stopped moving. Men approached us from all sides until we were surrounded by five men in dark snowsuits. I didn't care to ask them who they were or where they were taking us, I just fell into the arms of the nearest one. I let him carry me to a snowmobile, and place me onto the small raised seat behind him.

I slumped against the backrest as he crawled on in front of me, my legs straddling him. I held onto the handle beside me with my good arm and cried with relief under my goggles.

TWO

I DIDN'T REMEMBER MUCH of the trip, other than bouncing and jolting in the seat behind the driver. I clenched my teeth as the constant movement caused the pain in my shoulder to shoot through my arm. I wanted to cry out, tell him to slow down or stop, but there was nothing left in me to protest, so I merely held on and prayed for the ride to end.

It did end, eventually. When the vibrations of the motor died beneath me, tears fell from my eyes. The man reached over, took my arm and moved to pull me from the sled. I couldn't control the scream of pain.

"Are you hurt?" He shouted to me. The wind was still howling and I couldn't see anything that gave me the impression that we had arrived, though, to be fair, I couldn't see much more than the person in front of me.

I nodded, tears coming fast and hot.

"Your arm?"

I nodded again.

He looked me once over and reached his arm around my back and leaned down to get a hold of the back of my knees, sweeping me off my feet. I held onto his neck and let him carry me like a baby. Every muscle in me ached and I was so tired I didn't even care where he was taking me. I felt every one of his footsteps echo through my body, but for the first time in days I felt safe. I wasn't going to die on a frozen mountainside. I cared about nothing else.

WE WALKED THROUGH A door and I could feel the warmth hit me, making my cold skin tingle. I squinted with the sudden influx of light and commotion. The other girls were there, and it seemed as though everyone was talking at once. The man holding me didn't put me down as I assumed he would, but carried me through the crowd to a door at the opposite side of the room. It opened as we reached it and a woman came through. She was old and kind looking, with long white hair in a ponytail and wrinkles around her eyes.

"Jude? Is she ok?"

Jude. I had to remember that name so I could find him again and thank him.

"Take off my helmet."

The woman pulled the helmet off his face and I saw him for the first time. He was young, not much older than I was, and his sweaty hair stuck to his face in places and poked out in others.

"I think she's hurt, she can't move her arm"

"Let me find a wheelchair, I can take her to the clinic."

"It's fine, I can carry her."

She held the door open and Jude followed the woman.

It was bright and clean, with a faint smell of floral-scented cleaning products. Even though I didn't know where I was, it was a relief to be rid of the dingy, filthy warehouse that I had lived in for the past few days. My muscles began to shake uncontrollably though I wasn't cold. Still bundled in the warm parka and snow gear I had been given, I hung like a child in the arms of a man I didn't know. Though I knew enough to feel vulnerable, at this point I didn't care. This 'Jude' could have carried me anywhere and I would have let him.

The woman walked ahead of us and held open a swinging door that led into another brightly lit room that assaulted my nose with the pungent odor of disinfectants. He turned into the room once we were clear of the door and I could see we had entered the clinic, or what I assumed must be the clinic. There were four or five people in lab coats and scrubs, plus a variety of beeping machines and half a dozen cots. Jude laid me down on one of the closest beds.

"Whatcha got?" asked an older man as he hurried across the room toward us. He was kind of a dumpy fellow, thick around the middle and missing most of the hair on the top of his head. His thick glasses perched on the tip of his nose as he looked me over.

"I'm not sure," said Jude. "She's one of the helicopter crash survivors. She screamed when I pulled her arm, the right one." The old doctor clucked his tongue and began touching my arm through the sleeve.

"We need to take this parka off, but if it's what I suspect, that might be difficult. I'll need your help, Jude, and you too, Delta."

"Just let me know what to do."

"We need to get her upright, for starters," the doctor said.

I winced as they reached behind my back and pulled me upwards into a sitting position, and closed my eyes as I felt the layers being peeled from me one at a time. My hat and goggles came off first, followed by the fleece neck warmer, the static electricity making my greasy hair stick to my face. Someone unzipped the puffy red parka and they slid it backwards and down, off my shoulders and onto the bed, where it promptly slid itself onto the floor.

They didn't bother with the ski pants I wore, doing little more than unbuckling the shoulder straps and letting them fall. "That's better. It was the right arm, yes? Tell me, child, can you touch your ear?"

I nodded and lifted my hand, gasping when it stopped well before my ear.

The doctor nodded.

"As I expected. Broken clavicle. You're going to be in here for a bit." He turned to the woman. "I need to keep her, at least until the bones knit back together and she can move around a bit better."

Delta nodded and they both left, Jude still bundled in his thick winter clothing and goggles, his heavy boots thumping on the floor.

"I'll get you some pain killers right away," the doctor said.

"And I'll send over one of the nurses to help you get out of the rest of those clothes and into something more comfortable. I hope you're not attached to that t-shirt of yours, because it'll be a lot easier on you to just cut it off."

I shook my head. I had been living in this shirt for a week, I'd be glad to be rid of it.

As he left me, sitting there on the edge of the bed, something struck me. A doctor had come to see me, diagnosed me and proposed treatment, and not once had anyone asked me my name.

THREE

I STAYED IN THE clinic for over a week, cursing regularly, since even the slightest movement caused the broken collarbone to shift and grind against itself. I became accustomed to the shooting pains that coursed up and down my arm and dreaded the slow, shuffling trips to the bathroom. As promised a nurse had come to help me. She had brought a stack of clothes, cozy sweatpants and a comfortable flannel shirt that buttoned in the front. We had managed to get me dressed again, and she combed and tightly braided my hair before slowly easing me back onto the bed, where I stayed, moving as little as possible.

I hadn't seen any of the other girls I came with, or anyone else that I recognized for that matter. Though other than the clinic staff, the only person I had seen without winter gear on her face was the woman who had been at the door when we arrived in this place, and I couldn't remember her name. Typically the only people in the clinic were the handful of doctors and nurses that milled around looking busy. I spent most of my time watching videos or trying my hand at one of the crossword puzzle books that were lying around. Compared to the initial busyness of the clinic when I had arrived, it was almost peaceful.

"I think they're going to let you go back with the others today," said the kindly old nurse as she brought me breakfast. Her name was Edna, but other than that, I knew nothing about her. No one really talked to me, and I did my best not to draw their attention. I listened to their conversations in hopes of discerning where we were, or why I was here, but their conversation was as dull as the fresh beige paint on the walls.

"Really?" For the first time in a week I was a bit excited. I had noticed that my collarbone had stopped shifting and grinding in the last days, so it was thrilling to think that I would soon find my way out of this bed. They had fitted me for a sling, a black canvas one that attached snugly around my forearm and hung from the padded neckpiece with a series of straps and buckles. They had also allowed me to take a shower. I needed the nurse to help me wash my hair, but despite my lack of privacy I was thrilled to wash off over two weeks of filth and grime. It had been a kind of rebirth. Everything just looked better.

I picked up a piece of toast with my left hand and took a bite. I would be leaving the clinic. The thought brought alternating waves of happiness and fear, but I tried to push down that nagging feeling that something was terribly wrong and focus on the good. I ate slowly and methodically, wrestling with the foil cover on the yogurt and doing my best not to make a mess of myself.

My food was nearly gone when I heard a commotion on the other side of the curtain. Someone had occupied that bed since I arrived, but I had never seen the curtain open. Something was wrong. People were rushing around, their shoes squeaking on the hard floor, a level of panic mingled with their typical speed and professionalism. I didn't hear anyone say anything to confirm that feeling, but the air felt electrified in some way.

They said things I had heard before on the television medical dramas. From the shadows of my curtained room, I listened as they performed CPR, and shouted directions at one another. The machines beeped loudly and others were rolled into the space, clattering and squealing.

It felt like hours, but in reality it was only about twenty minutes before the activity settled down. A heart monitor was beeping steadily and the voices of the doctors dropped to low, hushed tones. The entire clinic breathed a collective sigh of relief. Whatever crisis had happened, whatever emergency had just taken place was over for now. A janitor dressed in dark blue coveralls and a hat pulled low over his face came through, wheeling his cart and picking up the discarded gloves and surgical gowns that littered the floor of the area beside me.

I waited in my bed—waited for a doctor to come and discharge me, for someone to come and take me to wherever I was supposed to be, but no one came. Someone forgot to bring me lunch, and dinner. As the clock continued to change, counting the hours and minutes, I grew restless. Staring at the walls, uncertainty overcame me. I contemplated calling for one of the doctors, or even getting out of bed to go see why they had obviously forgotten about me, and I was just about to, when Edna slipped through the gap in the pastel-striped curtains.

"Sorry child. It's been a busy day. We had a bit of a fright and it appears no one brought you anything to eat."

In her hands were a few granola bars and a small carton of chocolate milk. My stomach growled in appreciation. She placed them on the table and rolled the top of it over my lap.

"Am I still going to get to go today?" I asked.

She shook her head.

"I doubt it," she said. "The doctors are having an important meeting right now, and one of them needs to discharge you. Looks like you'll be here another night at least."

I nodded even though she had already turned and left.

The room was quiet and they had dimmed the lights as they had every night since I arrived. I pushed the button on the side of my bed to angle myself lower in hopes of falling asleep. The bed buzzed as my head slowly moved down into a more comfortable position. I picked up a granola bar, and holding it in my right hand, I used my left to peel the wrapper away. It had tiny chocolate chips in it and tasted like peanut butter. Chewing slowly I listened to the sounds around me, the beeping and humming of the machines next to me.

I reached back for the buttons and lifted the head of my bed back up to the highest position. I had been able to sit up from there without any pain, so I pushed the blankets back and swung my legs over the side of the bed and slid to the floor. My bare feet were cold on the hard tiles, but I moved slowly to the curtain beside my bed. I couldn't hear anyone on the other side, but still I peeked around the curtain first. There was no one there except for the patient lying still in the bed. I pushed back the curtain enough to slide between it and the wall, and crept over to the bed. I held my breath and hoped whoever this was wasn't one of the girls I had come in with. I didn't know any of them, but we had a strange sense of being in this together. .

It wasn't.

I stifled a gasp as I saw the face of the woman lying in the bed, tubes attached to her mouth and IVs dripping into needles in her arm. I knew who she was instantly. I had seen her face many times, so very many times.

It was Meredith Kroeker, the President of the United States.

FOUR

THE DOCTOR CAME AND discharged me the next morning. Standing behind him was the woman who had met us when we arrived.

"We haven't been introduced," she said. "My name is Delta, I'm in charge of you and the other girls you came with."

Delta waited for me to stand up and handed me a pair of slippers she had been holding.

"Come with me, we'll get you dressed and back with the other girls. They've been wondering about you."

"Is everyone else ok?" I asked.

Delta nodded.

"Nothing but some cuts and bruises and mild frostbite—I patched them up in the room and they're all fine."

Not all of them.

My thoughts drifted to the girl who hadn't made it out of the helicopter before it exploded. I felt a pang of guilt that I hadn't even noticed her in my haste to get out, much less tried to help. The other girls said she was unconscious, but it still haunted me. She was one of us—whatever we were.

I shuffled along behind Delta as she turned corner after

corner. The hallways seemed never ending and any time I thought I might have found some bearing we turned again and I was lost.

Delta walked a few steps ahead of me, and though I wanted to ask her all the questions that were swirling around in my head, I held my tongue. She seemed nice enough, but if they had wanted to tell me what I was doing here, or even where "here" was, they would have told me a long time ago. I watched as her long white braid swished back and forth in front of me as we walked. She was dressed in jeans and a wool sweater that hung down almost to her knees. We rounded the corner and she opened a door.

"Here we are," she said. "Don't worry; you'll learn where you need to go quickly enough." She held the door and we entered the room.

I had expected to see some kind of bunk area where the other girls were staying, but we walked into some kind of waiting room. There were chairs around the outside and a reception desk in the corner. There was a set of double doors to the left of the receptionist.

"Call me when she's done, and I'll come back and get her," Delta said to the young man behind the desk.

"Yes Ma'am," he said, not looking up from the computer. He pointed to a clipboard on the desk. "Fill this out."

I took the clipboard and the pen and sat down on one of the chairs. It was difficult and clumsy to write with my hand in a sling, but slowly I managed. It was a medical history form, pretty standard, but very detailed. There were four pages of questions to answer, boxes to tick and charts to fill out. I answered everything as well as I could remember. My mom was usually the one responsible for accounting for my medical history, so there was much I didn't know.

A lump grew in my throat when I thought of my mother, but I pushed it back. This wasn't the time. I didn't know what time would be the time, but I knew this wasn't it.

I paused at the last question. I had no idea what molecular radiation was, not to mention whether I had ever been exposed to it. Staring at the paper, I finally scrawled "no". Surely someone would have told me if I had ever been molecularly radiated.

Wedging the pen under the clip of the clipboard I handed it back to the receptionist. He took it without looking at me and flipped through the pages. Finally he stood and headed for the double doors.

"Come with me."

I followed him through the doors, down a short hallway and into another room. It was a doctor's office, complete with a paper covered exam table, and multiple instruments on a rolling table. He took a paper gown from a drawer under the exam table and handed it to me.

"Put this on, you'll need a full work-up. The doctor will be in soon."

It struck me as strange that I would have spent a week in the clinic only to be discharged and end up in a doctor's office. One would think if any tests had needed to be done they would have done them then.

It took me a full fifteen minutes to struggle out of the

sling and my clothing and then into the paper gown. I was slowly placing my arm back in the sling when the doctor came into the room. She wasn't familiar, she hadn't been in the clinic. She was perhaps forty years old or so, her hair black with only whispers of grey peeking out around the edges. It was pulled back in a tight bun. Her skin was a pale brown and perfect, not a blemish or a scar or a wrinkle.

"Good morning," she said, "I'm Doctor Harris."

She sat down on a stool and wheeled over toward the exam table. Pulling on a pair of gloves she glanced at the table of instruments. There were items I was familiar with, and others that I had never seen before, and couldn't even venture a guess as to what they were for.

"We'll start by drawing some blood." She reached over and secured a rubber tie tightly around my bicep and picked up a needle attached to an empty vial. "Make a fist."

She inserted the needle carefully into the vein in the inner part of my elbow and blood began to flow down the tube and into the vial. When it was full she replaced the vial with another, and another until finally eight vials of blood sat neatly on her table, each already labeled with the same number.

Then, we began a full and detailed physical. I had been to doctors before, but mainly they just measured my height and weight, maybe looked into my ears and eyes. This was vastly different. Every bone and muscle was poked and prodded, every orifice was examined. Nothing was private, no question too probing. By the end of it, almost two hours later, I felt so exposed, so vulnerable that it was a relief to be rid of the paper gown and be able to struggle into my clothing again. My hands shook as I dressed, reeling from the invasive examination. Tears formed in my eyes and I brushed them away, setting my jaw and breathing deeply to calm my nerves. Delta arrived at the door as I was trying to button the flannel shirt again with one hand.

"Let me, child," she said, waving her hand and coming toward me.

I recoiled, not wanting anyone to touch me.

She stopped, looked me in the eye.

"This is the worst part," she said quietly. "And it's over now. Let me help you."

I let her button up my shirt and she helped me attach my sling properly.

"Unfortunately we need to get you into different clothes in a few minutes, but I can help you with that too."

I followed her through a different maze of hallways, or perhaps they were all the same ones, I couldn't be sure. Finally we walked down a hallway I knew I had never seen. It was thinner and dimmer than the other ones. We stopped at a red door. Delta reached out and opened it, standing aside to let me go in. I walked through the door into a large room. In it stood four sets of bunk beds against the concrete block walls. There was no one in there, but I could tell there were people staying there. The blankets were ruffled and a few small personal items lay scattered around. Delta walked to a closet on the wall closest to us. She opened it to reveal a rod with a few dozen hangers. On each hanger was the exact same thing. She lifted out a hanger and handed it to me. It held a long simple sleeveless dress, made of jersey or some other knitted fabric and a long-sleeved woolen sweater that buttoned up to the top. Every piece was red.

The door was red, the blankets on every bunk were red, even the shoes lined up in the bottom of the closet were red.

"Do you need some help dressing?"

I nodded without making eye contact. She had underwear too, and a plain, stretchy sports bra. I had been wearing a bra for a few years now—mainly because all of my friends were—even though I didn't have much of a chest to speak of. The bra was a struggle, since there were no clasps. I had to pull it over my head and try to get my arm through without causing myself any pain. It was a relief to know that I had just recently showered. It would be a few days before I'd really need another one, so I wouldn't have to do this again too soon. I shivered at the chill as Delta finally pulled the sweater up over my shoulders. I didn't even move to try to do up the buttons, but just let her do it.

"I think the girls left one of the bottom bunks for you for now. Since you can't really climb, right? They should be coming back soon. Oh, and one more thing..."

Delta reached into a basket that sat in the closet and pulled out a red piece of fabric. As she unfolded it I could see that it was a tube, made of some kind of thin stretchy fabric. She walked behind me and pulled it over my head so it sat in a puddle around my neck. Then, she smoothed my hair back and pulled the tube over my head so one end revealed my face and the other end hung down, covering my hair. Deftly she wrapped my braid into a knot at the back of my neck and tied the end of the fabric around it securely.

"You can't show your hair," she said, by way of an explanation. "The girls will be back soon."

Delta left me standing in the middle of the room, covered in red from head to toe, with nothing but unanswered questions.

I DIDN'T HEAR THEM coming as I thought I would. A group of six girls tended to make a racket as they moved from place to place. I didn't know they were coming until someone opened the door. I had been sitting on a bunk, the one that looked the least used, waiting. They entered the room in silence, one behind the next. When the door clicked closed behind them they breathed a collective sigh.

I stood from my bunk to greet them, every one of them dressed identically to me.

"Hey, look who's back!" said one of the girls, rushing toward me as if to give me a hug. She stopped abruptly when she noticed my sling.

"What happened?"

The other girls gathered around.

"Um, broken clavicle, collarbone," I said.

"Ouch," said another.

"Been there," said yet another, "no fun at all."

It was difficult to recognize them by faces alone, one

girl, the one with the darkest skin stood out; I remembered her beautiful dark eyes from the warehouse and the helicopter—they reminded me so much of my sister. I glanced at the others looking for the only one I was sure to recognize, Pale-eyes was there too. She was the tiniest of the bunch, standing not much more than five feet tall at most, her dark curls a stark contrast to her eyes.

"Girls, we're so rude," she said, pushing her way to the front. "We haven't even introduced ourselves. I'm Kenzie."

One by one they introduced themselves, Shalisa, or Li as she preferred to be called was my height and had one blue eye and one green. "They thought I was some kind of devil when I came out," she said, and then whispered to me, "My parents are a bit on the superstitious side."

Freya was the tallest; she pulled her headscarf off while introducing herself. Her hair was so blonde it was nearly white.

"I'm Willow," said the girl with skin the color of burnished walnut. She pulled off her scarf too.

"Are we allowed to take these off?" I asked.

"Only in here," said another girl, she was a bit on the plump side and had eyes the color of caramel. "My name is Hazel."

"And I'm Margo," said the last girl. "Did no one explain the rules?"

I shook my head.

She snorted. "Better sit down; there are a lot of them."

"We don't have enough time," said Kenzie. "We need to be back in the kitchen in five minutes, she's just going to have to learn as we go." She glanced at me. "Hey, what's your name anyway?"

I hadn't realized I hadn't introduced myself. It had been so long since I said my name it felt funny coming out of my mouth.

"Rhea," I said. "My name is Rhea."

FIVE

Delta

"Status report?"

I doodled on my notebook. I hated these meetings.

"Delta," came the voice again. "Status report."

My head snapped up and met the scowling eyes of Nadia Black. She was running the meeting today.

"They are all together now, the one with the broken collarbone has been released by the clinic."

"And Meredith?"

I didn't know why I needed to give a status report on her, we all knew.

"Madam President is unchanged."

The women around the table nodded and made notes on their tablets. I watched their eyes for any sign of treachery and treason but saw none. They were good at what they did. At this table sat women who held all the power the United States had to offer. They controlled all three branches of the government, Executive, Legislative and Judicial. They were invincible and they knew it well.

Every single one of them stood to gain from Meredith's death. She was a wild card for them, the only one with a shred of morality. She was powerful and fair, listening both to the needs of the wealthy and the weak. She was an excellent President. The doctors didn't know what had caused her injuries, but there was nothing in me that thought these women didn't have a hand in it. Nadia was the most likely suspect. As Vice President of the United States, she would be propelled into the top seat in the country, a position she had coveted since the moment Meredith was sworn in.

The others weren't innocent either.

"Do you still believe these girls are suitable?"

I nodded.

"I have no reason to believe they were compromised by the crash in any way. Bones will heal, scrapes and bruises will fade." I said slowly. "They will all be well and healthy enough when the time comes."

I made sure not to mention any of their names. I knew them all, of course, but there was something about using a name that made them human, a fact that none of the women here felt the need to know. Humans have feelings, humans have needs, humans are not disposable.

Nadia nodded, tucking her hair behind her ear, revealing the tattoo that marred her face. The thin black line that stretched from the center of her forehead to her left earlobe was an ugly reminder to me, but a mark of accomplishment to her. Nadia was sterile, they all were. As society shifted to become matriarchal, women began to sterilize themselves to be considered on equal footing as men. They rose higher in their fields until nearly every business had a woman at the helm, every level of government had a female majority.

I sat, stiff in my seat, as we checked off all the notes on the agenda, ending the meeting with a long, rambling description of the avalanche protocols and a detailed description of the accumulation of snow on the mountain above us.

"Meeting dismissed." Nadia stood as she spoke, collecting her belongings and heading for the door. The others followed her, most likely to continue their business behind closed doors. I leaned back in my chair and glanced around the room. There were a few other senior staff members, key positions in the estate. No one spoke. No one dared to. One by one, everyone left the room, heading back to their jobs.

I stood, unsure if the creaks I heard were from the chair or my own bones. I was stiff from sitting so long. Jude was there when I made it to the hallway.

"The girl is fine," I said, knowing his question before he could ask it. He asked the same thing every day, and since she was moved out of the clinic today, he was probably more interested in knowing where she had gone.

Jude smiled.

"You know me too well," he said. A smile teasing at the corner of his mouth.

"I was young once too, you know."

"I doubt it," he said in a petulant tone.

"You're right," I said. "I came out of my mother a crotchety old woman."

"Your poor mother."

I swatted him at the back of the head.

"You'll do much better to forget about her," I said, as we walked together down the hallway.

"What are they going to do with her?" Jude asked.

"I don't know exactly, but they don't kidnap girls to give them puppies and marry them off to their staff. Whatever their plan, it won't be good for you to get attached."

Jude smiled. "Too late for that."

I knew it was. I knew this boy as well as I knew myself. I had been as close to a mother as he could have hoped for. Boys were seldom so lucky. He and his brothers—not by blood, but by circumstance—could have spent their lives on the streets as most of their contemporaries found themselves, if they managed to live that long. Instead they were here, safe, working hard, but fed and warm. They were my contribution to this world, such a tiny thing that I could do, but it made a difference and for that I was grateful.

Jude and his brothers—Red, Vaughn, Harris and Finn— were not the first family I had raised, but they were the ones who were with me now. I couldn't be sure where many of their older brothers were. I prayed for them all daily—listing them one by one, like the beads on a rosary—but every day I looked through the windows at the blowing snow and wasn't sure they were still out there somewhere.

I smiled and patted Jude on the shoulder.

"I just don't want you to get hurt," I said.

"I know."

He wrapped one of his long arms around my shoulders and kissed me quickly on the cheek before rushing down the hall ahead of me.

I watched him go, and I knew that he too had become a man when I wasn't watching. My only hope was that I somehow made him strong enough to face the trials that waited for him.

SIX

Rhea

"WE NEED TO KEEP our hair covered and our sweaters on at all times when we aren't in our room," said Kenzie in a whisper as we headed through the hallways. "Most of our work so far has been done in the kitchens, but they told us they'd assign us to other areas as needed."

I wasn't sure how much help I'd be in the kitchens, at least for a while. I couldn't wash dishes or cut things very well with one hand, and since my right hand was my dominant one, I wouldn't be terribly fast at anything.

My stomach growled at the thought of food. I hadn't eaten anything since my breakfast in the clinic.

"When do we eat?" I asked.

"After everyone else is done, with the rest of the kitchen staff."

"And don't even think of sneaking anything while you're working," Margo broke in, sliding up next to me as we hurried toward the kitchens. "I learned that one the hard way." She rolled her eyes.

"Don't listen too much to her," said Kenzie, as Margo pushed her way to the front. "They feed us well, we just have to wait a bit."

"Are there any other rules?" I asked.

"Oh, tons, but we can talk later, back in the rooms. Right now we need to work."

I followed the others through the big swinging doors into the kitchen. It was steamy and hot, but whatever was cooking smelled delicious. People were moving in every direction at once, some kneading bread, others stirring huge pots of soup or working over steaming griddles.

"Rhea, watch out!"

I turned in time to narrowly avoid being run over by a rack of dishes being pushed from the dishwashing area.

"I don't know how much use I'm going to be in here," I said.

"Oh, don't worry," said Willow, "we don't actually work that hard, we mostly set tables and sometimes we peel potatoes, or pick the stems off herbs. They don't ask us to do anything that might give us dishpan hands or would be dirty or dangerous in any way."

I could set tables. Not as quickly as I could with two hands, but I could do it.

We pushed through the kitchen, doing our best to dodge the people working in there, and walked through the swinging doors to the dining room. I caught my breath at the beauty of it. There were probably enough tables for about two hundred people, each surrounded by ornate chairs. Half of the slanted ceiling and one entire wall was made entirely of glass. The snow was still swirling outside and building up on the small ridges between each window, but I assumed that if it wasn't snowing the view of the woods around us would be breathtaking. I felt like we had walked right into a snow globe. The walls that weren't glass were covered in art, paintings, tapestries, and relief wood carvings. Even the floors were a beautiful, glowing dark hardwood, inlaid with intricate designs. This room had to have cost a small fortune.

The other girls were standing around a cart, each pulling out armloads of cloth—tablecloths, I gathered, as they began to sweep the fine, embroidered white cloth across each of the bare tables. It seemed a shame to cover them up; I had never seen such striking tables. I followed the lead of the other girls and we worked hard, setting each place with fine china, silverware and crystal stemware. It seemed so surreal, so overly extravagant and opulent.

"You're going crooked," hissed Li as she came up behind me. I had been arranging knives beside each plate. She quickly adjusted them so they sat in the proper spot. "You need to be careful. Everything needs to be perfect on these tables."

I nodded, trying to concentrate more on what I was doing, but it was difficult. Everything I saw gave me one more answer but a dozen more questions.

When we had finished setting the tables with dishes we began to fold napkins, which I found exceedingly difficult with one hand. Most of the ones I completed were unfolded and redone by the other girls, but at least for napkin folding we were allowed to sit. Eventually I was gently directed toward napkin placing, something I could do more easily. I was instructed on the proper way to place the napkins and, other than a few that were quickly adjusted by Freya, I did a pretty good job.

"Hurry up," called Margo. "They'll be coming in a few minutes; we need to get out of here."

"Why the rush?" I asked Hazel, who happened to be the closest person to me.

She shrugged. "We're not really supposed to be seen, by them."

"By who?"

"Everyone. Now!" yelled Margo.

I placed the last napkin and followed the others to the kitchen door, nearly knocking over one of the serving staff in the process, causing the water jug he was carrying to spill all over his white shirt and vest.

"What's wrong with you?" he snarled, dripping.

"I'm sorry," I reached for a cloth and handed it to him as he shook the water from his shirt in a futile effort to dry himself.

"Red, what happened to you?" asked another voice, as another boy rounded the corner, dressed the same.

Jude. I glanced up at him. Standing in front of me, with his dripping friend, was the one who had come out in the storm on a snowmobile, brought me back and carried me to the clinic. He looked much better than the first time I'd seen him, sweaty and disheveled. He had dark brown hair, with finger-sized curls framing his face. His eyes were brown around the outside but faded into the color of amber near the pupils. I stood, dumbstruck, wanting to thank him for helping me, but unable to form the words.

"Just an accident with one of the Sisters," Red said. "Jude, could you cover for me while I get a new shirt?"

"Yeah, of course, but hurry up."

Red handed his pitcher to Jude and left, leaving Jude with a funny grin on his face.

"Glad to see you're feeling better," he said, then turned back and disappeared through the doors.

"Rhea," I heard Kenzie's voice as I felt her hands on my good arm, dragging me with her. She pulled me into a corner. "Talking to the boys is totally against the rules; you're going to get yourself in trouble if you do that here."

"Do that here?"

Kenzie's eyes sparkled and she leaned over to whisper "You'll only get in trouble if you get caught. I didn't say don't do it... just don't get caught."

I laughed out loud as I followed her back through the kitchen.

"Where are we going?"

"When table setting is done, we plate the desserts," she said, then stopped abruptly to whisper in my ear. "Here's another important rule: Don't drip chocolate on your hands, or you'll have to lick it off."

She giggled at her own joke, and I couldn't resist giggling too.

"WHY DID HE CALL me a 'Sister'?" I asked as we loaded the last of the dessert plates onto a trolley for Hazel to push out into the kitchen for the serving staff.

"Because that's what we are, apparently," said Willow, pulling Kenzie toward her. "Aren't you getting the family resemblance?"

Kenzie laughed and swatted at Willow.

"No one has told us," said Freya, more seriously. "They also haven't felt the need to mention why we have to wear these strange clothes, or cover our hair, or stay out of sight. It's just what we are."

"Has anyone asked?"

"We aren't here to ask questions," answered Li in a way that made me think that was the only answer any of them had gotten.

"We can talk about it tonight," said Kenzie, "Back in our room. You never know who might be listening out here. Plus, it's almost time to eat."

I nodded. They all seemed so ok with everything, but I supposed they had been here longer. I came at the same time as them, but alone in the clinic I hadn't been able to absorb any of the information they had. I didn't yet know all the rules, or understand all the procedures. Perhaps getting a primer on all that might help me make sense of all this.

As promised they brought our food into the dessert area. There was a large island counter in the middle where we had done our work. Someone had wiped it down and everyone pulled over stools that had been standing against the walls.

"Here," said Hazel, smiling shyly at me as she pulled over

an extra stool. Her sweater hugged her more tightly than the rest of us. It seemed silly that all the clothes were the exact same size. Kenzie was so tiny that her dress skimmed the floor so she had to hike it up when she walked, though the same dress on Freya, the tallest of all of us, sat inches above her ankles.

"Thanks," I said as I hopped up onto it, joining the others at our makeshift table. The doors opened and two of the boys—dressed like Jude, though he wasn't with them—came in with trays piled high with food and plates. They didn't so much as look at us, but just placed the trays on the counter and left the room.

"They're always so pleasant," said Margo in an obviously sarcastic voice. "I do wish they'd stay."

The other girls laughed as they passed the food around. I had been so hungry earlier, but now my stomach churned and ached. Given this bounty of food, I could barely look at it. instead I just picked my way through a buttery soft roll. It smelled delicious, but tasted like sawdust in my mouth.

SEVEN

WE SPOKE IN HUSHED tones even in the confines of our room, speculating, collaborating. We sat on the floor between the bunks in our matching clothes, as if we were having some sort of slumber party and hadn't been taken against our will. Our work was done for the day and everyone had pulled off their headscarves as soon as we entered the privacy of our room.

"We only have a few minutes before our evening shower," explained Hazel.

"Our evening shower?" I asked. "We have to shower every evening?" I groaned inwardly. Showering and dressing was difficult enough with my broken collarbone, I had hoped to at least make it a few days before having to undertake that project again.

"Twice a day, actually," said Freya.

I didn't even know how to respond. At first I assumed Freya was joking, but I didn't see any of the telltale smirks or winks from the other girls that would have made it obvious that they were pulling my leg.

"Twice a day?" I repeated, incredulous.

Hazel nodded. "You get used to it."

"And you'd better do it properly too. I made that mistake,"

said Margo, rolling her eyes. "If you don't scrub properly they'll send someone to help you. That wasn't fun." She pulled her knees to her chest. I cringed.

"But how do they know?" I asked.

The girls looked at each other, each willing the next to answer. Finally it was Willow who spoke.

"They watch us."

"In the shower?"

No one met my eyes. I couldn't reconcile any of this in my mind. I had felt so vulnerable and exposed during my exam, but the idea of being monitored while showering just seemed like such an unnecessary invasion. I too pulled my knees to my chest and wrapped my arms around them, mirroring all the other girls in the room with me.

"They don't let men in though, don't worry," said Freya. "Usually it's Delta, and she doesn't spend as much time watching as some of the others."

She spoke as if that tiny fact would somehow comfort me; relieve me of the deep sense of intrusion. I was barely fourteen years old, the idea of being naked in a room with other people was almost too difficult to grasp.

"Are we all the same age?" I asked, trying to change the subject.

"Generally," said Margo, taking the bait. "Kenzie is the oldest, she's fifteen, same as Li and Freya. The rest of us are fourteen. Though, I guess we don't know how old you are."

"I turned fourteen a month ago."

Margo thought for a second.

"I guess you're the second youngest. Hazel turned fourteen yesterday."

I glanced at Hazel who was doing her best to curl up and disappear.

"Happy Birthday?" I said.

A weak smile appeared on her face.

"Not really, but thanks," she whispered.

Li glanced at a clock on the wall.

"Shower time," she said, without a hint of enthusiasm, her words nearly dripping with the same dread I felt.

I followed the lead of the others as they stood, pulled on their headscarves, helped themselves to another hanger of identical clothing and filed through the red door back into the hall.

IT WAS EVERY BIT as humiliating as I had assumed. I tried not to think about what we were doing, but it was impossible. It was difficult enough to manage a proper shower with my limited mobility, but knowing there were eyes on me, watching me—scrutinizing me—made it seem as though the clock stood still. We all showered in the same room, reminiscent of the typical men's locker room I had once seen on television. The whole room was white tile with a red band of smaller tiles about two thirds of the way up the wall. Eight shower heads protruded from the tile, spaced evenly across opposing walls. Delta stood in the entrance, where the floor was slightly higher, so as not to get her shoes wet. She seemed less than enthused about being there, but the fact that she was still unsettled me. The water was tepid at best. Not as warm and enjoyable as my shower earlier. I scrubbed myself as best as I could, taking care to follow all the tips the others had given me. I was the last one out of the shower and into the dressing room. Most of the others had dressed as quickly as possible and were likely back in our rooms by the time I got there—probably eager to forget and push away the sickening feeling.

I shivered beneath the large, thick towel I had wrapped around myself. It seemed like such a strange luxury to have such a plush thing. The towels we had at home were thin and threadbare in places, well used and seldom replaced. If I wasn't feeling so strange and vulnerable, it would almost be possible to enjoy the extravagance.

Hazel was sitting on the bench waiting for me. Other than her, the room was empty.

"Do you need some help?" she said, a flush creeping up from the red collar of her sweater to the bottom of the headscarf, giving the illusion she was entirely red from head to toe.

The independent and defiant part of me wanted to say no, but in fact I was somewhat relieved.

I smiled.

"I really do," I said, laughing to ease the tension.

"I thought you might, being hurt and all."

She smiled another weak smile. I was getting used to those smiles—the ones that never quite reached the eyes. I was smiling those smiles too—smiling, but never quite able to relinquish myself to it, never able to commit.

She held up her own towel in front of me, and respectfully watched the floor as I struggled into my underwear and stretchy sports bra. There was no one else in the room, but it was definitely more comforting to enjoy that modicum of privacy. Once I had pulled all my undergarments into place, she lowered the towel.

"We need to use this," she said, holding up a small jar of what looked like a thick lotion.

I raised an eyebrow at her.

She shrugged.

"It smells nice," she said, unscrewing the cap. I dipped my finger into the silky white cream. It did smell nice, floral but somewhat citrusy too, it reminded me of drinking lemonade on a fresh spring day when the trees were in bloom.

"We need to use it after every shower," she said. "We all usually help each other get the places we can't reach, and you can probably reach even less than the rest of us."

I nodded. It was all so ridiculous, why not add more?

I scooped some lotion and began to rub it into my arms and face while Hazel timidly applied some onto my back and shoulders. After a few moments, when I was well-buttered and softened and smelling like lemon blossoms, Hazel helped me slide the clean shift dress over my head and get my arms through the holes. Then she held up the sweater so I could gingerly thread my somewhat immobilized arm through the sleeve.

"Thanks," I said, as I slid my arm into the sling.

She just nodded and walked through the door. I secured my headscarf and followed silently.

There was nothing left to say.

WE HAD SOME TIME before our nighttime curfew. They called it that, even though we were expected to spend all of our spare time in our room. At exactly nine o'clock the lights would go out and we were expected to sleep, dressed in our red shifts in our red beds, behind the red door.

With nothing to do for amusement, we talked. One by one we told our stories—how we had come to be in the warehouse together.

My voice cracked when I recounted my story, the warm summer day when those two men pulled me from the tree and put me in the back of their truck. They went looking for Ember and my heart surged when they came back without her. I missed my little sister, I missed my family, and not knowing where they were or if they were safe in this storm gnawed at me. I had grown used to that ache, as if it was now a part of who I was.

"When do you think the storm is going to end?" asked Li.

"I don't know," I said, truthfully. It was all wrong, every bit of it. It didn't snow in the summer, and even in the winter, when snow was expected, it didn't snow for this long with such a bitterly cold temperature. I remembered the previous winter. Ember had wanted me to come play in the snow with her. She always wanted to build snow castles with moats and towers but I never wanted to. I was too old for princesses, I had told her. She went outside by herself and spent the entire afternoon building an elaborate castle, while I pretended not to care.

I did care, and I had no idea if I would ever see her again.

"I was on my way back from the grocery store," began Willow. "My mom needed some ibuprofen for my little brother, Xavier. He had been howling all night and he had a fever. My mom had been up all night with him and she thought it might be that he was cutting some new teeth. He's only two. I went to the pharmacy so she could rest a bit and was walking down the street when a truck pulled up and asked me for directions. The next thing I knew I was waking up in a shipping container in the warehouse. They must have knocked me out or something, but I don't remember. I don't even know what happened to the medicine."

Her deep brown eyes welled with tears.

"You'll see them again," Kenzie said, murmuring mothering affirmations as she wrapped her tiny arms around Willow, who crumpled into them. I knew the feeling. For days we had been segregated in crates and shipping containers like some unwanted cargo. We hadn't been allowed to talk to each other, and for many of us there was barely enough room to lie down to sleep. We were barely fed, hardly acknowledged and alone. We had survived a helicopter crash, and we were surviving a freak snowstorm, but I too needed physical contact—from someone other than the cold, callous doctor.

"Why would you even say that?" asked Margo, her voice

louder than necessary.

"Leave them be, Margo," Freya said quietly. "There's nothing wrong with a little hope."

"There's plenty wrong with it. We're in a hopeless situation. Our families are all probably dead out there and we were snatched from our lives and hidden away here. We're survivors in a hellhole. I'm not sure which would be better."

No one spoke. No one could disagree, but yet none of us wanted to openly agree with Margo. It did seem completely hopeless, but we were alive. I looked around the room, the only light coming from a single, dim fixture in the center of the ceiling, giving everyone the same haunted look, our faces pale against the sea of red. It was a shallow victory to be safe here. Yes, we were alive, but what of those we were taken from? What of them, and what of us? What were we here for? There was no indication of our purpose here in this stolen sisterhood, and yet here we sat, alive, safe, and warm.

EIGHT

THE LIGHTS WENT OUT at precisely nine o'clock. We had prepared ourselves to be plunged into darkness, so we were all safely in our beds. There was little light outside, but what there was reflected off the constantly swirling snow casting an eerie glow through the windows onto the walls around us. As my eyes adjusted I could make out the shapes of the other girls around me. No one spoke. It was against the rules.

I didn't know how anyone would know if we whispered into the night. The others said they might have bugged our room, or some other such nonsense, but it seemed unlikely to me. Why would they care what petty conversation a group of teenage girls were having in the dark?

And yet, I obeyed.

We all did. Even Margo, who I was getting the distinct impression sat on the edge where passive resistance met full-out rebellion. She didn't strike me as the kind of person who would sit still for long, blindly following the rest. She had a fire in her. Hazel, on the other hand, would follow until the day she died. I could see that she struggled with the fear and the unknown, but she would follow. The others fell somewhere on the spectrum between Margo and Hazel. Some of them, like Li, disguised her struggle with humor and jest, but as she lay in the bed near me, I could make out the silent sobs racking her body.

We all cried that night.

When we stopped crying the dreams came.

I lay awake in the room as one by one my companions slipped into tortured sleep. Some murmured and fought against unseen enemies, while others shouted in strangled cries. I knew what waited for me and was unwilling to let it take me, but eventually I too succumbed.

THERE WAS EMBER, RUNNING off to the kitchen to find us popsicles. I climbed down from the perch in the pecan tree where I sat, and leaned against the wide base of the trunk just where the sun met the shadow. I left my legs to languish in the warm sunbeam while my body cooled in the shade. I could see the light filtering through the leaves around me as they swayed in the gentlest of breezes. I breathed deep, relishing the smells and sounds of summer. The sound of the birds and the smell of lilacs permeated my dream to the point where it felt I could reach out and touch them. Mom had told me once that when she was younger lilacs had only bloomed in the early spring, but they were so popular that they created newer varieties that bloomed continuously through the summer. Everyone in our area had lilacs. Old Mrs. Everson had so many her backyard was a veritable jungle of flowers. White, purple, pink and yellow flowers took turns exploding into bloom and filling the air with their satisfying scent.

Ember and I loved reaching over the fence and pulling armloads of flowers off her plants before scampering off to our own home. She didn't like it, I knew, but she let us. Our backyard had no flowers. Mother worked in the government and had little time for such frolic. We had grass that Father mowed regularly after getting home from his own job as a laborer. I felt sorry for him when he'd come home, reeking of diesel fuel and covered in a thick layer of dust and grime from whatever task he had been awarded that day. The fatigue read clearly on his face, and yet, there he was, priming the lawnmower and pulling the cord to blare the sound across the neighborhood. He would shuffle as he walked, obviously exhausted, but yet he would do it, back and forth across the yard, snipping and manicuring the perfect green lawn.

The lawn was due for a mow, I remembered. It was long and soft as I raked my fingers through the thick green blades.

I didn't give any notice to the truck until it stopped in front of our house with the motor still running. I had my back to the street and turned to peek around the tree as two men stepped from the cab and started toward me.

That fear. That paralyzing feeling gripped me instantly. I knew instantly that they were up to no good. They were dressed in military-issue clothing, though not marked like the city and county patrols were. They were both clean-cut and had the look of soldiers, but they carried no identification whatsoever. Mother would have told us if someone was going to come today.

I stood slowly as they approached and inhaled as deeply

as I could as they closed the gap between us. I felt rooted in place. Every fiber of my being shouted at me to run, but one still small voice overpowered it all.

Ember.

She was too young, only eight years old. Whatever these men had come for, they would find in me, only me.

I clenched my fists and screamed as loudly as I could. The high-pitched noise cut through the silent neighborhood, shattering the peaceful stillness. A flock of birds took to flight from Mrs. Everson's peach tree. I knew Mr. Oliver across the street would hear me, peeking out from behind his curtains. He wouldn't help though. No one would help me.

But I could help Ember.

The men surged forward at my scream; one grabbed my wrist and pulled me toward him. I tumbled off-balance and fell into his arms, but kept screaming until his hand clamped down over my face. It was huge; it covered my mouth and my nose, cutting off the air. I couldn't scream but I could fight. With every ounce I had I railed against him, wiggling my body and slamming my fists over my head, aiming for his face but mostly falling short. I connected a few times and he scoffed at me like I was little more than an irritating mosquito. It was effortless for him to lift me off the ground and carry me toward the truck. The second man had gone inside. I fell limp as the man dropped me unceremoniously into the back of the truck. It was dark and windowless, no way out.

"Is your sister inside?" he asked firmly.

I lied instantly, praying the fear on my face would not betray *me*

"No. I was alone. She went to play with a friend."

He nodded and pulled the overhead door closed, plunging me into darkness.

That was the last time I saw the sun.

THE LIGHTS FLICKED ON and at the same time a bell chimed in the room. I had already woken up, my face wet with tears. The others began moving around me and from their faces I could tell I wasn't alone in my nightmares. I sat up in bed, pulling my blankets to the side and rising from the metal bunk. I reached beside my pillow to where my sling was crumpled, untangled it and pulled the straps over my head, securing my arm. The Velcro seemed oddly noisy in a room full of girls. No one spoke, each of us submerged in our own sorrows. We filed from the room, each pulling an identical sweater over our bare shoulders and a headscarf over our hair. No one bothered to knot them now; it was pointless for we'd be taking them off again in a few minutes.

For the second time in twelve hours we stood under the warm spray of the showers. The temperature was better today. I could still smell the cream I had covered myself with the night before, and as I washed myself it ran off my skin and down the drain. No matter. I would simply add another coat.

This time I finished more quickly, perhaps because I had more practice, and perhaps because I cared less about getting clean when I hadn't done anything to get dirty since the last shower. I wrapped the giant soft towel around myself and followed the others to the change room.

Some were applying the cream, filling the room with the sharp citrus and floral scent, while others were taking turns drying and combing each other's hair. Those with long hair pulled it back into braids to secure it tightly under their headscarf. Willow helped the others with their hair, as hers was too short to do anything with.

I sat on one of the benches and reached over to where one of the pots of lotion sat, dipped my fingers in and began to apply it to my legs. No one said much, but quiet conversation began to trickle from us. The shower had revived us—washed away the night and brought forth the day. Our tear-stained faces were gone, replaced with rosy cheeks from the warm water and steam.

I couldn't help but watch the others, but as I did, I noticed something strange.

"How come some of you don't have a cellutation tattoo?" I asked, my hand reaching to my own mark, an open circle, visible now on my right collarbone. I ran my fingers over it, feeling the lump of my broken clavicle beneath it. I had always understood it to be a standard inoculation, given to all babies upon birth to prevent most of the major diseases of the past. It involved a series of vaccinations that found and replaced cells that had the potential of developing into diseases like cancer, MS or ALS— diseases that had once plagued the population.

Kenzie was the one who answered. Perhaps they had this conversation already and I had missed it while I sat in the clinic.

"I was never cellutated," she said, pointing to her bare collarbone. "My family was part of a very religious sect, and they believed that death and disease we not ours to control."

This made no sense to me. What parents or societies would subject their people to the horrors of these diseases? Cellutation was a brilliant invention. It wasn't perfect of course; it had some side effects, especially when it came to procreation, but what good were lots of children if their mother could die early?

"There are four of us here who haven't been cellutated," said Willow, pointing at her own bare shoulder. "My family believed that health came from diet and exercise. I wasn't allowed sugar until I got here." She laughed. "There's only so much kale a girl can take,"

The others chuckled.

How kale would stop cancer I had no idea.

Four girls my age, all at risk for contracting those awful diseases—I had never really thought much about my own mark, it seemed as though everyone had them. It was standard after all. Yet, here, more than half of us didn't have the mark. Was that intentional or was it just that more people than I was aware of chose not to undergo the inoculations?

"I don't know why I wasn't inoculated," said Freya quietly. "No one was where I lived, and I didn't know about it until Margo explained it to me here." She winced as Willow pulled a brush through a snarl in her pale hair.

Hazel nodded along with Freya. Her collarbone was bare too.

I continued slathering myself in lotion, taking less care than I did the first time. We took turns holding up towels for each other so we could each get into our clothing with some small amount of privacy. Hazel held the towel for me again.

"Sorry I take so long," I said, struggling into my underwear.

She said nothing.

Willow, having finished everyone else's hair, came to me with the brush.

"May I?" she asked.

I nodded.

She was quick and thorough, her fingers dancing as they pulled my own amber-colored hair into a tight braid. I pulled the headscarf down over my head and left it hanging around my neck as she wrapped the braid around itself into a secure knot on the back of my head. She helped me pull the stretchy tube back over my hair, taking care to ensure no hair was visible on my forehead. She twisted the scarf at the back and knotted it in place.

"We need to get going," said Margo. "We're going to be late for breakfast."

I HAD ASSUMED WE would be setting the tables for breakfast before eating like we had the night before, but the counter was already full of food for us when we arrived. I joined the others, pulling the high stools across the floor to a place at our makeshift table.

"We always eat first," said Li, noting my confusion.

"Everyone else here sleeps later, and some don't bother with breakfast at all."

I couldn't see how anyone would skip a breakfast like this. Steaming bowls and platters heaped with food sat in front of us: scrambled eggs, oatmeal, pancakes, bacon, and fruit salad.

"Where are they getting the fruit from?" I asked. Surely there were no regular delivery trucks coming up the mountain to deliver it, and fresh fruit wouldn't last that long.

"It's a frozen mix," said Kenzie, "I saw it in the freezer."

"Tastes pretty good though," said Margo, helping herself to a heaping scoop.

We ate until we were full and the plates barely looked touched.

"Who eats the rest?" I asked. I doubted our leftovers would be served to those in the fancy dining room.

Willow shrugged. "The boys maybe? But we aren't allowed to be in here when anyone else comes."

Delta entered the room at that moment. In her hands was a small tray with seven disposable paper cups on it.

"I hope everyone saved room," she said with a hint of a smile.

I couldn't imagine eating anything else, but the cups were small.

The others laughed as she came around, each of them taking one of the cups from the tray. There was one cup left when she came to me. I glanced inside.

"Pills?" I asked.

"Vitamins," corrected Delta.

There had to be over a dozen of them—perhaps even as many as twenty—all different shapes and sizes and colors.

Hazel filled my empty glass with more orange juice.

"Cheers," said Margo.

"To health!" said Li, laughing as she raised her cup.

Delta left the room and I was about to open my mouth when Margo stopped me.

"Don't ask," she said. "We don't have a hot clue."

"It doesn't make any sense."

"We know."

I poured the vitamins into my hand and counted them. Seventeen.

"Don't bother asking Delta either," said Margo. "She's good with the 'how', but not so much with the 'why'".

The other girls chuckled as they downed the vitamins one after the other, swishing them down with sips of orange juice.

"You have to take them," whispered Hazel, concerned.

I nodded and placed the first few small ones in my mouth, the big ones would have to go down on their own. I felt them slide down my throat with a gulp of orange juice, and knew in that moment, I would never return to the Rhea I once was, languishing in the grass beneath the pecan tree.

NINE

THE DAYS BEGAN TO bleed together into a giant tapestry, each thread complementing the other but nearly indistinguishable from the last. We counted the days for a while, trying to keep track but it was difficult to gauge exactly what day it was. The snow had stopped blowing years ago yet nothing about the outside world had changed. Without the seasons it was difficult to tell, but since they celebrated most of the major holidays here, we had a rudimentary idea. We had been in this mountainside estate for over three years. Christmas had come again for the fourth time since we had arrived. It was always a festive time here, we were given tasks decorating trees that some brave soul had gone out and cut down. We hung garlands while they partied, and the smells of turkey and ham permeated the kitchens. We ate like kings when we had finished our work, and went to bed each night stuffed full of whatever delicacies they had.

Margo burped loudly on the bunk across the room. Li threw a pillow at her.

"Honestly Margo, do you have to be such a pig?"

"They feed us like them, why not?"

Kenzie shook her head and smiled slightly. She seemed

more down than usual. Christmas had been difficult for all of us, but in the last days the sun had come out, trickling daylight through the frosted windows. Perhaps there was hope.

"Are you ok?" I asked her quietly as the others chatted and joked around as if we were in some kind of pseudo-summer-camp.

"Today is my birthday," she said, "At least I think it is."

I wrapped my arm around her shoulders. I had been free of my sling for years now, and other than a lump where the bone hadn't quite come back together properly, I was feeling as good as ever.

I didn't want to ask if she missed her family, or if she wanted to talk about it. We had all talked ourselves half to death. Every one of us was in a similar situation, ripped from our homes and stranded here without so much as an idea why. I didn't need to ask her because I knew already. She felt the same things I did.

"Happy birthday," I said, pulling her small frame toward me and enveloping her into a hug.

"I'm nineteen years old today," she said, not because I didn't know, but more to hear the words herself.

We sat there for a long while, until Delta opened the red door. It was too early for our showers, but we all stopped what we were doing and readied ourselves for whatever task she was coming to bring us.

"Mackenzie?" she said.

Kenzie stood up, my hands dropped to the bunk.

"Come with me dear." She left the room and Kenzie followed, her eyes unsure.

This had never happened before. We were always together, and in fact we had been cautioned to never go anywhere by ourselves. I supposed following Delta wasn't really the same as going somewhere alone.

Kenzie didn't return. We waited for a while, had our showers and waited until the lights turned off. We didn't expect that she wouldn't come back. Even the next morning we assumed we would find her in bed with us, but when the lights came on and the bell chimed we could see that her bed hadn't changed from when she left it. It was still neatly made, exactly what one would expect from Kenzie.

She didn't join us at any time during breakfast, and when Delta came with our vitamins, she wouldn't answer any of the questions we peppered her with.

"She turned nineteen yesterday," I said to the others. "Do you think that has anything to do with it?"

It seemed like a rather large coincidence that they came for her on her birthday after we had been here for years.

"Could be," said Margo. "Though, unless we get some answers, we'll have to wait a while before we can confirm that. Who turns nineteen next?"

We all turned to Freya and Li. They were both fifteen when we arrived here.

"Me I think," said Freya, clearing her throat. "In February."

Li nodded. "My birthday is in May."

Mine was in June, but I was over a year younger than some of the older ones, I wasn't yet eighteen.

A chill swept through the room and suddenly the food I had eaten began to weigh heavily in my stomach.

"Does anyone know who these people are?" I asked. We had tried to have this discussion before, many times, but there was always a reason we didn't. Sometimes it was a fear of being monitored, or wanting to deny that the past three years were more than a dream. It was difficult for me to want to put a face to our captors, to the people who had taken us from our families. I felt like that would make it real somehow. I didn't want any of it to be real, even as days slipped into months and years. Denial was easiest. It was easy to deny since we didn't see most of the people who lived here. We lived in our own little bubble, set apart from the others. As I looked around, the other girls shook their heads.

"This is ridiculous," said Margo, standing up suddenly. "We need to know what's going on here, and I know how to find out."

She went to the door and stood on her tiptoes, peeking out the round window of the swinging door that separated us from the kitchens. Suddenly she smiled and with a sudden kick, swung the door open, reached out and pulled in a very surprised young man. His arms were full of dirty dishes, and he struggled to keep from dropping them.

"What in the blazes…" he said, regaining his balance. He looked up at the room of girls dressed in red from head to toe and his jaw dropped. He turned to leave, but Margo blocked his path.

"One more step and those dishes of yours are all over the floor," she said.

"I'm not supposed to be in here."

"Then answer some questions and you can leave."

He was close to our age, perhaps a few years older, tall and a bit gangly. He was the one I had spilled water onto. That moment seemed so long ago.

"What's your name?" asked Margo.

"Red," he said, "could you guys make this quick?"

"Do you have a girlfriend, Red?"

"Honestly?"

"Margo!" said Li, "get to the point."

Margo shrugged and laughed. "A girl can dream."

She focused her attention back on Red, he was growing more nervous. His hair made me wonder if the moniker "Red" was more of a nickname than his actual given name, since it was a rather shocking shade of red that blended in with the freckles that scattered down on his face and neck.

"Last question... who is in charge here?"

Red wavered and Margo stomped her heel into his toe.

"Leave me alone you menace!" said Red. "I honestly don't think you want to know."

"Who is it?" said Margo, leaning in to intimidate Red, who towered over her by a good six inches. "The mafia?"

Red laughed at that, a loud sudden burst which didn't make Margo look any more relaxed.

"Try again, sister. You have no idea what you're dealing with. Those aren't criminals out there. You have the honor of being hosted by a US Senator, the Chief Justice of the Supreme Court, the Chair of the Federal Reserve and the Vice-President of the

United States."

Margo stepped back in shock and Red took the opportunity to slide back out through the doorway, leaving us to absorb what he had said as the door swept back and forth to find its resting place.

I inhaled sharply. I couldn't believe I had forgotten. Everyone looked at me.

"I, I... I didn't even think..." I said.

Willow moved toward me. I stood suddenly and the stool I had been sitting on tipped over and fell to the ground with a bang. I was having trouble breathing and colors swam in front of my eyes.

"In the clinic... when I was hurt..."

"It's ok, Rhea, you can tell us."

"I... I saw Meredith Kroeker. She was unconscious."

The room was silent. I needed to sit down but my stool was gone so I collapsed to the floor. Willow dropped with me.

I didn't know what I had thought about where we were, but I knew it wasn't this. I knew the people who held us were rich, That was obvious. But to think we had been kidnapped by the most powerful people in the United States, and possibly the world, was beyond belief.

I DON'T KNOW HOW we got back to our room, but the next thing I knew, I was lying on my bed. The others sat around on the lower bunks too, silent and sullen. It was one thing to think that some bad guys came for us for some nefarious purpose, but an entirely different thing to learn that the people tasked with running the country, the people we needed to trust in times of difficulty were behind this. We must have misunderstood something. Governments don't kidnap fourteen and fifteen-year-old girls.

"Ok," said Willow, "We need to puzzle this out. Does anyone remember the names of any of these people?"

"Obviously Meredith Kroeker is here, She's the President, assuming she's still alive," said Li. "And the Vice-President is Nadia Black."

We didn't have any paper or pens, but we all did our best to commit everything to memory.

"There's no way we could guess which senator we're dealing with, there are too many of them," said Margo, "But I think the Chief Justice of the Supreme Court is Alexandra O'Claire."

I nodded. I remembered that name from a Politics class I had taken in school. "That sounds right to me too."

"Ok, we have three names," said Willow. "Anyone know who the Federal Reserve person is?"

I shook my head, and looking around I could see others doing the same thing.

"Her name is Vita," said a quiet voice. Hazel was curled in a ball on Freya's bunk with her back against the wall. "Vita Caruthers."

"Whoa, Hazel! Good show!" said Margo, "How did you know that?"

Hazel's lip quivered and a tear slipped from her eye and traced a path down her cheek. "My mother worked for the Federal Reserve. Mrs. Caruthers...Vita... was her boss."

We said nothing. What was there to say?

That ache that held us captive, that constant wrench in the pit of our stomachs wasn't going anywhere fast, and even the institutions we had been trained to trust were failing us. The world had frozen and we had survived. Even if it ever melted, it wasn't going to be the same world we left.

WE DIDN'T GET ANY more answers for more than a week. The lights had been off at least an hour by then, and I could hear the soft snores of some of the other girls. Margo and Hazel always seemed able to fall asleep much more quickly than the rest of us. I tended to spend a few hours every night tossing and turning in the dark and trying to settle my mind.

I heard the click of the doorknob turning and my heart leaped from my chest. I inhaled and readied myself to scream.

"Kenzie?" someone said.

Kenzie?

We hadn't seen her since the day Delta came to take her away.

"Shhh," she said, sliding into the room. She was dressed in a white robe with long sleeves and a white headscarf that mimicked the ones we wore, and she seemed almost ethereal in the dim light of the moon that filtered through the window. "I can't stay for long; I'll be in so much trouble if they find out, but I had to come here."

I stood to face her, standing across from her.

"What happened to your face?" I asked, gasping quietly.

She had a deep purple bruise on her cheekbone and a swollen cut on her lip.

She shook her head and covered her face with a pale hand. Her skin had barely more color than the dress she wore.

"Why did they take you?" Willow asked, standing to embrace tiny Kenzie in her arms. By now we were all awake and gathered around.

"I still don't know, but I think it's something big. They've been keeping me in the clinic, you know, where they did our testing when we first got here?"

I shuddered at the mention.

"I get injections multiple times a day, and I think they're doing some kind of testing on me. I don't know, but I needed to tell you."

"We were so worried," said Li.

"I don't think what I'm telling you will help with that, but I wanted you to know I was still alive."

"Of course you're alive, why wouldn't you be?"

"I don't know. Some of it hurts. I don't know what they're doing to me."

She wept there, a cloud of white surrounded by a sea of red.

"But the worst part..."

She reached her hand up to her headscarf and pulled it slowly off her head.

Her hair was gone.

Every last bit of her beautiful black waves were gone.

We gasped collectively and swarmed her, each of us reaching out to comfort her. It seemed like nothing in comparison, but there was something about that simple loss, some stripping of the girl we knew that chewed at our hearts.

We cried together.

Suddenly the door banged open again.

"Good grief, Mackenzie, you need to get out of here."

Delta was standing at the door.

"Thank your lucky stars I noticed you were gone before they did. If we're fortunate we can get you back before anyone realizes you left." Her voice was brusque and stern but in some small way, relieved. Kenzie pulled her headscarf back onto her head and rushed to Delta who pulled her through the door and out into the hallway.

"The rest of you, back in bed."

The door slammed behind them and we were plunged into darkness again. We stood there in silence for a few minutes, unable to move, unable to think.

As we crawled back into bed a siren shrieked through the halls and we looked at each other. Had they caught her? Had she made it back in time? We had no way of knowing.

I don't think I slept at all the rest of the night, and though no one spoke another word, I doubted I was alone.

TEN

FREYA WAS THE NEXT one to leave us. This time we wept together on the eve of her birthday.

"I wish I could cut it all off right now," said Freya twisting her fingers into her white-blond hair. "It would be easier doing it here with all of you than letting them do it."

We had no scissors or anything that could help her, so we remained silent.

After Kenzie left we had grown more diligent about keeping track of the days, so we knew for sure which day they would come for Freya. Margo had pocketed a pencil from the kitchen and had entrusted Hazel with keeping the calendar. It took her a few hours of laborious work to draw a yearly calendar on the wall, marked with each of our birthdays. Freya would be first, then Li, followed by Margo and Willow. I was second-last, and Hazel would be the final one. Kenzie still hadn't returned and we hadn't seen her since the night in our room. For a while we had tried asking Delta, but she was unwilling, or unable to respond to our constant questions. I could see the pity in her eyes—that spark that she wanted to tell us something, anything. We could wear her down eventually, I thought, but it was too much. Secretly I think we all preferred not to know.

"I don't think I can do this," Freya said softly.

"You can," said Margo.

"How can you be so sure?"

"Because you don't have a choice."

"I can die."

"You can, but you won't"

Freya shook her head. "You can't know that."

"If they had wanted us dead, they would have killed us a long time ago," said Margo, who by now had stood up and was pacing the tiny room. "But no, they fed us, kept us healthy, freakishly clean and gave us piles of vitamins that probably cost them a small fortune. What would be the point of all that if they were just going to kill us."

"I don't know," said Willow. "They could need healthy subjects for their tests, but how can we know the tests themselves won't kill us?"

That silenced Margo. Without knowing what they were testing for, there was no way to know.

Willow glanced at Freya and her mouth dropped open.

"Oh, goodness, Freya, I'm sorry! I didn't mean to say it like that!"

Freya shook her head.

"It was the truth."

"Can't we do something?" I asked.

"What do you mean?" asked Li.

"I don't know. I just feel so useless sitting here waiting to be herded off into some lab. Can't we escape or something?"

"We don't even know where we could go," said Willow. "That snow has been out there for years already, and it's cold. Really cold. Even the insides of the windows are frozen"

It was true. They had stopped using the main dining room recently because it was impossible to keep warm—the majority of the walls and a good chunk of the ceiling was glass. It was now being used as a kind of cold storage room, housing extra furniture from the other large interior room they had repurposed into the new dining room. It wasn't as opulent as the other room, but it was warm. Sometimes we would go into the old dining room after our kitchen work was done to spend a few minutes in a sunbeam. There was no other place we were allowed that had windows like that. No one seemed to care if we made ourselves into popsicles for a few minutes, as long as we stayed out of sight of those in charge. We now knew the schedule better, and as long as we could skirt around the important people, and reported for our duties and curfews no one paid much attention to us. Margo was the first one to go off on her own. She didn't do anything dangerous, but I think she just wanted to test the waters. She snuck off to the kitchen after our showers and before curfew, and came back with a plate of chocolate cake.

"The girls in the kitchen are really sweet," she had said as we took turns nibbling on the moist rich cake. "Terribly stupid, but sweet."

"I think Meredith Kroeker is still alive," Margo had told us. "They've been making purees in the kitchen for her, and they said something about a feeding tube. I heard some of the boys talking about the temperature. I don't think their thermometers even go low enough."

It was cold. Dangerously cold. I knew there were supplies and things we could use to brave the cold, but how could we get them? And even if we could, where would we go? It was a grim reality that there were probably a lot of people out there that weren't prepared for this, and if all the country's leaders were here with us... who was out there helping everyone else?

"Let's not talk about this," said Freya. "Can we talk about something else? Anything? Something happy. I need to pretend for a while."

No one said anything. It was difficult to think of something fun to talk about.

"Freya... did you kiss Red?" asked Margo.

Freya gasped and her creeks flushed. "Margo!"

Margo laughed. "You said you wanted to talk about something else."

"I didn't mean..."

"You did, didn't you."

Freya didn't say anything, but the answer was plain on her face.

"I knew it."

Freya had been sweet on Red since the moment Margo pulled him through the swinging kitchen door. Margo may have been the first to venture out on her own, but Freya was by far the most frequent. She usually didn't go far, she told us, just far enough to find a dark room or hallway to meet Red without Delta or anyone else noticing. She would come back to our rooms glowing and happy, a beacon among the dull drudgery here.

We all burst out laughing as Freya turned a deeper shade of red. Then the questions wouldn't stop.

"Was he a good kisser?"

"What was it like?"

"Are you in love?"

Freya giggled and for a moment I felt like we were girls again, schoolgirls at a sleepover, sharing about the boys in their class. If I couldn't feel that underlying tension and fear I could almost feel happy right now—but the fear would never leave me.

When we crawled into our beds that night, knowing tomorrow Delta would come for another one of us, we were sullen and somber. Any lightness we'd had earlier was gone, and the knot in my stomach tightened again.

THEN, FREYA WAS GONE too.

"And then there were five," said Willow as we all stared at the red door that had just closed behind another of our friends. There was nothing more we could say.

ELEVEN

"WHAT ARE YOU DOING?"

I knew the voice without turning around. It was Jude.

"Nothing much," I said. "It's just nice to feel the sun sometimes."

I was standing in the old dining room. I came here daily after we finished our lunch duties. It was the exact time the sunbeams passed out of the shadow of the trees and bore down directly on the room.

"It's freezing in here," he said as he sat down beside me.

I nodded. It didn't matter to me. I had my sweater, and the cold was invigorating sometimes. The others had gone back to our room, but I needed a few minutes alone. I had my sweater pulled tightly around me and I was sitting on a couch that had been covered in some old white sheets. All the furniture in here was covered, presumably to protect it from the sun or maybe dust. Whatever the reason it gave the room the appearance of not being a room at all, but rather a continuation of the rolling drifts of snow outside—and I sat in the middle of it, drenched in red like a splotch of blood dripped on a snowy path.

"What are you doing in here then?" I asked him, without

turning. I had come across Jude in the hallways a few times over the last months, but I had never been able to meet his eyes. I never knew quite how to feel around him.

I had celebrated my eighteenth birthday two days earlier. It was now June and still there was no reprieve to the cold, and no sign the winter might end. I still had another year before I followed my sisters into the lab. I had truly begun to think of them as sisters now, for what else were we? I wouldn't have called us friends, since it was unlikely my friends would have included someone as loud and bossy as Margo, or someone as delicately elegant as Freya. We were stuck together with no choice in the matter, and forced to love each other. Sisters.

Li had gone now too, and Margo, leaving only Willow, Hazel and I. We would have until October before Willow left us, and then it would only be Hazel and I until the following June. We tended to spend more time alone than we did before. None of us that were left were terribly animated people, so there was little lightness to our group anymore. Willow had withdrawn more and more as one by one the girls left us, and Hazel had never been one to add much to the conversation, so even though I didn't really know how to talk to Jude, I was thankful for a bit of company.

"To be honest, I saw you here," he said. "You stand out."

I wouldn't in another year. Then I would be almost invisible in here.

I nodded. "The red."

"That's not what I meant."

I didn't know how to answer, but I glanced up at him.

He was taller than I was, but not outrageously so. Sitting on the couch next to me, I could look him in the eye, though his legs stretched out in front of him farther than mine did.

He was watching me with a twinkle in his eye.

"It's not funny," I said, noting the way his lip was turned up and his eyes wrinkled at the corner with whatever amusement he was thinking.

"I'm not laughing," he said, suddenly stone-faced.

There were five of them that I had seen. Before Margo left she had taken a liking to Harris, and was nearly beaten by the patrol who found her out of our room in the middle of the night. She said it was nothing real, just some messing around—an amusement to keep her mind off the ever-nearing deadline. I didn't entirely believe her. She was Margo, after all. Under all her puffery and bravado she was a girl like the rest of us—a girl who needed to be loved, wherever she could find it.

Jude and Red were two others, as well as Vaughn and Finn. I liked Finn from what I could tell. He was the tallest and gangliest of the bunch of them, possibly four or five inches taller than Jude. He was a prankster, and the cooks in the kitchen were constantly yelling at him.

"It needed a bit more pepper," he had winked at me once in the hall as he ran from the verbal assaults being hurled at him from the kitchen.

"It was just an extra cup—barely a smidgen!" He had called back at the cooks as he laughed and ran.

"To be honest," Jude said. "I'm here on official business."

"Official business?"

"Well," he said. "Official business of the heart."

My eyes widened as I looked up at him again. His eyes were twinkling.

"Vaughn is quite... hm, what is the right word... yes... Vaughn is quite besotted with you."

"Vaughn?" I tried to hide the disappointment from my eyes. I barely knew Vaughn. I didn't think I had ever exchanged so much as a word with him.

Jude shrugged. "That's what he tells me."

"I didn't realize Vaughn had a voice."

"Mmm, yes, he does," Jude said, "but it only comes out with a bunch of blushing and stammering, especially when he talks about you. Hence the reason I'm sitting here and not him."

"Is he listening?" I said, slightly horrified that he might have snuck in here among the stored furniture.

"No, no," said Jude, "He's more likely to be cowering in his bunk. It's ok, I can tell him you're not interested in men."

I raised an eyebrow. "How did you know?"

He snickered.

"I'll let him down easy."

"Thanks."

We sat in silence for a few minutes.

"Do you know what they're doing with us?" I asked.

He shook his head.

"If you did would you tell me?"

"Probably. Unless they're grinding you guys up and making

you into soup," he said. "Then I'd let it be a surprise."

He said it with such a note of seriousness that it took me a minute to understand his words.

"Jude!"

He snickered.

"I know as much as you guys do," he said, "on your nineteenth birthday they take you to the lab. We deliver food there usually, but I don't see anyone, and no one tells me anything."
I didn't answer.

"I would tell you though, if I knew" he said quietly. "It's cruel to leave you in the dark."

"Thanks."

I let out a slow breath.

"Were you taken too?" I asked. The words were out of my mouth before I had fully formed them.

"Taken?" he said and shook his head. "No. All five of us were pages at the White House. Good job if you ask me. I've been doing it since I was a kid."

"Didn't you go to school?"

"Oh, sure, they had a tutor for all of us. I learned me some sums," he winked. "But no, I didn't go to a normal school if that's what you're asking."

"Your parents agreed to that?"

"I didn't have parents," he said. "None of us did. We're the only family we have, well, us and Delta."

"Delta?"

"Yeah, she raised us."

"At the White House?"

He lifted his hands in surrender. "Don't ask me. They run a 'don't ask, don't tell' policy over there. I assume you're familiar."

I nodded.

"Are you sure they didn't kidnap you?"

He laughed.

"Maybe if we were girls, but since we're male, it's more likely we were abandoned."

I didn't understand.

"Girls are far more valuable, obviously. Women hold all the power. Look at the balance here, it's the women calling the shots, has been for years."

I knew that, obviously. I knew that a long time ago the balance had shifted from a patriarchal to a matriarchal system, but I had no idea boys were being abandoned because of it. "The orphanages were full of boys, never girls. I guess we were some of the lucky ones."

"You feel lucky?" I asked.

"Sure. Without Delta and my job here, I'd be out there," he pointed at the snow. "Instead, I'm here, talking to you."

"I guess when you think about it like that..."

I didn't know where I would be if they hadn't taken me. I had no idea if my family had made it somewhere safe. It had been almost exactly four years now. It was unlikely that they would have survived unless they had found a place to go.

"I should go," Jude said, standing up. "I need to go break Vaughn's tender heart."

"Don't say it like that."

Jude laughed. "Don't worry, it's not the first time. Vaughn goes through crushes faster than a dog goes through bacon. Next week he'll be on to someone else."

I nodded. "That makes me feel special."

He laughed again. I enjoyed the sound of his laugh.

"Do you need anything, sister?"

"My name is Rhea."

"Do you need anything Rhea?" he repeated.

I started to shake my head, but then thought of something.

"Do you think you could find a deck of cards?" I asked. "It gets so boring, and the other girls don't talk much. Maybe I could get us playing something, or at least, I could talk to the Jacks or something."

Jude nodded. "I'll see what I can do."

"Thanks," I said.

He turned to leave.

"Jude," I said, stopping him before he could leave. "Thank you."

I wanted to say more, to thank him for taking care of me that first day, for being so gentle and being the first person that seemed to care whether I lived or died, but I didn't. I think he still understood.

TWO DAYS LATER THERE was a knock at the red door. We had just arrived back from our shower. No one knocked on our door. The only people that used it were us and Delta, and she never knocked.

I went to the door and opened it. There was no one there. I moved to close it when Hazel stopped me.

"What's that?"

I looked where she was pointing. On the floor, leaning against the door frame was a single deck of cards. I picked them up and on the box was scrawled

"Three girls, four queens, four kings and four jacks. Sounds like a party!"

I laughed and closed the door. A party indeed.

TWELVE

"WHAT ON EARTH ARE you doing, Hazel?"

We had been getting dressed after our morning shower. Delta hadn't bothered to stay until we were all dressed, she rarely did anymore. She completed her duty by watching us shower, though "watching" was probably a stretch. She sat in the corner and read a book.

Hazel had snuck back into the shower room once she left, and when she returned, she was carrying something.

"What is that?" I asked.

"Hair," she said.

Hazel had apparently gone over the deep end once and for all.

"Our hair?" asked Willow.

"Probably not much of yours," said Hazel. "Looks more like mine and Rhea's."

I gagged.

"You pulled our hair out of the drain?"

She nodded, nonplussed. It was as if that was a completely normal thing to do. Carefully she curled the slimy lump up in her towel and carried it back to our room. She smiled. I gagged again.

IT WAS FREEZING IN the dining room that afternoon, but I had borrowed an extra sweater and pair of socks from our closet, so I was warm enough. I had made myself a comfortable spot on one of the couches, where I knew the sun would linger longest. The deck of cards was in my pocket and I pulled it out, shuffling mindlessly and then laying out a complicated game of solitaire on the cushions beside me. I was leaning back on the armrest to savor the silence, when I heard the creak of footsteps on the hardwoods behind me. I smiled. It was no accident that I came here every day. Jude knew he could find me here, so I did my best to make myself available. He didn't always come, but when he did I enjoyed our conversation. It was nice to talk to someone else, someone not dressed in red from head to toe, someone who wasn't living and trying in vain to understand the same nightmare. He had a nightmare of his own, I knew, but we didn't need to think about it here. We could just be for a minute.

I turned my head to peek out over the back of the couch, ready with a witty remark.

"Sorry, am I disturbing you?"

It wasn't Jude's voice.

I jumped as I looked directly into the bespectacled eyes of a man who seemed about the same age as my father, perhaps a little older. He could have been the same age, since even my father would have aged some since the last time I saw him. He was balding a bit on top, and little squishy around the middle where my father had been lean and firm.

Before I knew it, I was on my feet, flustered, my playing cards scattering in a flurry to the floor. I had never seen this man before but I knew to the core of my being that we were not supposed to be having a conversation.

"I'm sorry," I said, dropping to my knees and frantically trying to gather the cards up. I knew I'd never get them all, but I could come back to find the rest later.

"No," the man said. "Don't go."

He hurried around the couch and dropped to his knees beside me, reaching to help collect the cards.

"Really," he said as he handed me a few. "I'm not trying to get you in trouble."

I watched him from the corner of my eye as he reached under the couch to pick up an ace that had slid out of sight beneath the draped sheet.

"Do you know how to play anything other than Solitaire?" he asked.

I nodded. I had been teaching Hazel and Willow how to play whatever card games I could remember. Our favorite was probably War, since it never seemed to end and required no scorekeeping, though it grew tedious after a few days. Not much better than endless games of "Rock, Paper, Scissors". I knew how to play a lot of card games, but for most of them the rules were a bit fuzzy, definitely not clear enough to explain them to others. I had always relied on my father to keep track of the score and remind me of the rules as we went.

"Do you know how to play Gin Rummy?" he asked.

I nodded again. It had been a while, but I had played it in the past.

"If you know the rules, I can play along, but I would need a refresher," I said, my voice soft and muted in the giant room.

"I'm an excellent player, myself," he said. "Though it's been a long time since I've had an opponent."

He took the cards from my hands and helped me to my feet. There was a table nearby, one that hadn't been needed when they moved the dining hall. It was smaller than most of the grand dining tables, but had a few chairs propped upside-down on top of it. He reached for a chair and set it on the ground, motioning for me to sit while taking down another one for himself.

"I think we have them all," he said as he flipped through and counted the cards with a speed and grace that mimicked my father. When satisfied, he began to shuffle them and smartly dealt us each ten cards for our hands.

I slowly slid them to the edge of the table and took a quick stock of my situation. I was seated in an ideal place, able to keep my eye on both him and the door to the kitchen. I'd see if anyone looked through and saw us. It wasn't likely there would be anyone in the kitchen at this hour. Lunch service was finished and they wouldn't need to start cooking dinner for at least another hour. I had fears Jude would come. As many times as we had spoken, I still didn't know how he fit into this whole situation, or where his loyalties laid. I knew he had been raised by Delta, and though I hoped his first thought if he saw me here was to ask me before running to her, I couldn't know for sure.

"What's your name?" asked the man, flipping through his hand, rearranging the cards into whatever pattern suited him.

"Rhea," I said. There was no sense lying about it.

"Pleased to make your acquaintance Rhea, My name is Simeon."

I nodded as I too glanced at my cards, quickly sliding some into place behind others. I had a good hand, a few small runs and some pairs that I could make into sets if I was lucky.

His name didn't strike me as familiar, but that wasn't unusual. No one other than Jude had even mentioned who lived here, and none of the information he told us was names anyway. Based on his expensive clothing I was sure he wasn't one of the staff here, making this meeting more dangerous for me than him.

"You might know of my wife," he said, "She's a senator, Tess McAllister."

The name was familiar, and did me a service. We hadn't known who the senator was, and now, at the very least, I could finalize our list of captors. I made a mental note and nodded.

"I've heard of her."

I picked up a card from the pile, sliding it into place beside another pair that matched it, and discarded one of my trouble cards.

"She's not terribly nice," he said, his voice low and steady.

I said nothing. There was no "right" response to that kind of statement. I was most inclined to agree with him, seeing as how I was taken from my family, but I was smart enough to know the folly in making those feelings known.

"Don't get me wrong, she's beautiful and powerful, and a long time ago I did love her."

I grew exceeding less comfortable with the one-sided conversation, and he soon noticed my stiff posture and flushed face.

"I'm sorry, Rhea. I didn't mean to drop that all so soon," he said, "It's just been so long since there was someone I could talk to, someone for whom every thought wasn't the next move of some unknown power struggle. I'm up to my limit in strategy and planning and scenarios. Don't mind my old soul, freeing a few demons."

He laughed, his voice light and free in the chilled air. It was cold enough in here that I could see his breath, though he wore nothing more than a crisp collared shirt.

"Aren't you cold?" I asked, feeling instantly embarrassed and wishing I could take the words back.

He looked up over his cards and winked at me.

"Apparently you have never met my wife," he said. "I'm no stranger to frigid temperatures."

I must have looked shocked.

"It's ok," he said. "It was a joke, you can laugh."

I forced a smile that I hoped looked more sheepish than terrified.

"Oh, darn," he said, glancing down at the gold watch that dangled around his wrist. "I had less time than I thought I did. I need to get going."

A sense of relief flooded through me. I hadn't seen anyone at the door. It was entirely possible I would make it out of here before anyone saw.

"Rhea, is there anything I can do to help you?" he asked suddenly.

Inwardly I cursed that he wasn't leaving.

"I'd like a one-way ticket home," I said before the words had formed fully in my brain. In fact, I just wanted him to leave.

The edges of his mouth turned down and I could see a kind of unknown sadness in them.

"I can't help with that one," he said, "Even if it was possible. We're snowed in here for a while. The scouts haven't found a safe way off this mountain yet, and I would venture to guess you know what happened to our last helicopter"

I nodded.

"Is there anything else? Do you need something that will help make your stay here a little more... comfortable? I see you have a deck of cards already."

"A book or two?" I asked. "We spend a lot of time doing nothing. It would be nice to read."

"That I can help with," he said, a smile lighting his eyes. He was an attractive man, or would have once been. His hair was dark, but streaked in places with bright silver, and it waved around his ears in a pleasing way. I liked the way his eyes crinkled when he laughed.

"Can we do this again?" he asked. "I've so missed pleasant conversation."

"I didn't say much," I said.

"I know, but maybe next time you will?"

I knew that if this was what he had in mind, I had little power to stop it.

"I won't get in trouble?"

"I'll do my best to prevent that from happening," he said in a deeper tone, as if he held some authority over the matter.

I knew he didn't, but nodded anyhow.

"See you again, Rhea," he said as he stood and left the room, leaving me alone at the table. He vanished through the doors, and for a moment I wondered if the last ten minutes had actually happened, my mind betrayed only by the doors, still swinging back and forth.

THE KNOCK AT THE door still startled us. I knew some books would arrive soon, but it was unnerving to know someone was on the other side of the red door and be unable to guess who it might be.

I opened the door and immediately looked to the ground, where I thought I might find a book leaning on the doorframe, as I had found the deck of cards. I saw boots, boots that were tapping impatiently.

Startled, I leapt back as a hand shot forward, grabbing my arm and pulling me into the hall. I yelped like a dog, unable to control my voice.

"Do you have any idea what you're doing?" a voice hissed

at me.

Jude.

I tried to free my arm from his tight grasp, but he wouldn't budge. I was fully in the hall now, and the door had closed behind me. I knew Hazel and Willow would be worried about my sudden departure.

"I don't know what you're talking about," I said.

He glared at me, his eyes holding a pointed look as he held up a stack of books.

"What on earth are you doing with Simeon?"

"Nothing."

He raised his eyebrows and waited.

"He showed up in the old dining room and wanted to play cards. What was I supposed to do?"

"Run?" he said, "Hide?"

"He didn't really seem scary," I said, remembering the uncomfortable time we had spent. I had been terrified at the time, but not of him.

"He's not the problem," said Jude, his voice even and firm.

"I know that."

"Do you?"

I nodded. I knew how dangerous it was. I had seen the bruises on Kenzie's face when she snuck out to tell us where she had gone, but what was I supposed to do?

"If you know so well," said Jude, "Maybe you should start by staying in your room."

His words stung, as intended. I had only been in the dining

room in hopes that maybe Jude would find me there. I had no idea Simeon would wander through the kitchen, to my knowledge he never had before. None of them did. How would I have guessed he would be the one to slide silently through the swinging doors?

I yanked my arm from Jude, defiant, and turned to face him, so I could look him squarely in the eyes

"I didn't do anything wrong."

He didn't respond, but handed the small stack of books to me. His mouth was open and I could see he wanted to say something, but was holding himself back.

I took the books and he backed away from me.

"Be careful, Rhea. You don't know what these people are capable of."

I let out the breath I was holding, and my shoulders slumped as Jude turned and walked away. The books felt heavier in my hands than they should have, carrying all the added weight of misplaced expectations and intentions. I leaned back on the door and watched him go. I wished I could run after him, I wished he could explain what he meant. I wished...

Suddenly my body lurched as the door opened and I found myself falling into the room in a heap of red fabric.

"Sorry Rhea," said Willow, giggling. "We were just worried and wanted to peek."

She reached down from where she stood at the door and helped me to my feet.

"Are those books?" Hazel asked, her eyes wide.

I handed them to her and brushed off a sore spot on my

tailbone. It would likely bruise from the tumble.

"Where did you get these?"

"Long story. I'll tell you tomorrow."

It was nearly curfew anyway, I didn't even care to know what books Simeon had sent Jude to bring to me. I didn't want to talk about any of it. I pulled the blanket back, let my sweater fall from my shoulders and tossed it on the empty bunk above me. None of us bothered to use the upper bunks anymore and the other girls weren't coming back. I slid between the red sheets of my red bed and yanked the red headscarf off my head as I settled it into a dent in my pillow.

The lights flicked off.

I wished everything was different.

THIRTEEN

IT WAS A WEEK before I bothered to look at the books Simeon had sent for me, which was strange because I had taken Jude's advice and had spent most of my free time in our room. Hazel and Willow spent a lot of time reading now, but for some reason I wasn't up to it. I had loved to read once. I would devour books from the library until towering stacks threatened to engulf me and Mother would tell me to take them back. Maybe it was because I had never felt fully satisfied—it was easier to spend my time lapping up the stories of others than making any of my own.

I was part of a story now and I didn't like it.

There was no chance of a happy ending, that was sure, and definitely no chance for a love-interest. I embodied none of the characteristics of a good heroine, but all of the struggles.

Finally, I was beyond bored. With a great sigh I rolled over in my bunk so I was lying on my stomach. We had kept the books on the bunk that sat beside mine, no one slept there. Willow and Hazel slept on the other side of the room. Neither of them was with me, which was odd, since typically it was me who would be found wandering the halls during our time off.

Reaching through the bars at the head of my bed I pulled

the books onto my pillow one at a time, enjoying the way they felt, greeting them like old, forgotten friends. They were all old, and well-read, some of them were missing chunks of the cover, or were dog-eared in places. There were five in total. I assumed Simeon hadn't been sure what to send for me, so had collected a mix. Two books I remembered from my childhood, books about children in a school for wizards. I had read them before, but would gladly escape to them again, though I was sure there were earlier books in the series that weren't there. It didn't matter much. I knew the story well, and they were long enough to keep me busy for a while. One of the books looked a little too "romantic" for my tastes, with a shirtless man on the cover supporting a buxom brunette as a horse reared in the background. This book too had been well-read, and had a tendency to fall open to the same pages. Uninterested, I tossed it onto the bed. The fourth book seemed intriguing, about a time long ago when men were in power and women waited for marriage and children rather than choosing their own destinies. I knew it had been like that once, but I had never really read a book like that. It seemed strange and foreign. I tossed the two child-wizard books on the other bunk too. I would read them later.

The fifth book was one I had never heard of. It was an old book, faded and worn and it wasn't very big, but when I looked at the cover I gasped. It depicted two women standing at a wall, dressed entirely in red with the exception of a strange white hat. They were shapeless, though I knew they were women. The title of the book was *The Handmaid's Tale*, by Margaret Atwood. Neither the title nor the author sounded familiar to me, but without even cracking the book open I knew Simeon was trying to tell me something, or better yet, show me.

I opened the book, leaving the other one unread on the pillow beside me, and began to read. I read until it was time for dinner service, and in every spare moment I had. When it was nearly curfew I sat up, looked at Hazel and Willow with tears in my eyes.

"I know why we're here."

"IT CAN'T BE TRUE," said Willow, "You've just been reading a book, it's fiction, Rhea."

We were whispering in the dark, unable to contain the revelations I had found in the book Simeon had sent. I had given them a quick synopsis, where women were arrested and made into "Handmaidens", women whose job it was to have sex with the "Husbands" to bear children for the "Wives" who no longer could due to some kind of pollution.

"But don't you see the similarities?" I asked.

"Sure, we wear red, just like them... But it's not the same. There's no way something like that could happen now."

I had looked at the date on the copyright page. It said the book had been published in 1985.

"See, that was decades ago," said Hazel. "That was back when men were in control, and had all the positions of power. Why would a society that placed all its hopes on women, steal girls from their homes and force them to have sex with men?"

I shook my head. "I know all of this, and it's not like I think it's exactly the same, but..."

I didn't know how to explain it any better. I hadn't told the girls where the books had come from, they had just assumed Jude brought them, like the cards. My gut feelings would have made more sense to them if they had known who really gave them to me, but I didn't want to tell them that. Jude knew already and he was one person too many.

"You heard Kenzie," said Willow, "it's medical testing. They need us to figure something out. If they had been taking her to breed with random men, she would have told us."

All of their arguments were sane and rational; perhaps I was letting my fear get the best of me. I so wanted to figure this all out, find reason in the madness, and maybe I had taken the few similarities between myself and that book and made them more than they really were.

"I don't know," I said, my voice barely perceptible in the quiet dark room.

"Neither do we," said Hazel. "But I definitely hope you're wrong."

FOURTEEN

HAZEL SLIPPED BACK INTO the room with a giggle, slamming the door behind her. I glanced up from my book. I had started reading a different one in hopes of taking my mind off the crazy comparisons I was making with The Handmaid's Tale.

She was close to glowing with some unknown delight, unusual for Hazel who was typically so shy, and spent much of her time living inside her head. It was interesting to see her so animated.

"What's up Hazel?" asked Willow, playing solitaire on the floor.

Hazel grinned and pulled a pair of scissors from the deep pockets of her sweater.

"Gonna kill us all?" I asked.

"Better," she said, walking over to her bunk.

"What could be better than that?" asked Willow.

Hazel didn't answer, but dropped to her knees and began rummaging under her bed. None of us owned anything, and the only things we had that didn't go in the clothing closet were the books and the deck of cards.

"What are you looking for?"

Again, she said nothing, but pulled something out, and settled onto the floor cross-legged with a triumphant smile on her face.

In her hand was the ball of dried-up shower-drain hair.

"Hazel! Honestly?" said Willow, the disgust plain on her face.

"What are you doing with that?"

Hazel studied us seriously. "I think we need one tiny little spot of joy in our lives," she said.

"You've got problems if that's your idea of joy."

She rolled her eyes.

"The joy comes in what I'm going to do with it," she said with a wink. "Rhea, pass me one of those books... the trashy one."

I tossed it over to her and when it landed on the floor it fluttered open to the same page it always did.

Hazel took a great amount of pleasure carefully tearing out one of the pages from that section.

"Hazel! First collecting drain hair, and now destroying literature?"

"It's a stretch to call this literature and you know it."

She had me there.

Carefully she laid the page on the floor and holding the clump of hair, she began to cut, chewing on her lip as she concentrated, reducing the hair to a pile of dust that collected on the paper.

"Are you going to tell us what you're up to?" I asked finally.

Willow and I had been exchanging confused looks.

"I'm adding a bit of spice to dessert tonight," she said, snorting with laughter. "You might not want to partake."

IT WAS FAR MORE difficult to get the dessert plated these days, since there were only three of us now, but we managed. It was peach cobbler with whipping cream, and a sprinkle of love from the sisters in red. It did seem somewhat cathartic to pull the prank, and as disgusting as it was, I had to hand it to Hazel. She really pulled it off. We could barely contain our laughter as Finn stopped in to collect the final tray. Willow had warned the boys, the only people who had been friendly in this place. It wasn't meant for them, after all. When the last of the desserts were sent out, we prepared a clean set for them and for ourselves.

"I wish I could just march in there and tell them what they're eating," said Hazel.

"You wouldn't make it to the door before running away, you mouse," said Willow.

"Hey, I never would have thought she'd be the one to enact any kind of revenge," I said as I spooned some cobbler into my mouth. "They broke her. Who knows what she's going to do next."

She blushed and ate a heaping spoonful of whipped cream, gleefully enjoying our dastardly deed.

We heard the scream and the gunshot.

For a moment, no one breathed.

Willow's spoon paused at her open mouth, and I watched in slow motion as the cobbler slipped from it and splattered on her lap. There was a tiny window on the swinging door that led to the kitchen, and we could see a commotion outside as, like us, the cooks and serving staff tried to understand what was happening.

Hazel was as pale as the peeling plaster walls, stark against the red of her clothing. Even Willow's dark skin seemed stark and ashen. We didn't move. People rushed back and forth past the window, never in a consistent direction. Which way would we go? Where had the sound come from?

The door burst open as we sat, stunned and paralyzed. In piled Jude, Finn, Red, Vaughn and Harris, each of them clutching butter knives. Finn reached out, slammed his hand onto the light switch and plunged us all into darkness.

"Get down, all of you," whispered Jude, beckoning us to the wall where they were crouched below the window on the door. Harris quietly slid the lock into place and we all huddled on the floor together. It didn't escape my notice that Hazel had slid in next to Vaughn and was clutching his hand.

"What's going on?" I asked, as loudly as my terror would allow me. I had never heard a real gunshot before; its sound was as foreign to me as the roar of a lion, reserved only for television—and the scream. The scream would haunt me. It was a woman. That much I could tell. Beyond that, I only knew of three females who were definitely safe.

"I'm not entirely sure yet," said Jude. With his back on the door he slowly slid himself up until he could see through the window before dropping back down. "It happened in the hallway, not the dining room, so I doubt it was anyone important."

"Important? What's that supposed to mean?" I hissed.

"You know what I mean. A big player, a VIP," he said, rolling his eyes. "They were all still enjoying their delicious desserts."

Finn snickered. "Nice one by the way."

"I have to ask," I said. "Butter knives?"

Red shrugged. "Short notice. Better than nothing."

I had to agree with him there. I was just glad they ended up in here with us. The commotion had died down in the kitchen and while there were still excited voices, it didn't seem like a dangerous situation anymore. We stayed where we were, straining to hear something through the door, until someone knocked sharply on it.

Jude slid up to peek through the window.

"Delta," he said, pushing away from the door and turning to unlock it.

I slid away from the door too, but stayed on the floor.

Delta came inside and closed the door behind her, taking quick note of who was in the room. She didn't seem surprised to find the boys here with us; perhaps it was her that told them to come here.

Without a word to any of the rest of us, she reached out and pulled Harris into her arms, holding him tightly.

"No," Harris said, repeating the same word over and over again. His eyes filled with tears and I had a sudden realization.

"Margo?"

Delta nodded and my throat constricted, making it hard to breathe. Why would someone shoot Margo? What could she have possibly done?

"Finn, Jude, take the girls back to their room, quickly," said Delta, still holding Harris, who seemed more and more like he might fall down as the seconds ticked by. "Vaughn, and Red, get Harris back to his room, and stay with him until I get there."

The boys obeyed without question. I rose to my feet, dumbfounded, unsure of what this all meant. Where was Margo going that was worth risking her life? What possibly could have been the reason to shoot a defenseless girl? Finn reached down to help Willow and Hazel to their feet. They were both still pressed against the wall, cowering in the shadows. They both seemed as stunned as I felt, and we moved like we had lead in our veins.

I felt Jude take my arm and lead me through the open door into the kitchen. The light seemed brighter than necessary, blinding me. I let Jude lead me, unaware of our direction. I could hear dishes clattering as life seemed to return to normal. The giant dishwasher swished and steamed, oblivious to our tragedy.

Everything seemed too white, too clean—such a harsh contrast to the darkness I felt inside me. We left the kitchen, stepping out into the hallway. It was then that I saw her. Someone had covered her upper body with a white sheet or a tablecloth, hiding her face. A puddle of blood had formed beneath her and the white fabric was sucking it up, spreading a deep red stain across the fine white folds. Her hands were pale, and like Kenzie, she was dressed in a spotless white dress. The red blood seemed so out of place, such a blow to the idea that—for whatever reason they had taken us—at least we were safe. I inhaled sharply and the room began to swim. Everything was white, the light, the tiles, the walls, her dress, and yet the red blood ruined it all. Nothing here was clean and fresh, it was all tainted, stained, hidden.

I looked down at my own dress, as deep a shade of red as the blood seeping from Margo, the life drained from her.

I heard the screams, haunting and awful, before I realized they were coming from me. My legs collapsed beneath me and I fell to my knees, unable to stand any longer. I felt Finn push past me with Hazel and Willow, rushing toward our rooms. I saw Jude's face, and could see his lips moving but I couldn't understand his words. Frustrated, he stood, yanked me up by the arm and swung me over his shoulder. I stopped screaming and began to sob, tears flowing up my forehead and into my hair as I bounced upside down on Jude's shoulder as he ran through the halls.

THEY DIDN'T COME FOR us like I thought they would. Everything was normal again and we were expected to fulfill our duties just as we had since the moment we arrived. I stood under the hot shower that evening, trying to feel the heat and wash the day away, but I felt nothing. If I could have made the water hotter I would have—in hopes that I could feel something. Even pain was preferable to feeling nothing.

I turned the knob, and with a squeal and a rattle the water stopped. I stayed under the showerhead until the water stopped dripping on my head.

Jude had carried me back to my room and laid me gently

on the bed. My headscarf had fallen off at some point and I could tell my hair was loose. I hadn't bothered to braid it in weeks, the scarf held everything in place anyway. He was angry and I didn't know why. In my haze I could see his silent argument with Finn. They were shouting, but I couldn't hear anything but a constant ringing inside my head. I saw Delta, her calm face, her rationality. She sent them away, Finn pushing Jude through the door ahead of him.

They were all gone.

Three of us left in a room with eight beds. I was starting to think the girl who died in the helicopter might well have been the lucky one. We hadn't seen any of the others in months, how could we be sure they were still alive? I had been operating under the assumption that our presence here was useful for some unknown reason. They had taken care of us, fed us, kept us healthy, for what? To be gunned down in a hallway?

My muscles began to ache and I was starting to feel dizzy. I needed to sit down. I reached to the hook and took the giant soft towel that was hanging there. Wrapping it securely around myself, I headed for the change room. Willow and Hazel were gone already so I scooped my clothing up in my arms and opened the door to the hallway. It was against the rules to leave the shower area without dressing first, but I didn't care anymore.

The air was cool against skin still hot from the shower. I hadn't even bothered with my shoes, so I could feel the cold tile against my warm wet feet. I dripped all the way to the red door. I was about to open it, when I realized there was someone there.

Sitting in the shadows beyond the door was Jude.

"It's not right," he said. "None of this is right."

I didn't bother to answer. It was obvious to him how I would respond anyway. I stood, facing the door, my hand on the knob, water dripping off of me into a puddle on the floor.

"I heard them talking," he said. "They have some kind of plan." He stood up, moving toward me. I felt vulnerable in nothing but a towel, but he didn't seem to notice. "I promise you, Rhea, I will find out what they're doing."

He reached toward me, and brushed a lock of wet hair from my face. In one quick motion, he folded me into his arms, kissing me lightly on the forehead.

"I promise."

When I opened my eyes he was gone, the feeling of him still lingering on my body, the touch of his lips on my face. My hand trembled on the doorknob, and it felt as though I had to try a few times to get it to work. Finally I opened the door and slid inside, leaving the dream, and re-entering reality.

FIFTEEN

Delta

I KNEW FROM THE moment they summoned me that they needed someone to answer for this. I wasn't sure exactly how it was my fault that Margo had made such an irrational decision, but someone needed to take the fall.

"I'm disappointed, Delta," said Nadia, not even looking up from her tablet.

"I'm sorry."

It was the only thing I could say.

"We're down to six girls now, and only two who bear cellutation marks, so I've decided to make some changes."

I nodded.

She held out a piece of paper.

"From now on you will follow these procedures. Our testing must succeed and if there are any other mishaps like this one, I will hold you personally responsible."

I took the paper and read it slowly. My heart sank. I glanced up at the women before me, hoping one of them would show some kind of remorse, some hint of humanity, but none of them met my eyes.

HOURS LATER I FOUND myself in the clinic, watching the deep breaths of the President as she lay on the gurney. Her hair fanned out around her on the pillow. There were six or seven machines attached to her, and a variety of tubes and wires that crisscrossed the bed. She looked healthy, despite what she had been through. The doctors still hadn't been able to figure out exactly what it was that caused the cardiac arrest, though I knew in my heart that Nadia had something to do with it.

I reached out and slid my hand over hers—resting mine gently on her soft, warm hand.

The doctor slipped through the curtain with practiced silence. I barely heard her come in.

I didn't look at her.

"Do you want me to wake her up?" she asked.

I shook my head.

"Not yet."

I needed Meredith, but she was safest the way she was. They had tried to kill her, of that I was sure. They needed to get her out of the way, but I needed her more.

The doctor nodded and this time I heard her leave, calling out stats to one of the nurses to put in Meredith's chart.

I knew she was safe here. I smiled.

It was going to be more difficult now, but I would find a way.

SIXTEEN

Rhea

"DO YOU STILL HAVE those scissors, Hazel?" asked Willow, pulling off her headscarf. Her hair had been progressively getting longer. What began as a tight pixie cut had expanded into a mass of black curls. We had no mirror, so she just made a face as she ran her fingers through it.

"In some ways I'll be glad to be rid of this," she said.

It was Willow's last night with us, and while I feared for her there were moments I was jealous of her. I wasn't sure what was worse, facing my fear, or spending another few months unsure of what I was actually afraid of.

Hazel nodded and slid the scissors from their hiding place under her mattress; she moved to hand them to Willow. Willow waved her hand.

"I'll slice off my ear. You do it."

Hazel froze.

"I... I..." she said.

"Give them to me," I said.

Willow sat on the floor in front of my bunk.

"Get rid of as much as you can," she said. "I don't want to give them the pleasure."

I began to snip away at her thick curls. The scissors weren't terribly sharp, so I could only cut away small chunks that fluttered to the floor in tiny dark piles. It was a long time before I finished cutting away any last bit that was long enough for me to grip. Willow ran her hands over her head.

"That's better," she said.

I wished I had her courage. I wasn't sure how well I would do if someone else cut off my hair. It was a piece of me. A completely inconsequential and superfluous piece of me, yes, but every time I had looked in the mirror at myself, it had been there.

"You look nice," said Hazel with tears in her eyes.

Willow burst out laughing.

"Of course I do," said Willow, with a confidence I'd never be able to muster. "I've always been fabulous!"

Hazel tried her best to smile, but her face didn't cooperate.

I wanted to laugh with her, enjoy these last hours with Willow, but it was hard to find anything to laugh about, or smile about for that matter. We had been here for almost a year and a half, and slowly all of our friends had been taken, one by one, for reasons unknown to us. It was painful to bear that loss again and again. We assumed our friends were still alive, though we had no contact with them.

Except Margo.

My throat constricted at the thought of her. I still saw her blood seeping through the white cloth every time I closed my eyes.

Willows face fell. "You guys need to quit it," she said.

"I'm sorry, Willow," said Hazel. "You know how hard this is."

Willow reached out her arms and pulled us both into a hug.

"I know," she said. "I've stood there with you until now, and I did the exact same thing, but today, I want to do something different. I need something different."

"Tell us," I said.

Willow's face was serious and her voice went quiet, in case anyone was listening. I strained to hear her.

"I need you two princesses to suck it up and laugh with me."

I couldn't help myself.

I laughed.

"GIN," I SAID, KNOCKING on the table.

Simeon shook his head and grunted.

"I've created a monster," he said. "We need a new game, something I'm better at."

I smiled. I had beat him the last nine games we had played, but who was counting?

"Chess, have you played chess?" he asked.

"I was the all-state champion in school," I said.

His jaw dropped.

"Seriously?"

I laughed, "No," I said. "I've never played."

His laugh boomed out over the piles of stored furniture.

"You had me going," he said.

It wasn't hard.

We played cards at least three times a week, and other than Jude, no one had been the wiser. I saw his face through the tiny window into the kitchen, frowning at me whenever he saw us in here together, but I mostly ignored him. I knew it was dangerous to be seen with one of them, but Simeon was discreet and who would see us here? No one needed to know, and at times I welcomed the break.

I knew he must know things about why we were here and what use they had for us, but I was reluctant to ask. We had an easy relationship, simple camaraderie. We played cards and talked about the weather, which was pretty much always the same.

"You're a smart girl, Rhea," he said, collecting the cards and reshuffling them. "And pretty too."

I flushed as red as my headscarf.

This was new.

"Thank you," I said, my voice meek and quiet.

He laid the cards on the table without shuffling. I could feel the blood rushing through my face, hot and frenzied. He reached his hand under the table and I could feel it rest on my knee, stroking it gently. I wanted to pull away, to run, and even though I physically could have, I felt completely trapped.

His hand released my knee and he pushed his chair away from the table. I stared at my lap as he stood and walked behind me. I couldn't see him anymore, but I knew he wasn't far. I held my breath as I felt his hands on the sides of my head, pulling my headscarf back, releasing my hair in a tumble of waves down my back. His hand gripped the back of my chair and he lowered himself to his knees behind me and began to run his hands through my hair.

"Oh, I love the way you smell," he said, burying his face in my hair, his breath hot against my neck.

A tear slipped from my eye, and I brushed it away hastily. Was this his plan all along? What was his plan? I could feel his hands stroking my hair, my face, my neck. I wanted to scream but nothing came.

Suddenly his hands gripped my shoulders and I heard his breath sharp and ragged behind me. I pinched my eyes shut, unsure of what I was hearing. I didn't want to know, I didn't want to understand what he was doing.

"Rhea," he whispered.

I tried to shut him out.

"Rhea," he whispered again, and then I heard a thump as his body hit the floor.

I jumped from my seat and turned around. His eyes were wide and panicked—his skin pale. He was clutching his chest and struggling for breath.

"Simeon?" I said, startled.

"Help," he said.

"I'll find someone," I said, looking frantically for my headscarf. Not seeing it, I made a move to dash for the door.

His hand gripped my ankle before I could run.

"Please," he said.

I dropped to my knees beside him; trying to remember the

first aid I had been taught. Nothing came.

His hand reached for me, he gestured me closer.

I leaned forward and he laid his hand on the side of my face.

"Tell," he said, snatching a quick breath, "Tell Jude I love him. I always have."

"Jude?" I said.

His hand slipped away from my face, and I could see the light leave his eyes. I watched him in silence as he died.

"Rhea? What are you doing?"

Tears fell from my eyes as I looked up to see Jude towering over Simeon's body. I didn't know what to say, what to feel. So many emotions rushed through me, each different and impossible to make sense of.

I opened my mouth to speak, but before anything came out, Jude dropped to his knees beside me, fumbling for a pulse and listening to Simeon's open mouth.

"Move over," he said, leaning over the older man, "Help me get him onto his back."

Simeon's lower body was twisted, so I moved to where his legs were and tried to pull them straight, while Jude pushed at his hips.

He knelt beside the man and began compressing his chest.

"Rhea, do you know CPR?"

I nodded, which wasn't entirely a lie. I had learned it once, though right now I was having trouble remembering my own name.

"Get up to his head and start breathing for him."

I paused.

"Now!"

I hurried around Jude's body, his muscles tense as he pushed his hands into Simeon's chest in a steady rhythm.

"Push his head back, lift his chin," said Jude, sharp and quick with his directions. "Now, good strong breaths."

I plugged his nose, holding it as if it was a smelly sock, and cringed at the thought of pressing my mouth against his.

"Now!" said Jude, "If you can't do it, move out of the way."

I took a deep breath and pressed my mouth against Simeon's. It was warm and wet. I exhaled with as much strength as I could.

"Again," said Jude.

Time stood still as we worked, occasionally switching places as we grew fatigued. After what seemed like hours, I saw Jude lean back on his heels. I continued compressions and waited for him. He did nothing.

"It's over," he said. "We did all we could, but it wasn't enough."

I kept my rhythm going, unable to stop, unable to let someone die. Tears fell from my face and my hair swayed back and forth in time with my aching arms.

"It's over, Rhea," Jude repeated, his hands reaching to my shoulders to gently move me to stop. I flinched at his touch.

I stopped.

"What happened?"

I shook my head, unable to speak.

"We need to get you away from here," said Jude. "They can't know you were with him when he died."

I knew his words were true, I wasn't supposed to be with any of them period, and being found here, beside Simeon's lifeless body would mean trouble for both of us.

"He said something Jude," I said, my voice shaking. "About you."

"About me?"

I turned and looked him deep in the eyes. I wanted to stay in those eyes, I wanted to melt into him and stay there forever.

"He said to tell you he loved you, and he always had."

Jude's face twitched.

"Why would he say that?" he said, stunned. "I barely knew him."

I shrugged.

"I thought you would understand," I said.

He stood, shaking his head.

"That makes no sense."

I stood up next to him, and before either of us could say another word, I knew we weren't alone any longer. My hair hung loose around my shoulders as Jude and I turned simultaneously to face the door. Standing in the kitchen door was Tess McAllister.

Simeon's wife.

SEVENTEEN

WORRY HAD GNAWED AT my insides since the moment Delta closed the red door behind me. I couldn't read her, though I doubted she knew much more than me. Simeon was dead. Our efforts to resuscitate him had failed, and having been found with Jude, standing over his dead body had been damning. Any hope of making it through this slid through my fingers like beach sand. In that moment, Tess saw me as treasonous, no matter the truth. The rebel inside me wanted to shout at her as she turned slowly and walked from the room, the picture of her dead husband obviously seared into her brain. They had made this happen, not me. They had taken me from my home, from my family and they had caused this. I said nothing. I couldn't find the words. As angry and hurt and scared as I was, I couldn't manage even the slightest rebellion. I had allowed Jude to bring me back to the red door, herding me inside like some illicit contraband that needed to be hidden. I had run with him, trying in vain to pull my headscarf back over my trailing hair. He spoke to me, but I didn't hear the words, I felt nothing other than our feet pounding down the hallways.

Once inside, I had crumpled onto my bed, trembling like a

frightened cat, cornered without escape. I had felt Hazel's hands on me, heard her murmured consolations. I didn't know how to tell her what had happened.

I knew from Delta's face when she arrived that I was in trouble. Hazel tried to make sense of it; I could tell the cryptic words Delta used made no sense to her. They made sense to me.

They were deciding what to do with me. She would come back when she knew.

"What happened?" asked Hazel as the door snapped shut behind Delta. For the first time I heard the scraping sound of a lock being turned from the outside.

I lifted my tear-stained face to meet her eyes and shook my head.

How could I explain the moments that had passed so quickly, yet had forever imprinted themselves on me? Simeon's hands stroking my hair, his cries for help, Jude's strong shoulders working to save his life, a last breath and whispered messages, Tess' face—visions which would haunt my dreams forever.

"They're going to kill me," I said, my voice hollow and thin. I was sure of the words I spoke yet they sounded foreign and distant to me.

"Why would they kill you?" Hazel asked.

"They killed Margo."

"We don't know what happened."

"She's dead. We know that much."

"If they wanted to gun you down in the hall, they would have done it already," said Hazel.

She was right.

They were planning something worse for me.

THEY LEFT US THERE for two days. No one brought food, but we drank water from the bathroom sink to soothe the raw edges of our hunger. We had no cups to drink, so we just craned our necks to fit our heads beneath the faucet and drink from the tap. It was never cold, and had a distinct mineral taste that I remembered from drinking out of the hose at my uncle's farm. It was a far cry from the purified water they had for us to drink with our meals, but it was water. We wouldn't die of thirst.

It had taken me a few hours to calm down enough to tell Hazel the story from the beginning. She had listened patiently, nodding and gasping along with my words.

"I'm sorry Hazel," I said as I sat back down on my bunk.

"For what?"

"This. Being locked in here."

"You didn't kill Simeon," she said. "You did nothing wrong."

"I did plenty wrong. I never should have let any of this happen."

"We haven't been in control of our circumstances since these people dragged us off in their trucks," she said, flipping the pages of the book she was reading. I had tried to read too, but none of the words would stick in my brain long enough for me to make sense of sentences and paragraphs. I found myself rereading the same passages so many times I could recite them, but still had no basic level of understanding. Instead I had taken to pacing. Hazel said it made her nervous, but she had chosen to ignore it. I had no more power over my fidgety energy than I did over our circumstances. It was easier to succumb than fight.

Of all the possible outcomes I could imagine, being left to starve in a room to ponder your fate seemed significantly worse than whatever punishment they could dole out. I needed closure, and if that meant death, so be it. There was something so excruciating about waiting.

"Can't they just come here and get this over with?" I said.

It had been my refrain since Delta locked us in here.

Hazel nodded. "They will."

I raised an eyebrow at her passive form ignoring me from her bed. She flipped a page before speaking again.

"At the very least, they'll want to kill us outside so our bodies will freeze and we won't stink up the joint."

"You are not helping," I said, resuming my pacing.

She was helping. We both knew that—just like we both knew that our morbid senses of humor were our lifelines, admittedly tenuous, but still anchoring us to hope.

We both heard the noise at the door at the same time, the jingling of keys as someone beyond the red door thumbed through a keychain to find the right one.

My chest ached as I realized I was holding my breath. I inhaled deeply as the lock slid open and the knob turned.

Delta entered, dropping her keys into the pocket of her thick sweater.

"You got lucky, Rhea," she said. "Thank whoever you need to that it was just Simeon that died."

"Just Simeon?" I asked.

Delta smiled.

"You might think Tess would be grieving, but you haven't met this women. She feels rather irritated and somewhat inconvenienced."

"Inconvenienced?" asked Hazel.

"He was her husband," I said. "If my husband..."

Delta walked to me, reached out and lifted my chin to look her in the eye.

"Keep that," she said sternly.

"What?"

"The exact thing they can't grasp. None of those women in power out there understand the partnership of a man and woman. There is no love in those relationships. That is why Simeon found you in the first place."

"For love?"

"To have a connection. Tess is incapable of seeing anything other than her own ambition. Simeon was nothing more than a necessary accessory."

I shook my head. Simeon had never spoke of their marriage, and while I was jealous of the power-couples in the estate, I now felt nothing but pity.

"How sad," said Hazel.

Delta nodded, her face suddenly distant. "I wanted better for him."

Hazel and I exchanged a glance. I wasn't the only one who heard that.

"Delta?" I said.

She snapped back to us.

"Yes?"

"You wanted better for Simeon?"

Delta grimaced. "I had hoped I didn't say that out loud, but he's gone now, there's no harm in telling you. Simeon was my son."

Delta moved past us and sat on one of the empty bunks. I could see the lines of grief etched on her face.

"I didn't give birth to him," she began, "but he was my son."

Hazel and I sat on the bunk too, one on each side, like children waiting for a story.

"Boys haven't been valuable for some time, and I found Simeon and his brothers, not his real brothers, but there were four of them and I always called them brothers. Simeon was the oldest."

"What happened to their families?"

Delta shook her head.

"Nothing. They just wanted girls."

"They abandoned their children?" asked Hazel.

Delta nodded. "It wasn't unusual. The orphanages never had girls in them."

"What about Jude and Finn and the others?"

"I raised them much later, once Simeon and his brothers

were older."

"Are the other ones here?"

"No," she said. "Only Simeon. I don't know what happened to the others when the frozen days hit. I can only hope they found somewhere safe. I think they were prepared for catastrophe, but there is no way of knowing."

She stood suddenly.

"We need to go," she said.

"What's going to happen to us?" I asked.

"Nothing that wouldn't have happened soon anyway," she said. "They've decided to ignore your ages, and you two will join the others. They said you'll be more secure there."

Relief flooded through me. Of all the possible scenarios I had imagined, merely pushing us on had never even registered.

"They need you, Rhea. They were supposed to have eight girls, four cellutated, and four not. Two are dead now, and you and Shalisa are the only two who have the mark. Tess wanted to kill you. She pushed for it, but none of the others agreed. Whatever they are doing, you are more important to them than Tess' pride."

I nodded.

I moved to follow Delta to the door.

"Wait," I said. "Can I ask you something before we go? I don't know if I'll have another chance."

Delta turned back to me.

"When Simeon was dying, he said something about Jude... that I should tell him he loved him."

I knew from the look on Delta's face that she knew why he had said that.

"Jude didn't understand, but do you know?"

Delta nodded and a single tear traced a path down her wrinkled face.

"Simeon was Jude's father."

I had a hunch that was the case, but I hadn't understood the situation.

"He was born well before Simeon met Tess, his mother died when Jude was a baby. We made a promise never to tell him because Tess hates Jude. She tolerated having him around as long as he didn't get any ideas about his status. Simeon asked me to raise him with the other boys I was caring for."

"Like Red and Vaughn..."

"And Harris and Finn," Delta finished for me. "That way he could be close by."

"He had been under his father's eye his whole life and never knew it?"

"Yes, and now that Simeon is dead, that could put him in a difficult spot. Tess has already threatened me." Her voice was barely above a whisper. "He can't know, otherwise his safety can't be guaranteed."

She gazed at me with pleading eyes.

I couldn't tell him.

I nodded.

I couldn't jeopardize him either.

EIGHTEEN

Delta – eighteen years earlier

"I DIDN'T KNOW SHE had a baby," said Simeon, watching as the little boy explored the book they had given him.

"Does Tess know?" I asked.

He shook his head. "Not yet. I'll tell her... when the time is right."

"You need to tell her, Simeon."

"I know."

"You won't be able to keep it a secret here, not with all these people."

After years of threats against the government, many of the leaders and their families were now housed at the White House, including Simeon and his wife, Tess, a senator. It was easier to monitor and protect the key players if they were all in one place. The secret service had expanded to cover the additional housemates and for the most part, there was room enough in the large house for everyone to live. There were no other senators living there at present, but Tess was lucky enough to have connections.

"There are already four boys with me," I said, "What will people say when they notice one more?"

"That you have a heart of gold?" Simeon said, his brows rising, eyes pleading.

I couldn't resist him, and he knew that. I also couldn't resist these little boys, abandoned and left behind in a system where they had no value. I hadn't been able to resist Simeon either, at the time.

Now my child—this man—was bringing me his son, and asking me to do it all again, because he knew in his heart that I would do anything for him. He knew me well.

"What's his name?" I asked.

"Mariah called him Jude. She wrote it in a letter before she died."

I remembered Mariah. I didn't like her much but Simeon was smitten. If I had to be honest with myself, I didn't like any of the women Simeon brought home, Tess the least of them. I felt a pang of regret at disliking Mariah so much. At least she had more sense than Simeon's mother, and didn't just abandon her son, or leave him to die. So many girls these days did that. The orphanages were full of boys, devalued and unappreciated, and that didn't even include those who aborted their pregnancies once they knew the gender.

I reached down and picked up the boy from the floor. He was strong and sturdy, with a thick mop of curly brown hair and the most beautiful amber eyes I had ever seen. They glowed almost golden.

"Hello Jude," I said softly. "My name is Delta."

He nodded. I wasn't sure if he could speak yet.

"Would you like to come and meet my other boys?"

He nodded again.

"Don't tell him," said Simeon as I turned to head back to my quarters. It was going to be tight, the rooms they gave researchers were small, and it was already tight with the four boys I had in there. Simeon had been the one to get me that job, and I was thankful for it. I could do my work and was afforded a certain level of anonymity. As long as I could send in my findings on a regular basis, they were all content to leave me alone.

"He's going to need to know eventually," I said. "You are his father Simeon."

"I know," he said, "Let me do it, when the time is right."

"You need to tell Tess though."

I couldn't condone him keeping secrets from his wife.

He nodded, though I could see from his expression that he wasn't really planning on doing that any time soon either.

He turned and left, and once more, my life had changed.

NINETEEN

Rhea

Hazel held my hands as they led us through the darkened hallways. Neither of us knew quite where we were going, but we didn't need to speculate. We knew what would meet us at the end. Delta was in front of us and a large man walked behind us. I saw that he was armed when we left the room, but I hadn't turned to glance at him since. The only thing that gave away his presence were the heavy footfalls of his boots on the tile floor.

Delta pulled a set of keys from the pocket of her wool sweater. They jingled in the quiet space, the tiny sound grating at nerves that were already on edge. She opened the door and motioned for us to go in. We entered the room together, hit instantly by the sterile smell of disinfectant and chemical cleaners.

She followed us into the room and closed the door behind us. I sighed, relieved that she had left the man outside. The room was empty, save for a large mirror on the wall that probably hid others who were watching us, and a short bench. Everything in the room was white, and the red of our gowns stood out like the puddle of blood that had seeped from Margo. I tried to push the memory from my head.

"You will need to change," said Delta

She motioned to a bench in the corner, where two small piles of white fabric lay. They were smaller than I expected, having seen both Kenzie and Margo's long white gowns. Hazel and I walked slowly to the bench and lifted up the items. They were both made of stretchy material, and reminded me of the bathing suits Ember and I would wear when we jumped through the sprinkler. There was a short top, barely more than a sports bra, and some small stretchy underwear-like shorts.

"What happened to the gowns?" Hazel whispered to me.

Delta answered for me.

"There have been some changes," she said without elaboration.

I pulled my headscarf from my head and began to change. There was no need for privacy or modesty, we had lost that more than a year ago. Hazel did the same beside me.

I finished dressing and stared at myself in the mirror. I was plumper than I remembered, my body filled out from the rich foods and sedentary lifestyle. I had been built like a child when I came here, but now I looked more like my mother. My hips had widened and my breasts had filled out. I scarcely recognized myself. My blonde hair hung down my back, shiny and lush. Even my eyes were different. They had always been a pale violet, almost grey, but now they had deepened.

"It's all the vitamins," said Hazel, her voice barely above a whisper. She too was looking at herself, drinking in the person she was now, and trying desperately to remember who she had been before.

There was a set of doors beside the window, and they opened with a sharp metallic sound. I glanced over to see two women in white lab coats enter the room. They motioned for us to come with them. I glanced at Delta, and she nodded in their direction.

"I'll come see you shortly," she said.

We followed the women through the doors into another equally sparse white room. This time two chairs stood in the middle of the room. Between them was a small table of tools.

Our hair.

"Please sit," said one of the women.

We obeyed. The metal chairs were cold against my thighs and back.

A shiver ran up my back as I heard and felt the scissors clip through my hair. They were sharp and took large clumps at a time. Hair fell onto my lap in thick blonde waves, making a circle around the bottom of my chair. I felt a tear slip from my eye as I felt the buzzing clippers shave my head to the scalp. I could hear Hazel crying softly beside me, but I didn't turn to look. She was too far away from me to hold her hand, and there was nothing I could say to ease the pain in her that I knew I was feeling myself.

It's just hair.

The words, however true, were empty and faint.

The clippers stopped and I felt a brush sweep the hairs from my neck and shoulders. There were no mirrors in this room. For that I was thankful. I didn't want to see myself yet.

The feeling of air on my scalp was foreign, and I resisted

the urge to run my hands over my head, knowing that if I did I would start to cry. I could pretend for a while that it wasn't real, that none of this was. I could pretend until I knew I could control my emotions. I didn't know what they wanted from me, but I knew I wouldn't give them the satisfaction of seeing me crying and broken.

I bit my lip firmly as we moved to yet another room.

This one had a deep pool in the middle of the room. It was big, perhaps the width of three bathtubs and double the length. There were handrails beside the steps that led into the clear water. In the middle of the water stood a woman in a white jumpsuit, it looked to be made of the same material as our suits, but covered her from neck to toe. Even her fingers were covered in fabric.

"One at a time please," said one of the women, scrolling through her tablet.

I glanced at Hazel, and she pleaded with her eyes.

I nodded.

I walked toward the pool and stepped into the water. It was warm, but it sent tingles through my feet. As I went deeper, the tingles crept up my legs. It began to feel like pins and needles, slowly morphing into a consistent burn. I made it to the bottom of the pool and stood beside the woman in the pool.

"What is this? Why is it burning?" I asked, not expecting a reply.

"It's a disinfectant. Now please go under," she said.

"Under?" I asked as she placed her hand on my head and pushed me down into the pool. I had barely enough time to suck in a deep breath before my head was engulfed by the burning liquid. She held me beneath the surface and I could hear her counting, her voice strange and hollow through the water.

The searing sensation increased as every part of my body was overwhelmed and consumed by the liquid. My lungs screamed for breath and just as I began to feel dizzy, I was pulled to the surface. I inhaled and gasped as hands held my shoulder and pushed me back to the stairs and out of the pool. The air seemed colder than it had been when we entered the room.

Hazel glanced at me, confused as I stood there, swaying and dripping, thankful that the burning sensation had subsided.

"It's not fun, but you can do it," I said. "Get a good breath before you go under."

She nodded. I could see her wince as she stepped into the pool.

I closed my eyes and shivered, my teeth chattering. They offered me no towel or robe, but the liquid dried so quickly, I could understand why. Before Hazel came out of the pool I was as dry as I had been when we came into the room.

Hazel came out, gasping and coughing as I had, but fine.

The final room they took us into had two gurneys in it. They had no mattresses, but rather a hard molded-plastic surface. No one spoke, or touched us, but both Hazel and I knew that we were supposed to lie on them. There were bright white lights shining down on the beds, and I was glad to discover they were warm. I sat on the cold surface, drinking in the warmth of the lights that seemed so familiar, yet so distant. I hadn't felt the heat of the sun on my body in a long time. Even the direct light in the dining room didn't have this warmth and strength. I laid down into the molded bed—that seemed to fit me perfectly—and let the light wash over me. I closed my eyes and breathed deeply.

"I'll need to give you a few injections," said a voice, a new one, distinctly male.

My eyes fluttered open to see a small man with thinning hair and thick glasses standing beside me. He wore gloves that covered his arms to his elbows and most of his face was swathed in a mask. He had a tray beside him that held a number of instruments, including a few full syringes. Even beyond the protective clothing that he wore, I recognized him as the doctor who had helped me with my broken collarbone when I first arrived.

I nodded.

I could feel his hands on my arm and I tensed. The needle pierced my skin and I could feel the liquid he injected sliding into my body.

"Goodnight," he said, and the world went black.

TWENTY

Delta

I watched the girls through the windows as the night fell on them and they joined the others. I had hoped that Nadia would change her mind about keeping the girls in suspended animation while they conducted their tests, but it was too risky, they had said. They couldn't afford to lose another subject.

"It will all be worth it," a voice said from behind me. I didn't need to turn to know it was Nadia. She watched the testing regularly.

I nodded. I didn't want to say how I didn't understand how conducting medical tests on young girls could ever be worth it.

"What are you doing to them?" I asked.

"Changing the world."

"That's pretty ambitious."

"I know."

"The world changed almost five years ago," I said.

"I stopped in on Meredith," said Nadia, ignoring my statement.

My heart skipped a beat and I held my breath.

"The doctors don't know when or if she'll come out of the coma."

I nodded again.

"She's a sick woman," I said. "I wish we could find out what happened to her."

"Yes, but it's likely that we'll never know."

I did my best to keep my face blank.

I motioned toward Rhea and Hazel, who now lay still on their gurneys.

"So, what are you doing with them?"

Nadia smiled.

"Making children."

"Children?"

She nodded.

"I didn't know you were fond of children."

"I'm not," she said. "But the reality of the situation is that a very large chunk of the population is probably dead by now. If there's any hope of us making it out of here, we'll need to start growing some more people."

"Growing more people? You sound like you're talking about carrots."

"Well, we can't very well build them in a factory, not yet at least. If that was the case I'd skip right over the child phase and build adults."

Nadia's feelings on children were no secret. They were a necessary evil, and apparently until recently, they weren't all that necessary either.

"I guess since the girls are sleeping now, we don't have a whole lot of use for you, Delta," said Nadia.

My throat grew tight. It was my job to watch after the girls, keep them calm and make sure they took all their vitamins, ensure they stayed clean and illness-free. With them being put into some kind of suspended animation, I had become obsolete.

"I'm sure you can find something for an old woman to do," I said.

Nadia smiled. "I'm sure we can."

I heard the door open and close behind me and it was as if Nadia had taken all the oxygen out the door with her. I pressed my hands against the glass and leaned forward until I could rest my spinning head on the cool, smooth surface. I stayed there until I stopped shaking. I was an old woman, after all. There was little Nadia could do to me that wasn't going to happen sooner or later anyway. I had been lucky so far, being able to follow Simeon from the White House to here, safe from the cold. I would be lucky again, and if not, perhaps that would just be another kind of luck.

When the room stopped spinning I walked toward the door opposite the one Nadia left from. I pressed the numerical buttons in the correct order and stepped through the door as it opened. It was another room, similar to the last, lit only by the light coming in from the window. Beyond the glass I saw what I knew would be there. Four more girls dressed identically to Hazel and Rhea, each in their own sealed compartment. There were six compartments in the room, two were still empty. The light through the clear glass made each girl seem to glow with a slight blue tint. They were motionless—asleep. Machines moved slowly between them, feeding them, providing their brains with oxygen, giving them the vitamins they needed to stay alive. It was difficult to tell which girl was which from a distance, but the one on the far right stood out. She was smaller than the others, and had a petite dainty figure. Kenzie.

I held my breath as I looked at her tiny body, a bulge growing in her midsection. It was still small, but out of place on her diminutive frame. She was pregnant, by the looks of it, perhaps five months along. She would have known she was pregnant before they made her sleep.

Whether any of the others were pregnant, it was difficult to tell, but at the very least they were still alive.

I knew who I had to talk to, the only person who might know what to do.

"SHE'LL BE AWAKE IN a few minutes," said Dr. Murray, taking the syringe from the IV lines. "She'll be a bit groggy, but that should pass quickly."

"Are the doors locked?"

She nodded. "It will look suspicious if anyone tries to come in here, but at least it will give us enough time to put her back under. I'll have the medications ready just in case."

"Thank you."

I watched in silence as Meredith's eyes began to twitch. A soft groan escaped from her parted lips.

"Meredith?"

The President's eyelids fluttered for a moment and then

opened.

"Delta?" she said in a whisper.

"It's me."

"I was just having the most wonderful dream."

"It's from the medicine, you know that."

"I know," she said, "It was delightful though. They could have made that stuff so it was just black, just death, you know, but it makes me dream so nicely."

"I'm sorry to wake you up." I said.

"Don't be. I can dream more later."

"Probably."

"Why did you wake me up?" she said. "What has my wicked step-sister been up to?"

Meredith and Nadia weren't actually step-sisters, half-sisters would be more correct, since they shared the same father. They looked nothing alike—Nadia was tall and fair, while Meredith bore the dark rich complexion of her mother. They didn't know of their relation until they were adults, and their wealthy, high-class mothers made the mistake of attending the same party as their mutual former fling. A bit of alcohol and some loose tongues splashed the secret all over the tabloids. It was merely coincidence that they had both entered into the political arena, and held the Presidential nomination as a team. Nadia was furious, but Meredith had laughed it off, saying it made sense, since they loved each other and fought like dogs anyway. The public seemed to like their vicious camaraderie, or at the very least, wanted front row tickets to the inevitable implosion, so Meredith won the Presidency with Nadia at her side.

"I'm not entirely sure, I thought you might have some insight."

"Well, we know she wants me dead. Is it something else?"

Meredith coughed.

"Could you pass me some water?" she asked, "I haven't spoken in a while. How long has it been?"

I reached for the pitcher of water on the table next to the bed, and poured her a glass. I knew she would be thirsty. She always was, so I had learned to come prepared.

"I visited you last four months ago,"

"Is it safe for me to wake up yet?"

I shook my head. "I don't think so."

"Oh well, hopefully I can continue that dream of mine."

"The girls, Meredith. What was the plan for the girls?"

Meredith's eyes flitted back to me.

"I tried to stop it."

"I know."

"They want to change everything."

I nodded, encouraging her to keep talking.

"I don't remember the details, but I know they wanted to find a way to combat the cellutation infertility."

Cellutation, while being an incredible advancement in medical technology did have the side-effect of being hazardous to fertility. People were less likely to die from some of the most difficult illnesses, but as a trade-off, it also made it very difficult to reproduce.

"This doesn't seem like basic testing anymore," I said. "There's something else going on."

Meredith shook her head slowly.

"Nothing that they've told me."

I heard the sharp rapping at the door and my stomach dropped. The curtain swished to the side revealing Dr. Murray with a syringe at the ready.

"Delta, get in the other room, quickly, I can handle this."

"Delta," said Meredith as Dr. Murray squeezed the plunger of the syringe, injecting her IV lines with the medicine to keep her in an induced coma. She whispered something that I couldn't hear.

Her eyelids dropped as I pulled the door closed. The room was dark, so I left the door open a crack so I could see what was going on. I heard the doctor walk to the door with enough rush to make the people on the other side feel important, but not so much that it seemed she was hiding something.

"Can I help you?"

"Why was this door locked?"

"We were changing Madame President's clothing and bedding, we didn't want someone to come in while she was... indisposed."

Nadia walked to Meredith's bedside, where her half-sister and competition lay peacefully sleeping.

I knew the medicine took a while to take full effect, so I hoped Meredith could lie still long enough.

"She hasn't woken up yet?" asked Nadia.

"Not yet. We took a new brain scan this morning and everything appears to be fine, so she could wake up at anytime. For now, however, we must insist that she not have visitors. Without knowing what caused her coma in the first place, we don't want her to be exposed to any unnecessary contagions."

"Of course," said Nadia, "Anything for my sister."

Dr. Murray turned to push back the curtain so Nadia could leave, and as she did, I saw Nadia's hand reach out and snatch the empty syringe from the tray. I held my breath and tried to swallow any unintentional screams as she stabbed Meredith in the arm. I exhaled slowly as it registered that Meredith didn't flinch at all. Nadia pulled the syringe from her arm and laid it gently on the table before following the doctor from the room. A tiny drop of blood beaded on Meredith's skin where the needle had punctured her.

In no more than a few slow deep breaths, I heard the door lock and Dr. Murray came back to the bed motioning to me that it was safe to come out of the room.

"What did she say? She said something before she fell asleep again," I asked.

"I didn't catch it all, but she said something about a girl named Isis. Find Isis."

Dr. Murray picked up a piece of gauze and wiped the blood from Meredith's arm as if she had done it a dozen times. She didn't seem surprised at all at what Nadia did, but rather just went about her business as if nothing had happened.

"She does it every time she comes in here," she said,

noticing my confused look. "For a while poor Meredith looked a bit like a pincushion. Thankfully Nadia doesn't come around as often anymore."

"Is she aware?" I asked, thinking how horrible it would be to be awake and aware of pain, even in a sleeping body.

She shook her head, her thick, red hair braided tightly. "I don't think so; she has never mentioned it to me, at least."

I watched her as she peeled the crinkly paper off a bandage. It was difficult to look at Dr.Murray sometimes. Coralie would have been about her age by now, a young woman, a mother maybe. When she passed, I thought that the pain would never go away. At times the thought of her didn't enter my mind, but whenever her memory visited me the pain was as fresh and real as the day she was taken from me.

A sob built in my throat, threatening to choke me, so I quickly nodded to Dr.Murray and made my way from the room into the cold, stale air of the hallway. I longed for fresh air, and toyed with the idea of going down to the garages in hopes of finding a few breaths. They would wonder why I was there though, since I had no reason to be. I inhaled deeply to quell the familiar heartache. So many boys I had raised, and yet none of them would replace that little girl.

TWENTY-ONE

Delta- 25 years earlier

I STARED AT THE pile of pink clothes on the bed. There
wasn't much, not enough by far. I had known I'd need to buy
more soon, but I thought I'd wait until she was born, until I had
a tiny, squiggly, fussing baby. It's not like I had a pile of money to
spend either—my parents had basically disowned me—and even
though I had all the opportunity in the world, opportunity without
money was no better than a wish on your birthday candles. I was
supposed to finish my education, supposed to do a lot of things.
Instead I was an idiot, an idiot who got herself knocked up by
some guy she'd never see again. Now I was paying for it.

Coralie.

My chest tightened as if someone had wrapped me in a
towel and was slowly twisting the ends, constricting, binding me
until I could no longer breathe.

She didn't deserve to die, that perfect little person. She
deserved better than me.

I closed my eyes and waited until slowly the feelings
subsided enough that I could breathe again. They weren't gone,
and I had doubts they'd ever truly leave me. Grief is a sticky,

cantankerous bastard. That wasn't right either, Coralie was a bastard and there was nothing wrong with her. Nothing. I inhaled slowly, testing the bounds of my lungs. Still the hollowness prevailed, but there was no substance on earth that could fill it. It was only two days ago, but the moment I saw the nurse's face I knew. I was sweaty and spent, tears of fear and exhaustion already stained my cheeks, but I knew that all the pain and trial would be worth it when I held that child in my arms. They had rushed her from the room so quickly, before I could hear her cry. The nurse told me that was normal, something about fluids and needing some help. I waited impatiently for them to bring her back.

Instead, I was offered a bundle of pain wrapped in a flannel blanket.

In the yellow room with faded daisies painted on the walls, my heart broke.

I held her until all warmth had left her. I doubted it was even her own warmth that clung to her tiny body, but mine— leftovers from being inside me. When they took her I didn't protest. There was nothing left in me.

They moved me to another wing of the hospital, they said it would be easier for me than being surrounded by the babies in the labor and delivery ward. That room was dim and grey, a perfect match to my mood. The yellow daisies were gone and I didn't have to look at their sunny faces. The nurses moved around me, but I didn't see them. Food came and went, untouched and I barely moved.

At some point I must have gotten dressed again, or perhaps they dressed me, because I could remember sitting on the edge of the bed with my running shoes on. Someone else must have tied them for me, because I don't think I could have bent down that far. A nurse was filling out my discharge papers and I watched as a lock of her grey hair kept falling into her deep brown eyes. Her hands were wrinkled and brown—not soft and pale like my mother's—but for some reason that calmed me. I wondered how they would feel stroking my hair, or wiping a tear from my face. These were things my own mother had never done. My breasts ached. They said that would go away soon.

She glanced up at me, probably noting the hollow ache in my eyes.

"You're going to be ok, sweetie," she'd said.

I nodded. I didn't believe a word of what she said, but what else was there to do?

She clucked her tongue softly as she finished her paperwork. She stretched out her legs and stood up, pushing the rolling table away as she came to stand beside the bed.

"You just need to keep moving," she said.

I ducked my head and mumbled, "When can I stop?"

Her coarse brown hand held mine and she tucked a strand of loose hair behind my ear.

"When you find a place you want to be."

I placed the last of the tiny clothes into the big paper sack I had gotten from the grocery store on the way home. I had saved up some money in anticipation of buying diapers, and I knew

I should spend it on some food for myself, but I didn't feel like eating. A loaf of bread and a carton of eggs was all I bought. The bread sat on the counter now, and the eggs in the tiny fridge in the kitchen. I had laughed at the landlord when she called the miniature fridge and hotplate a "kitchen". It was less of a kitchen than I had in my dorm room, and we weren't allowed to cook in our rooms. Everyone still did. But this apartment was all I could afford, so I took it anyway. It was only one room, a double bed in the corner and enough room for a pull-out couch I found and paid some teenagers five dollars each to move up here for me. There was a table with 2 chairs and a bookshelf where I had put all my unused college textbooks. They were supposed to inspire me to go back, but there was no way I could pay to finish my education, not without the support of my family. I could survive, and to be honest, that seemed like enough of a challenge.

I snatched my keys from the hook by the door and carried the sack of clothing into the hallway, locking the door behind me. I had summoned enough courage, but I knew that if I sat around much longer, I wouldn't be able to hold onto it. I didn't need to go far; the donation bin was on the corner. I frequented it often, but usually at night, when people were less likely to notice that I was often taking more than I left. The daylight seemed to betray my mood. I would have preferred a gentle rain, as clichéd as that was.

A tiny voice inside me whispered that I should keep these clothes. It had taken me a long time to collect them, after all, and I was only 24. I could have more children someday. I knew I couldn't though. I couldn't leave this bag in my apartment, knowing the clothes tucked inside belonged to Coralie.

The donation bin was filled more than it usually was. They tended to come fairly regularly, to keep people like me from pilfering through the charity offerings of the rich people who lived on the other side of the park. Either someone had recently moved, or they hadn't come to collect the donations, but the bin was full and there were boxes stacked neatly on the ground around it. My heart lightened slightly. Perhaps there was something I needed— something from the ever-growing list of things I kept in my head to someday make my life easier. I did spot one thing right away, a blue laundry basket with only one cracked slat. I was lucky to have a washing machine in my apartment but a laundry basket seemed like a luxury. I picked it up with my free hand, leaving the stack of fabric inside it. I could always use towels, or blankets or sheets, or whatever they were. I juggled the laundry basket against my hip as I took a deep breath and laid the baby clothes on the pile.

That was when I heard it.

At first I thought it might be a rat or a mouse, that tiny muffled noise. I could hear children playing on the playground nearby, and cars driving down the road behind me, but yet that tiny noise caught my attention. I heard it again, and this time it sounded more like a cat. I moved a few boxes and heard it again. My hands shook as I lifted the lid of the box. Deep inside I think I already knew what was inside but I didn't breathe until I saw it.

A baby. A tiny, perfect child with rich brown skin wrapped in a blanket, tucked in a box and discarded with so much unused stuff. I didn't need to check if it was a boy or a girl. No one abandoned girls. When I had seen Coralie was a girl on the ultrasound, I had started getting letters from social workers, urging me to give her a shining future, allow rich families to adopt her. I couldn't give a girl the future she was capable of, they had told me. I had ripped up all those letters.

I was one of the lucky ones, I supposed. Cellutation made it more difficult to conceive a child. To be honest, I hadn't even thought it possible, knowing all the people in my parents' circles who hadn't been able to have children on their own. I hadn't even thought of using birth control that night, it just didn't seem necessary. I couldn't even remember the last person I had known who had a child of their own. Adoptions were much more prevalent. With enough money, it was possible to find a child. I could have sold Coralie—though they never really called it that— and lived comfortably. Boys weren't so valuable. It didn't make much sense to chance getting a boy by having a child of your own. They hadn't yet mastered any kind of gender selection yet, though the governments promised they were coming soon. Why take the risk of getting a useless boy, when you could just drop a bundle of cash and get the girl you actually wanted?

He squirmed and fussed as the light spilled into the box. The sun had started going down, but it was perhaps around suppertime. He looked as though he had been sleeping, so he couldn't have been here long. I lifted his warm, wiggling body from the box, taking care to keep the blanket wrapped tightly around him to keep out the cool breeze. I pressed him to my chest, as naturally as I had held Coralie and turned slowly, looking for someone who might have inadvertently left him here. I knew better, of course, but the unfulfilled mother in me couldn't believe it. He was a boy, but he was a person too. I carried the bundle across the street to the park where there were a cluster of benches that faced the donation bin. I would wait there; perhaps his mother would have second thoughts and come back for him. The cool wood of the bench shifted as I sat and the child began to squirm with more vigor. I could feel him searching for something, fussing as I held him. As his squeaks and grunts turned into wails, I could feel a chill against my breast. I looked down to see a wet spot growing on my shirt.

He was hungry. Of course.

I unbuttoned my shirt and pulled the blanket from around him and threw it over my shoulder, hiding us from any curious eyes. My hands shook with some mixture of grief and terror. I knew what I needed to do but it seemed too conflicting. My need to help this child warred within me against the feeling that I was somehow betraying Coralie. This milk was made for her, not this strange child. But she was gone, and it was of no use to her either.

I held the child close to me and I could feel the moment he latched on—his desperation and greediness. I tensed, unsure of what to do. Tears flowed from my eyes and I could do nothing to stop them.

We sat there together for a long time. He fell asleep on my shoulder with a contented sigh when he was done and I kept vigil, waiting for parents I knew would never come. The sun was gone by the time I allowed myself any kind of rational thought. My hands had been shaking for an hour now. Not because of the cool breeze, but a mixture of grief and fear. I felt like I was filled with butterflies, smashing into each other in a frantic search for the way out. I couldn't control my shaking any more than I could control the stars that were starting to wink in the darkening sky.

I could take care of him. Who would know?

My neighbors knew I had been pregnant, they wouldn't think twice, and I had some money saved up anyway, not much, but it would give me some time to figure out what to do about working. I had a part-time job doing the books for the property management firm that owned the building where I lived. It paid the rent but not much more. They had told me I could work from home once my baby was born, and had even supplied me with a tablet I could use. I'd need something else if I was going to take care of a child, but I had a bit of time to figure that out.

Looking at the quiet, sleeping face of this child, nothing else mattered. I would find a way. He deserved better than being left in a box on the side of the road, and to be honest, I needed him almost as much.

Clouds had begun to gather and as I stood from the bench, the wind began to blow and the familiar smell of rain stirred my senses. I wrapped the baby in his blanket and hurried back to the donation bin. The park was empty now and the streets were nearly deserted. I had already taken something of such value from that pile, but I needed to see if there was anything I could use. I filled the laundry basket with blankets and any baby clothing I could find, tucked the child into it, snuggled in the warm fabric and lifted the basket. It was heavy, but I wasn't far from home. I would need to hurry to get there before the rain started.

I paused for a second and turned back. Opening the bag of Coralie's stuff, I dug to the bottom for the few bottles and a rubber squeaking giraffe toy. Leaving the rest, I tucked the items into the basket and headed for home.

The rain started just as I ducked into an alleyway. It was a shortcut I had taken often, away from the prying eyes of neighborhood gossips. It was dark and the alley wasn't well lit. I didn't see the boy until he stepped out in front of me.

"Who are you?" he asked.

He couldn't have been more than thirteen, badly nourished and completely filthy. He had long hair that hung in stringy waves to his shoulders, covering his eyes, and I noticed, with a gasp that in one of his hands he held a small pocketknife.

"I don't have any money if that's what you want," I said.

"I don't want your money," he said, a slight waver in his voice blowing holes into his bravado.

"What do you want?" I asked.

"Where are you taking the baby?"

"Yeah!"

The second voice came from behind me. I didn't turn, but based on the pitch, it too seemed to come from a boy.

"Shut up, Amos. I told you to sit tight."

"But, I wanna know what she's doing with him too!"

"Amos..."

"I'm taking him home," I said.

"And?"

I rolled my eyes. "I'm going to cook him up like a turkey dinner, what do you think? I'm going to take care of him, you ninny."

The boy softened.

"Oh."

"You're not the woman who left him there," said the small voice behind me.

"Amos, honestly!"

I turned.

"You saw who left him?"

The boy nodded.

Part of me wanted to ask about her, to glean whatever small tidbits of information I could from these boys, but the truth was, I already knew more than enough about her.

"Don't worry... he's safe with me. You boys should get home before it starts raining."

"Oh, we don't have a home."

The older boy didn't even put words to his exasperated howl.

"You don't have a home?"

The younger boy pushed a hand through his greasy hair and spoke as the older one alternated between rolling his eyes and staring daggers. "Well, we did, but they didn't feed us all that well."

I glanced up at the gathering clouds and at these two

boys who were looking less and less like hoodlums and more like children.

"Come with me." I said. I didn't even think before the words came out of my mouth. All I knew was that I couldn't leave them out here in the rain.

"WHAT'S HIS NAME?" ASKED Amos.

"I don't know," I said. "I hadn't really thought about it yet."

The rain was pouring down outside, and a howling wind was making the tree by the window scrape its branches across the wet glass. Amos was clean and dressed in one of my t-shirts and an old pair of running shorts while I had his own clothes in the washing machine. It had been a hassle to get him to agree to a shower, but the chill in the air outside had persuaded him. Now, as his hair dried and his face had been purged of the thick layer of grime, I could see the pale freckles on his face. He had dark hair, and seemed to be some sort of mixed Asian descent, though it was rare for anyone to not be of mixed descent these days. I myself could trace my familial roots back to nearly every continent. I had initially thought they might be brothers based, I supposed, only on their ages and their combined filthiness. Once they were inside in the light I could see they looked nothing alike. Simeon had a sort of undetermined brown hair, the kind where you knew he had been born blonde, but it had darkened over the years, riding that middle—mousy—line between blonde and brown.

He was in the shower.

Thunder clapped outside.

"How about Thunder?" Amos asked.

I laughed.

"I don't know if many people want to be named 'Thunder'," I said.

"I would," said Amos.

Of course he would. Boys want to be strong and what was stronger than thunder?

"Thunder is a dumb name," said Simeon as he came out of the bathroom, drying his hair. He too was dressed in one of my college t-shirts and shorts. I wasn't sure if my little washing machine would get their clothes into an acceptable state, but it was the best I could do.

"Is not."

Simeon just rolled his eyes.

Amos played with the baby while I quickly scrambled up some eggs and made some toast. I couldn't remember the last time I had eaten, and as the buttery smells permeated the small apartment, I realized I was ravenous. I cooked the whole carton of eggs into one steaming, scrambled pile and dished out heaping spoonfuls into the mismatched dishes on the counter. The boys were hungry too, I could tell by the way their eyes widened as I handed them each a bowl of eggs with a piece of toast balanced on top. If I hadn't handed them a fork I was sure they would have just dug in with their hands. As I waited for my toast to pop I shoveled a few hot spoonfuls into my mouth too. They were probably the best eggs I had ever eaten.

I leaned on the wall by the window with the hot plate balanced in my hands. Simeon and Amos were at the table and the baby cooed and gurgled in the laundry basket on the floor between them.

The rain kept pouring down the window, cleansing the world like the hot showers that had changed these boys from hoodlums into the children I saw before me.

Rain could do that. It could wash away what nothing else could. It could erode through solid rock and nourish a seedling all at the same time.

"Rayne," I said, my voice quiet and pensive in the small space. "His name is Rayne."

TWENTY-TWO

"DID YOU GET ANY diapers?" I asked Simeon as I fumbled for my shoes. They were ugly and frumpy, but they were comfortable shoes and that's all I cared about.

Simeon shook his head. "The drugstore didn't have them on sale this week, but I checked the flyers and I think FoodMart has them the cheapest.

"'Kay, I'll pick some up after work then. I fed Rayne already, so he should be good until bedtime, and there's a bottle in the fridge for that. Simeon, keep working on those math problems I gave you. You too Amos, I'll check them when I get home."

I could hear Simeon sigh. He always did when I gave him homework, even though he and I both knew it was for his own good. None of them would amount to anything if they couldn't catch up with other kids their age. The orphanage hadn't bothered to educate either of them.

"Bye Delta!" said Amos with a grin. We had cut his hair and it now spiked in every direction in a most adorable way. I tousled his hair as I opened the door.

"Don't do anything stupid."

Simeon snickered, and Amos nodded with wide eyes as if I

had just bestowed upon him the secrets of the universe.

I closed the door behind me and waited for the metallic scratching of the chain sliding into place. We had figured out a way to survive and though the last months had been tricky, we were settling into a routine. I did my property-management job in the morning from the apartment while Rayne napped or played. Simeon and Amos used that time to do a paper route. It gave us some extra cash. They were friendly with the people on their route, so as an added bonus, they usually finished the week with a stack of extra coupons that weren't going to be used. We saved and clipped them religiously, poring over the sales flyers to get the things we needed at the best possible price. I had a second part-time job at a diner down the street from the apartment, and the boys cared for Rayne while I was gone. At thirteen Simeon was just barely old enough to babysit, but I made sure to check in on them when I could. I didn't like leaving them, but we needed the money. Amos was eleven, we had guessed, though we couldn't be entirely sure, since he didn't know when his birthday was.

I did my best to keep the money from their paper route in a cookie jar above the fridge. I didn't know how long they were going to stay with me, but I wanted them to have some money whenever they decided to start out on their own. We all worked hard, and somehow that made it all work for us.

I GOT HOME LATE that night. I was more than ready to kick of my shoes and hop into a hot shower. The diner had been busy and my pocket was full of tips I had made. It had been a good night, but an exhausting one and I was ready to wash off the diner grease and fall into bed. I knocked lightly on the door, my signal for the boys to unlock the chain, and let me in. Simeon would be awake—he always waited up for me—but with any luck Rayne and Amos would both be asleep.

I heard the chain slide back and as the door clicked open I sighed. Amos was still up, holding a very awake Rayne in his arms.

Simeon closed the door behind me. I had a paper bag full of takeout containers. Herb, the cook, always saved some food for me, stuff he couldn't sell, or had been sent out wrong and needed to be remade. The boys always appreciated the cold french fries, but today I had their favorite, a club sandwich that someone had ordered. Herb had put mayo on it, even though the ticket said not to. Sometimes I was sure he made orders wrong on purpose, especially club sandwiches.

"Herb sent some food," I said, as I plunked the bag on the table, dropping my keys and the plastic package of diapers beside it. I kicked my feet, one after the other, and let my clunky shoes fall to the ground. "Didn't Rayne go to sleep?"

"He was asleep, but, um, Amos woke him up... accidently," said Simeon.

The boys shared a glance I didn't understand, but that was nothing new.

I sunk into the couch, and reached my hands out. Amos handed Rayne to me. He was gaining weight. In the months I'd had him, he had turned into a pudgy, giggling boy. I smiled as he snuggled into my shoulder, obviously tired. He would fall asleep right away, I was sure, and I liked nothing better than when he did so in my arms.

I groaned as I stretched my feet.

"Can one of you pass me some milk?" I asked. Rayne was already starting to feel heavier as his body relaxed into mine and his breathing deepened. "And go ahead and eat something if you want, Herb screwed up a club again."

Simeon went to the fridge and filled a glass of milk for me. Amos sat on one of the kitchen chairs and stared off into the room.

"Not hungry?" I asked.

"We're ok," said Simeon. "Right Amos?"

"Yeah."

"Then put the food in the fridge, you can have it tomorrow."

I yawned and drank my milk while the boys seemed restless.

"Do you want me to go to bed so you guys can pull out the couch?"

I forgot I had been sitting on their bed.

Amos jumped up from his seat, and Simeon quickly shook his head, glancing at my bed.

"No, just stay there, we're fine."

Rayne had recently outgrown the laundry basket we used as his bed, so he and I usually shared the double bed, while Simeon and Amos took the pull-out.

"Why are you two acting so weird?" I asked quietly, to avoid disturbing Rayne, whose breathing had turned into light snoring.

"We..." started Amos.

"Just might be hungry," said Simeon, cutting him off. He dug into the bag and pulled out one of the cardboard take-out containers. He flipped it open and pulled out half a sandwich, handing it to Amos, and took the other half for himself.

I smiled and enjoyed cuddling with Rayne while the boys ate. They didn't really seem all that interested in food, but they were boys. Boys could always eat.

Yawning again, I stood and headed slowly over to the bed to put Rayne down so I could go have a shower and join him. I pulled back the covers and gasped when I realized why the boys had been acting so strange.

"Why is there a toddler sleeping in my bed?"

I turned to face Amos and Simeon, both looking a bit sheepish.

They looked at each other before Simeon spoke.

"We found him."

"I assumed as much, but why is he here?"

"We went for a walk," started Amos.

"Ok," I said, waiting for the part that explained the child in my bed.

Simeon sighed.

"Sometimes we walk past the orphanage," he said. "You know, by the back."

I sighed. I knew where he was going with this. The back door of the orphanage they had come from was a kind of "anonymous drop off" spot. People could drive down the alleyway, leave a child there, no questions asked. It was touted as a safe way to find new homes for children, but it was really just an easy, hidden way to dump unwanted kids, mainly boys.

I let them continue.

"We saw a car drive up and leave him on the step and drive away."

A tear fell from my eye. Not for the unwanted child, but for the two who stood in front of me. Six months ago they had cornered me in an alley with a knife to take care of an infant they didn't know, and here they were, doing it again. For children who had also been unwanted, there was no hurt or bitterness left in them.

"The guy who left him didn't ring the bell, so when the car drove away, we just walked up and took him."

"We can pay for him, kids that size don't eat much," said Amos, his face hopeful. "I can take him to the park sometimes, and teach him his letters."

He spoke like he was trying to convince me to get a puppy.

I laughed.

"Fine, we can keep him, but taking care of two little guys is going to be a lot more work."

"We know," said Simeon. "We just couldn't leave him."

"I know what you mean," I said, looking down at the boy in the bed, his dark curls spilled out over the pillow.

"Just promise me something?"

They nodded.

"No more kids."

I WOKE UP TO Rayne gurgling in the bed next to me. I had been able to lift the other little boy and get him closer to the wall so both Rayne and I could still manage to sleep in the bed too. I could feel the sunlight pouring in through the window, warming my face. I rolled over and groaned, opening my eyes to see a little round face, framed by dark curls staring back at me.

"Hi," I said, my voice soft.

He just stared at me.

Rayne wiggled on his back between us, and the boy looked at him and poked him in the nose.

"Baby," he said.

"Yes, that's a baby," I said, moving his hand away from Rayne's face. "Gentle."

He nodded. "Gentle."

I didn't know when kids hit different milestones, but I guessed this boy was about two years old.

Amos and Simeon were still asleep. They usually slept a lot longer than Rayne did, so I did my best to spend some quiet time with Rayne each morning in bed.

I wasn't sure if that was going to work out terribly well with a new toddler in the house, but for now, it seemed ok. I watched as the child touched Rayne's face gently and leaned forward to give him a kiss. Rayne giggled and babbled away, as interested in this new person as I was.

"Do you think he has a name?" asked Amos from their bed. I looked out over the blankets to see both of the older boys watching us.

"I don't know," I said. "I assume he'd have one, but whether he could tell us what it was, I'm not sure."

Amos came over and sat on the bed beside him, leaning against the wall.

"What's your name?" he asked.

The boy pursed his lips and scowled.

I tried a different approach.

Gently touching Rayne, I said "Rayne."

Then I reached across the bed to touch Amos. "Amos."

"Simeon," Simeon said, patting his chest, understanding what I was doing.

Then I reached out and lightly tapped the boy's chest with my finger.

"Who is this?"

A smile lit his face as understanding flashed across it.

"Lie-us."

"What did he say?" asked Amos

"Lie-us?" I asked.

The boy nodded.

"Linus?" asked Simeon.

The boy frowned and shook his head. His dark curls bounced.

"LIE-us"

I exchanged looks with the older boys, unsure. I doubted his name was Lie-us, but I couldn't figure it out.

"Elias?" asked Simeon.

The boy's face shone and he laughed

"Lie-us, Lie-us," he said, clapping.

"Elias," I said. "Nice to meet you, Elias. Would you like some breakfast?"

"Breskfust," he said, nodding.

I rolled out of bed and pulled on a sweater. The nights were getting chillier and I hadn't wanted to turn on the heat just yet. The sun would warm the apartment during the day, and paying for heat could wait a few more weeks.

Simeon crawled into the space I had vacated and dangled a toy over Rayne, who laughed and kicked and wiggled, completely smitten by his older brothers.

It was going to be a new adjustment having Elias here, but we had figured it out once before, and we would again. From what the boys told me, or more often didn't tell me about the orphanage, I had no regrets about taking Elias in.

I mixed up a pot of oatmeal and dished it into bowls to cool. There was even some brown sugar, a luxury we couldn't have every day, but it was a special day. Our family was bigger, and that was reason to celebrate.

TWENTY-THREE

Rhea

I could feel the warmth of the sunlight on my back and the thick mat of grass beneath my belly. I didn't need to open my eyes to know exactly where I was. The blossoms were in full bloom on Mrs. Everson's peach tree—I could smell them from where I was—a hint of sweetness mingled with the green smell of freshly-mowed grass. I could hear Ember playing nearby, singing some kind of nonsense song that I used to sing with her when she was little. I was surprised she remembered all the words. I rolled over onto my side to see where she was. When I opened my eyes I could see her across the backyard, her dark hair loose and moving slightly with the summer breeze. She was singing, and seated in the grass between her thin, gangly legs was a child. A neighborhood child perhaps? I didn't recognize her, and couldn't remember anyone new moving in. The little girl was laughing and clapping as Ember sang to her, her pudgy legs pumping with delight at the silly tune. Her hair was golden, almost white, and the sun shone through it, giving her hair the image of a glowing halo.

"That's beautiful," said a voice from behind me.

I turned my head to see Jude. He was lying on his back in the grass, next to the matted section I had just vacated. He too was watching Ember and this child.

I nodded.

"Do you know who the little girl is?"

He looked at me, perplexed.

"Your sister."

"Well, of course, Ember is my sister, but the other one?"

His eyebrow raised. "The other one?"

I turned back to see Ember, alone in the grass, picking at the blades and tying them into tiny knots of grass.

"Where did she go?"

"I don't know what you're talking about, Rhea."

Had I imagined it? A dream maybe?

"Did I fall asleep here?"

Jude shrugged. "Maybe. I almost dozed off myself a few times."

He sat up beside me and pulled me toward him, his strong arm wrapped around my waist. I could feel his chin against my neck, burrowed in my hair. I leaned back, enjoying the sunlight and relaxing into his embrace.

"I just want to freeze this moment," I said.

"But not literally, right? I've had enough of the cold."

We both laughed. It seemed funny though I didn't really know why.

I could feel his warm breath as he gathered up my hair into a clump and slipped it over my shoulder to reveal the soft curve of my neck. He landed his kisses there, lightly at first, little more than a whisper.

I closed my eyes, enjoying the moment.

When I opened them again, Ember was gone.

My stomach lurched.

We weren't supposed to leave the yard, yet I didn't see her anywhere.

"Ember?" I called, but no sound came from my mouth.

Jude's kisses were becoming more persistent and I was torn between forgetting about my sister and relishing his attention, but the gnawing feeling didn't go away. Something was wrong. Ember.

I tried to shout her name again, using every breath I had, but still nothing filled my ears but the chirping of birds and the leaves rustling in the slight breeze. I pushed away from Jude, scrambling to my knees.

"I need to find my sister," I said, I could feel my mouth move but still there was no sound. His hands grabbed me and pulled me back—angry and insistent. I struggled to free myself, still scanning the yard in search of Ember.

Finally, I gave a good yank, pushed myself away from Jude and turned to face him, ready to scold him for ignoring my pleas. My words caught in my throat when I found myself face to face with Simeon.

I screamed.

This time I heard it.

TWENTY-FOUR

Delta

"JUDE I NEED TO talk to you," I said as I passed him in the hallway.

He nodded and followed me into one of the less-used halls.

"What happened to Rhea?" he asked as the glass door clicked shut behind us, cutting us off from the traffic of the main thoroughfare.

"I'll explain in a bit, but I don't exactly know yet," I said. "I know where she is and that for now she is safe, but I need your help figuring it out."

Jude nodded.

"Do you know if there is a girl named Isis here?"

The name hadn't sounded familiar to me, but I didn't spend as much time around the estate as the boys did.

Jude bit his lip, a nervous tick he'd had since childhood. "I don't think so," he said, "But I know who would know."

I nodded. "You're right. Go ask Finn. Bring him to my room when you find him."

If there was anyone in this place who would know everyone it was the resident social butterfly. While Finn tended to concentrate his efforts on the youngest and most beautiful of the girls, he had a certain knack when it came to names and faces. It was brilliant almost. If he had been born a woman, opportunities would have been endless for the handsome young man, but instead he was a page. Destined to wait on the heads of state rather than be one.

Jude hurried away in search of Finn, his shoes squeaking on the marble tiles. I should have just followed him so I could talk to Finn as soon as we found him, but Jude would be faster on his own, and it was likely that he'd need to check a number of places. I was still an active woman, but I knew I would only slow him down.

Part of me wanted to go back to see if anything had changed with the girls—they had probably moved Rhea and Hazel into their tanks by now—but what could have possibly changed in the hour since I left them? They wouldn't know I had come, and they couldn't acknowledge me, but I still felt that I was somehow abandoning them, leaving them alone in that stark room in those horrible glowing tanks. They were barely older than children.

I knew I needed to go back to my room. Jude could find Finn quickly, and I didn't want to leave them waiting for me. If Isis was here somewhere, Finn would know, and they could tell me where to find her. I didn't even know what to ask her if they did. Meredith hadn't given me much information.

The hallways weren't terribly busy in the staff quarters. Almost everyone would be busy doing something at this time of day. Because the girls would usually be off to the kitchen to start plating the food for dinner, this had always been a quiet time for me. I opened the door to my room and walked inside, turning on the light.

It was a tiny room, with enough space for a single bed, a small, square bedside table with a lamp and a comfortable chair in the corner. My belongings were stashed in a small closet behind the door. I didn't own much, just the clothing I had been issued when we arrived at the estate. I hadn't had time to collect many personal items before I needed to board the helicopters, but I had managed a few, some books, some photographs. I spent as much time as possible in this room, and I exhaled as I absorbed its familiarity. I came here to get away from everything else, the dull ache that ate away at me as I did my work.

My job here had never been terribly enjoyable, the girls deserved more than to be stolen from their lives and pushed into someone else's idea of their future. I had been a participant, though if I had a choice that too might have been different. It was impossible to push back against such an abuse of power. So while yes, I was a participant, I stayed my guilt with the knowledge that I was an unwilling, and at times unhelpful participant. I remembered the stories my grandmother had told me when I was young about my grandfather. She would always tell me stories while she cooked, the smell of Indian spices permeating the sunny kitchen. She loved almost any kind of food, her favorites were vegetable curries, but she had a serious soft spot for the cabbage rolls and borscht she learned to make when she met my grandfather.

He was a German citizen who was drafted by the Nazis in

the Second World War. He had objected from the start, but their choices were minimal—serve or die. With a widowed mother and several younger siblings to care for, death wasn't an option, so he put on the sickening uniform and did his very best to be the most incompetent soldier anyone had ever met. At the first possible opportunity, he got himself captured by the allied forces and spent the rest of the war comfortably surviving in a Canadian prisoner-of-war camp. It was there that he met my grandmother, the half-Indian, illegitimate daughter of a Russian diplomat. She had been running from the German forces when she too found herself captured.

There were times that you fought—she would tell me—but fighting sometimes means dying, and sometimes dying just wasn't an option. There were other times when you rode the current, allowed it to take you to where you needed to be, and let it tell you the right moment to lift yourself up, plant your feet in the river mud and fight back. Fighting a battle you can't win is pointless, but sometimes if you wait, you will find the one you can.

That's what I was doing. Riding the current had brought me here. I was safe—for the time being—when I could have perished with countless others. I was fed and clothed. I could ride the current until the world thawed, unless I was needed sooner.

I didn't need to wait long for Jude and Finn. I could hear their footsteps and knew it was them well before Jude's light knock.

"Come in," I said, and the knob turned. Jude's head popped around the corner.

"I found Finn," he said as he opened the door, "and someone else."

Behind Jude I would see Finn's lanky figure fill the frame of the door. In front of him, he pushed a young woman in a wheelchair. She looked nervous.

They came into the room, pushing the girl to a stop, her chair and mine facing each other. Finn closed the door behind them, and he and Jude both folded themselves up and sat cross-legged on my bed. I didn't bother to chide them for putting their dirty shoes on my sheets. I was more interested in the girl.

"Isis?" I asked.

She squirmed uncomfortably in her chair and glanced at Finn who nodded his encouragement. I could tell she didn't fully trust me.

Nodding, she dropped her eyes to her lap.

"I don't go by that name here though."

"Why?"

"It's ok, you can tell her," said Finn. "We can trust her."

Jude and I shared a glance at Finn's use of the word "we". He just shook his head slightly, as if to tell me this wasn't the time. I didn't need to do much more guessing when I saw Finn reach over and take her hand.

"I use the name Rebekkah here," she said. "It's my middle name. Too many people knew who I was if I used Isis."

"Who are you?"

"No one. A ghost. A disappointment."

Finn shot her a look of disapproval. He obviously didn't

agree with her personal assessment.

"Finn?"

He blushed. "We've become... friends."

"I can see that," I said. "Isis, sorry, Rebekkah... there are things I don't understand, and while I was trying to figure out what they were, someone told me to find you. Unfortunately, I also don't really know what questions to ask, but I have a feeling you might know the answers anyway."

She nodded slowly.

"I know more than they want me to."

Finn squeezed her hand and she smiled, her affection for him shining through her fear, if only for a second. I didn't say anything hoping my silence would force her to fill the empty space. It worked.

"It started a few years ago. I was engaged, and my fiancé, Aaron, and I were planning our wedding. We had it all worked out, and had so many plans. But Aaron didn't make much money, and I hadn't saved much, so when I heard about a place that needed a young woman for a medical test, and paid well, I jumped at it. This woman had invented some kind of..."

"Serum," said Finn quietly, helping her find the word.

"Yes, some kind of serum that made it easier for girls to have babies. I wanted to have babies, but none of my sisters had been lucky yet. It paid really well... like, really well. I could have paid for our wedding and we probably could have had enough for a big down payment on a house or something."

I held my breath. I knew part of this story, but I had never imagined it would be told to me this way. Elias had worked there. His boss, a woman named Nova, had invented the serum. I didn't know how it worked, though I had visited the MedTech lab a few times.

"So how did you end up here?" I asked. Other than Elias, Simeon and me, there were no connections that I knew of from here to MedTech, and I knew Simeon didn't know anything about what Elias did.

"Well, about a week before I was supposed to go in for my appointment, a big black car pulled up to the house. This woman got out,"

"Nadia," said Finn.

"Yeah, but I didn't know who she was then. She came to the door and just walked in like she owned the place. She didn't even bother knocking. My dad was a bit weirded-out by the whole thing. She told me they needed me to do a service for my country. They needed the serum and I was the only way they could get it. They offered me even more money to go, get the serum, and then come back to their lab and let the scientists check my blood and see if they could figure out how to make a copy."

"They threatened her," said Finn, angered by the story, even though he had obviously heard it before.

Rebekkah nodded. "They said if I didn't agree, they'd come back and make my life miserable, send Aaron off to the military, cut off my dad's support payments, anything they could do." Tears had begun to gather in her eyes.

"I couldn't let them ruin our lives, I couldn't. I agreed and they left an envelope full of cash. A 'deposit' they said. Aaron came over later, and my dad explained it to him. He acted like we won the lottery, but it just wasn't sitting right with me. I didn't know why they couldn't just go ask for the serum, why they had to steal it. Why I had to steal it for them. I kind of freaked."

"You did the right thing, 'Bekks," said Finn quietly, still holding her hand.

"The morning I was supposed to go to MedTech, I called them and said I wasn't coming. Aaron was so pissed when I told him. Not only would we be losing the money from them, but also from the woman, though, I never really believed she would pay me anything anyway. She doesn't really strike me as a trustworthy person, you know?"

"I've noticed that myself," I said.

"Aaron freaked out, and we had this huge fight. He was really mad, but he agreed to go with me to the government lab and tell them I wasn't going to do it. It was already really snowing when we got there, and thankfully she wasn't there, so I told her assistant. It took a while, 'cause they told me to wait, but it just kept snowing and snowing. I was waiting on the second floor landing and I don't know what happened, but suddenly people were running everywhere. They were all going crazy and there was screaming. There were so many people, and they were all pushing and shoving..."

Tears had started flowing steadily from her eyes, and she didn't bother to wipe them away. I reached over to my table and pulled a tissue from the box, handing it to her. She took it and just crumpled it in her lap.

"She got pushed over the rail," said Finn. "That's why she's in a wheelchair."

Rebekkah nodded, her face wet with tears.

"How did you end up here?"

She took a deep breath, trying to steady herself.

"The assistant found me, I was kind of in and out at this point and I don't remember everything, but I remember him telling me to hold on, and then running to get someone. I think I passed out, but when I woke up, people were putting me onto a stretcher, and taking me up the elevator. It seemed like we were in the elevator forever, and I didn't recognize anyone in there, except for that assistant, and..."

It was starting to make sense to me. "Meredith Kroeker?"

"Yes, the President."

It was unlikely Nadia would have told Meredith what she was up to, so it was probably a fluke that she was even at the lab that day. She wouldn't have left a helpless girl to die. Meredith wasn't like her sister.

"They took me onto the roof, and it was so cold. They put me in a helicopter and some of the other people got in. The president said she would take the next one, and they started to take off. Finn, you tell the rest, I can't."

Finn reached over and pushed some of her dark hair from her face with a tenderness that seemed out of place on my social butterfly.

"Aaron showed up on the roof, must have taken a different

elevator, or maybe the stairs. Anyway, he ran past Meredith and grabbed onto the ski of the helicopter as it was taking off. The pilot tried to land again, but the winds were too strong and everything was icy, and he fell."

Rebekkah nodded and blew her nose into the tissue.

"They brought me here. Once my back was better they put me to work folding laundry and ironing sometimes. Dr. Murray came to see me once and told me the President said to stay out of sight as much as possible, though people don't really pay much attention to me anyway."

"Except Finn," said Jude loudly, shooting an elbow into Finn's ribs. Finn reached one of his long arms around Jude's neck putting him in a headlock and pulling him off balance on the bed.

Rebekkah just shook her head at their roughhousing, a smile creeping back onto her face.

"So, you two are together?" I asked her.

She blushed. "He's a fine young man," she said.

"If he wasn't, you tell me and I'll set him straight."

Rebekkah smiled at me. "That won't be necessary. Finn knows better than to mess with me."

I could tell we were going to get along just fine.

TWENTY-FIVE

AFTER THE BOYS AND Rebekkah left, I stayed in my room. I missed dinner, but I wasn't hungry anyway. The pieces had fit together, and even though there were still some empty spaces in the picture I was building, I had a pretty good idea what Nadia was up to. The question was how far she was planning to take it. She hungered for power and control, and if it was at all possible that she could grasp it, she would try.

Thankfully time was on our side. Nadia didn't have the serum that Elias had been working on, and whether it even still existed was impossible to say. Elias had started at MedTech right out of college, and had worked there for about three years before they had a working prototype. Who knew how long Nova had been working on it before that. Part of me hoped the serum had been destroyed, but I couldn't hope for that. Elias wouldn't allow their work to be destroyed, so if it had perished, there was a good chance he had also. I refused to believe that.

From what I knew from the status reports, no one had found a safe way off the mountain yet. The heavy snows had built up and there was no way of knowing when a seemingly safe path could be wiped out by a single avalanche. Perhaps one or two people could be lucky enough to make it, but not everyone. We were safe here, and they couldn't yet risk the loss of the heads of state by being reckless.

Nadia was a terrible person but she wasn't hasty. She was calculating and detailed. She wouldn't move until she had everything lined up so that her plans couldn't fail. We had time, but I didn't know how much.

TWENTY-SIX

"WE NEED TO DO something," Jude said. "This isn't right."

I couldn't disagree with him.

News had spread in the estate about the success of the program. The first child had been born healthy. I had watched Kenzie's body grow and change over the last months until I was sure her tiny frame would burst with the strain. It was a boy. Nadia was frustrated, but since they had still not perfected gender selection, it was still the luck of the draw. She needed girls, uncellutated girls to raise for her infant factory. She couldn't find more teenagers, and no one knew if there were more anyway, so she had decided to just breed some herself. It would push her plan back a number of years, but as long as the sisters could keep having children, she would succeed.

Both Willow and Hazel were now obviously pregnant, and as soon as Kenzie's body recovered, they would impregnate her again. It was also possible Freya was pregnant too, but her body had miscarried her first at about four months, and they had needed to start over.

Neither Rhea nor Shalisa had conceived yet. Their cellutation inoculations had made it much more difficult, and while the scientists were working on a way around that, they had yet to be successful.

I was glad the ultrasound machine had mysteriously become unusable. Several parts had gone missing and as long as we were stuck on the mountainside, with no supply chain, it was impossible to find replacements. Without the ultrasound machine, it was impossible to tell what gender child the girls were carrying. This irritated Nadia to no end, she would have preferred to cut her losses and abort a boy halfway through, so she'd be able to try again right away, but she was stuck, and there was no way around it.

I was sure one of the boys had done it, but I didn't know which one and I'd never asked. It was safer if I didn't know. I had been there when Nadia had found out the child was a boy. She threw up her hands in anger and stormed out, shouting over her shoulder to get rid of "it".

I scooped the child up in my hands before anyone else made a move and stalked out the door, letting people believe I was just following orders. Instead I found my way through the hallways to a small room at the very end of one of the wings. The little boy was now safe with Rebekkah, and I knew that between her and Finn they would take care of him. People paid very little attention to Rebekkah, and Finn was so well known around the estate that he could get in and out of just about anywhere. He could find and pilfer any of the supplies they needed.

"None of this is right, Jude," I said. "But we can't afford to be rash."

We were eating dinner in the dining room. It was unusually quiet, as it typically was when Nadia wasn't getting what she wanted. Most people tip-toed around her as it was, but today it seemed everyone was unusually meek.

"We just need to watch and pay attention, and we'll figure it out."

"Ride the current?" he asked, his voice holding a biting tone that earned him a raised eyebrow.

He didn't apologize and I didn't make him. It wasn't worth it. I wanted to be impatient too, but I knew the difference between speed and recklessness. Moving too soon would be reckless.

I lifted another spoonful of soup into my mouth. The food had been getting progressively less flavorful as they moved from mainly fresh and frozen to a synthetically-based diet. There was still some fresh food from the miniature farm that took up most of the upper level, but it was declining. A memo had circulated and we were told to be prepared for this. They could keep us alive for another twenty years with the freeze-dried and synthetic stores they had, but we were cautioned not to expect the same standard of living forever.

I sincerely hoped we were not going to be here for another twenty years.

Luckily within their synthetic food stores, they had a large quantity of powdered infant formula. Red had managed to "adjust" the computerized inventories and no one was any the wiser when twelve large cans went missing. They were all safely stored under Rebekkah's bed and would get the child to the point where he could start eating more solid food, which was much easier to find.

I wanted to ask one of the boys if Finn and Rebekkah had named the boy yet, but in the middle of the dining room, surrounded by people was not the place to do it. I ate slowly and watched the people, looking for any sign that things were changing, that our situation was getting less stable. I had instructed the boys to keep their eyes and ears open too. Nadia had been playing her cards close to her chest, but she couldn't do anything alone, and not everyone was as tight-lipped.

"Our time will come, Jude," I said as I sipped the last spoonful of soup. "And when it does, I promise you I will have something for you to do."

I HADN'T GONE TO see Meredith in months, not since pulling together the pieces of Nadia's plan. I knew I needed to let her in on what was going around, but I had been procrastinating. I argued with myself that she had a level of oblivion that I longed for. There were days I would trade places with her if given the chance. To be able to sleep through this nightmare would be a blessing, especially since she didn't have much power at the moment. She had been elected by the citizens of the United States, though one could only guess how many of those citizens were still alive. She had very little support in the estate, so she was safest where she was.

In contrast, I walked the halls with all the knowledge, and even less power. I knew I needed her strategic mind, but I felt nothing but remorse each time I woke her up to tell her how terrible the world had become.

"Delta, I need to talk to you," said Dr. Murray as I made my way into the clinic.

She nodded at the other nurses, who hastily made their way from the room. Once the room was empty, and I could hear nothing but the quiet beep and hum of Meredith's monitors, she sat down on one of the chairs and beckoned for me to do the same.

"Meredith's condition is precarious," she said, her voice low enough that I needed to strain to hear her. "Her body is starting to reject the medications I use to keep her in this state. At some point in the near future I won't be able to control it anymore."

I nodded.

"What does that mean?" I asked.

Dr.Murray took off her glasses and pinched the bridge of her nose, rubbing her fingers in small circles to alleviate whatever pain she was feeling. She had aged in the past months. She was no longer the energetic, young doctor that had come to work for Meredith. She now wore the strain of secrecy and silence on her face. She had always been pale, but now looked almost ghastly. Even her hair had lost its typical luster. I reached out and placed a hand on her knee.

"I can wake her up today, and most likely get her back under, but I think this may be the last time," she said, her voice weary and weak. "And after that I don't know how long she will stay that way. It could be days, or weeks, or months. Once her body fully rejects these meds, there will be nothing I can do."

She didn't need to say more, I understood completely.

Meredith would be at risk.

"You have gone above and beyond, Shayna." I rarely called Dr. Murray by her given name, but it suddenly felt appropriate. She needed comfort. She had been stretched too thin and it was evident that there was very little left for her to give.

She nodded and replaced her glasses.

"I can wake her up now if you want."

"Thank you," I said as I went to lock the door. I didn't think Nadia came here as often anymore, judging by the lack of bandages on Meredith's arm, but I wasn't about to risk it now. I was ready with a glass of water when Meredith woke up.

"Delta," she said, her lips dry and parched.

I pressed the button to raise her to a sitting position.

"I was just having the most wonderful dream," she said.

"Yeah?" I didn't really want to know about it. I hadn't found myself in any dreams that could be considered wonderful. Thankfully she didn't elaborate.

I held the glass to her lips and helped her drink from it. Her body was wasting away, I could tell. They fed her intravenously, but there was little that could be done about her deteriorated muscle tone. She would need some physiotherapy to get her back to her former strength.

"What's happening?"

I filled her in on what I had learned from Rebekkah and the things that had been happening since she was last awake.

"Almost six years," she said wistfully. "When is this going to end?"

I didn't have an answer for her, no one did, nor did she expect one. We all had the same thoughts, and for the majority of six years, she had been completely unable to express them.

"Were we wrong to keep you like this?" I asked.

She pondered for a moment then shook her head.

"Nadia tried to kill me once, and frankly I'm amazed she hasn't just taken me out while I slept, but this has been the safest path for me."

"It's not going to work forever," I said. "Dr. Murray says your body is rejecting her medications."

"It's not surprising," said Meredith, "The body has a remarkable capacity to heal itself."

"You're going to wake up at some point, and there will be nothing she can do about it."

She took a deep breath to steady herself.

"Then we will deal with that when it comes."

I frowned.

"Delta, none of us are promised much in this life, and those of us who have held power know how fleeting it is. I won't go down without a fight, I promise you that. Just let me know when and where I need to plant my feet."

TWENTY-SEVEN

THE NEXT TWO CHILDREN were girls, and it was the first time I had seen Nadia crack a smile in years. It wasn't a happy smile, or an excited one. More like the kind of smile a crocodile would give you once it had half a gazelle shoved down its throat, but at least it wasn't the fiery rage we were used to.

"Freya and Kenzie are both pregnant too, and now that Willow and Hazel have completed their two-month recovery, they'll be getting them ready to try again," I said to Rebekkah, as I came to visit little Jonah. He was growing rapidly, a testament to how well they were caring for him. They had laughed when they told me his name.

"What better name for a child who is stuck in the belly of a whale?" Finn had said.

Rebekkah had laughed with him as she had cuddled him. She had been a natural mother, and they all complemented each other better than I could have hoped for in their thrown-together family.

I visited them regularly, unable to keep myself from little Jonah's smiles. Even at eight months old, he seemed to understand his predicament. He was a quiet child, happiest on his mother's lap as she wheeled herself around the tiny room. Rebekkah had grown up so much in this time too. Motherhood suited her, and strangely the situation suited Finn too. I had never expected him to settle down with anyone, preferring the chase of many to any one girl.

"You and Finn are doing such a great job, Rebekkah."

"It's not like we had much choice. I couldn't have Jonah's life on my conscience."

I knew the feeling.

Jonah played happily on her lap with a tiny bunch of knotted rags she had made for him. It was a rather ingenious toy, with pockets and hidden places for him to hide his pudgy hands, and little places he could peek through. He was starting to grow hair like his mother, dark waves against his pale skin. There was much about his look that differed from Kenzie, though, and at times I wondered who was fathering these children.

"He asked me to marry him," said Rebekkah, her voice barely more than a whisper, as if she wasn't sure what my reaction would be.

My face felt strange as the smile broke through.

"Nothing would make me happier, Rebekkah."

"Really?" she asked, her eyes searching my face for some sign of deception.

"Why would I lie?"

She shrugged and dropped her eyes from mine. "Since I ended up in this chair, most people have written me off..."

She paused, just for a second, but I spoke before she could

continue.

"Whether or not you can walk matters nothing to me," I said leaning forward to lift her chin with my hands. "Any girl who can stop Finn in his tracks, has something so precious that he, and I, would be fools to dismiss it."

She smiled. Jonah reached up and put his hand on mine, and we both held her face.

"You will be my first daughter." I said smiling. Jonah smiled too.

She looked confused.

"What about Tess?"

I snorted. "She was never my daughter," I said laughing. "She might have married my son, but she had no need for me, nor I for her. But if it makes you feel better, you can be the first daughter I ever liked."

She nodded. "That'll do."

THEY MARRIED A MONTH later, in the viewing room that looked out over the sisters. We met in the middle of the night, so Jonah could be present without anyone seeing him. It felt right to be together. Finn knelt next to his bride, while Jonah slept on her shoulder. They made vows to each other while I stood in witness with Red, Vaughn, Harris and Jude. I tried not to be distracted by the six girls, silent and unmoving in their pods, but between the heartfelt words being spoken by Finn and Rebekkah, and the abomination that was taking place on the other side of the glass, I found myself more emotional than I ever let myself be.

When Finn and Rebekkah kissed, sealing their pact to each other, I could no longer hold it in. Tears streamed from my eyes. I felt Jude wrap his arms around me, and I let myself cry.

TWENTY-EIGHT

I WASN'T ABLE TO save the next boy that was born. Nadia had given strict instructions to the doctors to terminate boys at birth. She had no use for them. By now she had three little girls that were being cared for in a makeshift nursery by some of the older laundry and kitchen women. Freya's son was gone by the time I heard he was born, but I was there to witness Freya's death.

"What happened?" asked Red, grief-stricken at the news.

I knew he and Freya had been friends at some level before they took her into the blue. That's what we called it now: "into the blue." Their young skin was bathed in blue light and surrounded in glass. We couldn't call it a hospital, or a clinic, because that was where people got well, this was something entirely different that deserved no proper name.

"I think it was just too much for her body," I said, my voice sounding hollow and detached. I didn't want to be the one to tell him, remembering too vividly the time I spent with Harris after Margo died. "She had suffered two miscarriages and then the full-term pregnancy was the breaking point."

His face crumpled and I waited for him to begin to cry, but nothing came.

"They tried to save her," I said, knowing it would be no consolation, since they were the ones who had put her there and subjected her body to constant trauma. They had truly done everything they could, but there was nothing that could be done to stop the bleeding. She died less than an hour after her son.

I reached out to Red, hoping to bring him some level of comfort but nothing could bring back the years he had watched Freya through the glass.

He jerked away from my touch.

"Don't try to make me feel better," he said, almost growling. I could see the fire of his hair echoed in his eyes, and it scared me.

"Red, you need to..."

"I need to do nothing!" he said, the volume of his voice raising with each syllable.

I didn't know what to do. I had never seen him in this kind of grief-induced fury before. He had always been somewhat hot-headed but it was rare that I wasn't able to keep him at a simmer.

"Just wait here... don't do anything just for a minute."

I left the room, closing the door behind me. I heard the splintering crack of wood and I knew he had broken a chair. I understood grief, but this rage frightened me. I didn't know how I could settle him down, nor did I know if I truly wanted to. If I was really truthful with myself, I wanted to be angry too.

Vaughn was the first person I spotted.

"Vaughn, run to the clinic and get Dr. Murray. Tell her to bring a sedative."

He didn't question me. The terror on my face was enough

to make him drop whatever he was doing and run.

Jude was probably the nearest to where we were. He would be in the kitchens right now. I shouted his name as I hurried through the halls, oblivious to the strange looks I was getting, and not really caring. He heard my calls and ran out to meet me.

"What's going on?"

"Freya is dead," I whispered to him. "And Red..."

I didn't need to say more. Jude was off at a run. My fear alone was no match for his youth and vitality—unable to keep up, I let him go and rushed after him as quickly as my much-older legs could take me. Vaughn and Dr. Murray had met Jude at the door to Red's room. Jude and Vaughn were the first through the door and together they were able to pin Red face-down on the bed. Dr. Murray filled the syringe she had in her hands and amid Red's cursing and shouting, she pressed the needle through the skin on his arm and slowly pushed the plunger. He spat at her, and shouted threats at Jude and Vaughn who were doing their very best to keep him still.

The sedative worked quickly, and within moments Red began to relax. Vaughn and Jude rolled him over and lifted him into a more comfortable position. He was asleep by the time they arranged a pillow under his head and pulled a blanket over him.

"How long will that last?" I asked.

"Not very long, said Dr. Murray. "Perhaps an hour or so? I only gave him enough to give you time to make a game plan. Why was he so angry?"

"One of the girls died this morning, she was... a friend of his."

Dr. Murray nodded.

"Hopefully when he wakes up, he'll have settled down, but I don't know him well enough to say for sure. If you need me again, I'll bring something a bit stronger."

"Thank you, dear." I said. "Thank you for coming so quickly."

She didn't say anything else. There were no words of comfort left to be spoken. All of our wells were dry.

As Dr. Murray started off down the hall, I called to her and moved to catch up. Red was snoring, and Vaughn had left to finish whatever it was that he had been doing when I pulled him away.

"I think it's time that we act," I said in a low voice to her.

"What do you have in mind?"

TWENTY-NINE

Jude

MY HANDS SHOOK.

I had never seen Red act that way before.

I knew he held feelings for Freya, but it seemed like something inside him had snapped, and that scared me. Was the same thing going to happen to me one day? I too felt trapped in some sort of cage. Unable to think, unable to act, plagued by feelings I had for a girl who couldn't return them. I understood that fury. I felt it inside me, but so far I had been able to control it. Delta told me I needed to ride the current, but nothing seemed more difficult than inaction.

I sat on Finn's bed, my back against the wall, and legs sprawling out over the worn quilt. Red and Finn were assigned a room together, but Finn rarely came to it anymore. He had Rebekkah now, and spent his nights with her.

There were splintered pieces of the only chair in the room scattered on the floor, the remains of Red's rage. I should pick them up and dispose of them, but I didn't want to. I didn't want to do anything but fix this stupid situation we were all stuck in.

Rats in a maze.

No way out.

I envied Finn.

I hated Nadia.

I pitied Red.

Part of me wanted nothing more than to wake him up, hatch a plan and change this whole freaking thing to our favor. We knew how to get to the armory. Red could get us in there. He could get us anywhere. We could take out the key players before they knew what hit them and then we could take control. We just needed to keep the doctors alive long enough for them to wake up the girls and then we would all get off this malignant mountain.

There was a chance they would fight back. We might get hurt, or die, but what was worse? A quick death on our feet, fighting for something—or a slow, suffocating death waiting for something that was probably never going to happen?

"Jude?"

I wanted to stay in my rebellious mood, but something in her voice made me turn my head.

She stood in the door, and there was a spark in her eyes that I hadn't seen in years.

"There's something I need you to do, but I need to tell you something first."

I nodded and she came into the room. I moved my leg so there would be room for her to sit on the edge of the bed.

"You asked me once a long time ago who your father was, and I told you I didn't know."

I said nothing.

"I wasn't telling you the truth, Jude. I knew your father

very well."

No.

I refused to believe it.

The moment the words spilled from her mouth, the moment they reached my ears I knew the answer to the question I had always known but refused to acknowledge.

I shook my head, letting the momentum of the movement rattle through me.

"No," I said. "It's not possible."

The words Rhea had told me came flooding back into my mind. I had pushed them away a long time ago, refusing to acknowledge that possibility—refusing to acknowledge that Delta had lied to me for so long.

"I couldn't tell you, Jude, as much as I wanted to. Tess isn't your mother, and she has hated you since the moment she knew about you. We were all sworn to secrecy because of her. If we had told you, we would have been putting you in danger."

I could barely hear her, the blood pulsed through my head and I felt the fury rise up in me again. Clenching my teeth I fought it back.

"Why would you tell me now?" I asked—they were the only words I trusted myself to say.

"Because I need you to do something, and I'm not sure I'm ever going to see you again."

"YOU'RE GOING TO NEED a lot of supplies," she said, her

voice low.

I nodded, my blood was rushing through every vein with a strength I hadn't felt in a very long time. I could feel the adrenaline coursing through me, pushing me through every step.

I was leaving. I needed to get off the mountain, find more people and figure out a way to get everyone else out of here. I was pumped. I had every reason to start a war and I was going to figure out a way to do just that.

There were snowmobiles in the garage, and enough fuel to keep me moving for at least 24 hours. I hoped I didn't need much longer than that to find someone else. I moved through the estate like a panther, from shadow to shadow, collecting things I needed. Finn brought me a knapsack full of food—military-issued, freeze-dried rations that took up minimal space, but held maximum nutrition. I found as much cold-weather gear as I could, and stuffed a few extra clothing items into the bag. I had snowshoes, a helmet, some flares, and basic first-aid supplies that Harris and Vaughn had been able to scrounge up.

I was just about to head to the garage when I heard noises echoing down the empty halls. The sound of shouting and commotion drew my attention before I heard what I dreaded: gunshots. I ran toward the noise, hoping I was wrong about what was happening. Finn caught me before I made it too far and pushed me back.

"Is it Red?" I asked, out of breath.

Finn nodded.

"He must have woken up and left his room when we were

finding supplies for you."

"Why was no one watching him?" I hissed.

"Same reason you weren't, getting you out of this place."

"We need to stop him."

Finn shook his head and herded me in the opposite direction.

"It's too late for that," he said.

I fought back against him.

"He's going to get himself killed."

"You're right," said Finn, "And I'm not about to let you go down with him."

I stopped pushing. He was right. I didn't want to say it, but I knew he was. Red was doing exactly what he needed to do, but what I needed to do was something entirely different.

"Say goodbye to Rhea for me."

I had planned to go back and see her one last time, but the commotion was the perfect cover for me. I needed to leave now.

Finn slapped my back as I raced back to hastily don my outdoor clothing and together we ran to the garage. He carried a set of snowmobile saddlebags that were stuffed with some of the bulkier items, and I was dressed for the cold and wearing a backpack full of food.

The garage was empty; all of the security personnel had been diverted toward the commotion Red had caused. The snowmobile I was going to use sat filled with fuel and ready for me to go.

"Jude," The voice at the door was sharp, and I turned to

see Delta, pushing a wheelchair with a woman on it. She too was dressed for the cold and already wearing a helmet.

"I have a passenger for you."

My heart lurched. I knew I shouldn't ask now, I couldn't let my emotions distract me until I had gotten us off and far away from here.

I just nodded. I didn't trust my voice not to give away my mixed emotions of hope and dread.

"She's very weak, so she'll need your help."

I nodded again, and lifted her from the chair, and seated her on the passenger's seat.

"Do you think you can hold on?" I asked, trying to see through the mirrored lens of her snowmobile helmet.

She nodded.

I slid my leg over the seat, turned the key and pushed the ignition. The snowmobile roared to life as Finn raised the garage door. I didn't turn back as we sped out of the estate into the blinding white snow. I didn't want to see their faces as I left. I didn't want to know how scared they were for me. I was scared enough for all of us.

THIRTY

Delta

WE WATCHED HIM DRIVE away until they turned the corner and were gone. If I knew Jude, he would stay at breakneck speeds until they got to the bottom of the mountain, or at least far enough away to get a significant head-start. As the whine of the snowmobile faded into the distance I realized it had been replaced by a different sound. It was faint, indiscernible, but as I stood there, it began to grow. It was a rumble, slowly building until the garage around us started to rattle. I looked at Finn in horror.

Sirens began to peal, their harsh screeches overpowering the dark rumble. It was coming.

"Close the garage!" I shouted, but he had already started pulling on the door. I ran to help him and together we got the heavy metal door closed and bolted.

He grabbed my arm and he pulled me, stumbling, along with him into the estate.

Neither of us needed to say the word we were both thinking.

Avalanche.

It had been our greatest fear up here once it was apparent how much snow had fallen. As safe as we were on the mountain, there was one hazard for which we couldn't prepare.

Finn and I ran through the building, shouting to anyone who would listen. Whatever had happened with Red was over, and people were milling about, not anxious to get back to work. As we ran, we could feel the vibrations getting stronger until that rumble we heard sounded like the roar of a lion, so loud it echoed in our ears and rattled our bones. Panic spread like a lit fuse and as people screamed and shouted, the building shook.

It was upon us.

We were plunged into darkness.

Then silence.

THIRTY-ONE

Jude

WE HADN'T MADE IT far when the avalanche started. Whether it was as a result of the howl of the snowmobile or just a lucky coincidence, I had no idea. Whatever started it, it was now over. The deafening roar had silenced, and the snow had ceased its descent down the mountainside.

It had been a fast and harsh ride. My passenger held on for dear life as we raced to flee the stampede of snow. I had managed to cut across the path of the avalanche and find a higher slope where the sliding snow couldn't touch us.

We sat there, staring in disbelief as the estate disappeared before our eyes, enveloped by the same thick white snow that had surrounded it.

I dismounted from the sled and walked to the edge of the hill where we had stopped. Pulling off my helmet, I surveyed the damage. Trees were tilted at strange angles, and some were broken and buried altogether. How could any of them have survived?

"That was a bad one."

I turned to see that my passenger had taken off her helmet and I dropped to my knees in the snow with a mixture of shock and disappointment. I had hoped I was taking Rhea to safety, but I knew it sounded too good to be true. Sitting on my sled was Meredith Kroeker.

"We have avalanche protocols... but..."

I could see by the strained look on her face that she didn't need to finish her sentence. I knew the answer. I doubted anyone had survived, or if the estate had managed to survive the initial impact, it was unlikely they'd be able to dig themselves out before running out of oxygen.

"I know you hoped I was Rhea, and I'm sorry about that," she said. "I wish I could have helped you get her out of there too, but that would have been more dangerous for all of us."

I set my jaw, determined not to let my face betray me.

"Where are we going?" I asked, my voice rough and angry-sounding, but I preferred that to sounding weak and discouraged. I realized no one had really told me much of anything. "You guys seem to have a plan so it might be time to let me in on it."

Meredith nodded.

"Delta had mentioned she has a son, Rayne. She told me where he was most likely living, if he survived of course. We thought it would be prudent to find him."

"Prudent? Nothing about this is prudent." I spat out the words like filth.

She raised an eyebrow at me but said nothing more.

"If we're going to make it down this mountain in one piece, you're going to have to hold on tight," I said, climbing back onto the sled.

"On the plus side, we don't have anyone chasing us

anymore," said Meredith, replacing her helmet.

I had to give that one to her. Knowing there was no one following us would make the journey easier, but I had a feeling this was only the beginning.

I would get us down this mountain, and after that I would think about what had happened up here. I couldn't process it now. I wouldn't.

THIRTY-TWO

Delta

THE EMERGENCY LIGHTS FLICKERED to life. They were battery-powered and not useful for anything more than minimal lighting, casting an eerie glow onto the terrified faces around us. Finn was still gripping my hand, and I couldn't be sure if it was for my benefit or his. As the PA system crackled, I breathed a sigh of relief. We had all been to the seminars for emergency-preparedness and so far, everything was following the proper course.

"Attention residents," we could hear Nadia's voice over the intercom. She sounded slightly rattled, but every word she spoke was business. "We have enacted emergency protocols. All non-essential services are to report to the dining room for new work-assignments. Skeletal staff will be required in the kitchens. Only military-issued meal packs will be served for the foreseeable future. Medical services, please report to your stations to care for the sick and injured, and everyone else, thank you for remaining calm."

A loud screech followed her words until the intercom clicked off.

People stared at the speakers for a moment and then began

to move. We all knew where we were supposed to be.

"Finn, you should get to the dining room and find the others. They'll need you guys."

He nodded. "Can you go check on Rebekkah?" he whispered.

"Of course."

I was part of the emergency medical services. I had been well-trained in first-aid, and could place a band-aid with the best of them. Dr. Murray would be expecting me, but she would understand a quick detour.

I made my way through the hallways, stopping only at a supply cabinet to retrieve a few emergency candles and a flashlight. The living quarters didn't have emergency lights in each room—they weren't really required. It was assumed that in an emergency everyone would help out and only return to their rooms to sleep. There was an excellent chance Rebekkah and Jonah were sitting together in the dark.

"Rebekkah?" I asked as I opened the door. Jonah was fussing a bit and I could hear her whispering to him.

"Delta?" she said, her voice came weak and trembling out of the inky blackness.

I closed the door behind me before flicking the switch of the flashlight, illuminating their pale, scared faces.

"Oh thank goodness you brought us a light. I wasn't sure what I was supposed to do with Jonah in the dark."

"The batteries in this won't last forever, but I have a few emergency candles that you can use" They were big candles in glass jars and I had two of them. "These should last for a few days altogether. Hopefully by then the lights would be back on."

She nodded.

"I'm going to get Dr. Murray to give you a medical record to excuse you from emergency measures, ok?" I continued. "Probably something psychological so they wouldn't expect you to spend any time in the clinic."

She nodded, waiting for me to finish.

"Finn?" she asked, her voice strained.

"Oh sweetheart, I'm sorry. I should have said that first. He's fine. He was with me when it happened and I sent him off to get his work assignment. He asked me to check on you."

Rebekkah exhaled slowly, turning her chair toward the bed so Jonah could crawl off her lap and find his toys. With enough light to see Rebekkah, he would be more content.

"Thank you for coming," she said, "but we're ok here now if you need to go."

I nodded. Dr. Murray would be wondering where I was, and I needed to go to the clinic to see if anyone had noticed Meredith's disappearance.

"I'll come back in a few hours with some food, ok? It's unlikely they're going to let Finn leave whatever job they have him doing They're going to need all the able bodied help they can get."

Rebekkah nodded. "Of course."

I closed the door behind me and left them there.

The intercom crackled again, and I heard the operations manager's voice looking for anyone with electrical experience. The generators were down and they needed to get them going again to restore power. I hurried to the clinic, unsure of what I would find, but as long as it wasn't Nadia I would be happy.

NADIA WASN'T IN THE clinic that day and I didn't see her for weeks. Dr.Murray and the nurses had closed the curtains around Meredith's bed and arranged some pillows under a blanket. They had somehow rigged her monitors to still beep and hum regularly, so unless someone was really looking closely, it was unlikely that they would notice there wasn't a real person in there. Nurses included the pillow-person in their rounds, taking accurate notes of the pillow's blood-pressure and oxygen levels.

There were very few injuries. The building had withstood the impact of the avalanche and other than a few minor cuts and bruises from the panic, our work was peaceful.

I heard about Red in tiny snippets from everyone who came into the clinic. Second only to the avalanche, his mental unraveling was a hot topic. He had died, that much I knew, even before anyone told me. I could feel it. He had killed two security guards and shot Tess in the leg and grazed Alexandra in the shoulder before a guard shot him in the back. He had been on his way to Nadia, and mere seconds away from his goal.

I cried for him when I was alone in my room at night and prayed that Jude had made it safely away on the snowmobile with Meredith.

"Do you think they made it?" asked Dr.Murray, as if she

read my thoughts. It wasn't difficult. My thoughts had been the same—tumbling and flowing through my head—since the moment we had decided to get Jude and Meredith out of here. It wouldn't have been hard for her to guess.

"I don't know," I said, wishing I could be less honest with both her and myself. It didn't feel like Jude was gone—not in the same way I could feel Simeon's loss, or Red's—but I had seen their corpses, I had been party to their deaths. Would I feel it the same while a glimmer of hope still lived in me?

"FOUR DAYS," FINN MOANED, "Four days of digging, and all we have is air."

"Air is important," I said.

"So they tell me."

I knew how tired he was, how hard they had been working. I had visited them once as they slid bucketfuls of snow down the ventilation shafts to be melted and used elsewhere in the estate. One bucket at a time they had dug out a tunnel long enough to reach the fresh air so the air systems could circulate the oxygen properly and we wouldn't all die down here.

"Go home to your wife, Finn," I said, shooing him from my room, "before you and your smelly clothes fall asleep on my bed."

He muttered something unintelligible and stumbled out the door. I wondered if he would make it back to Rebekkah before falling asleep. Vaughn and Harris were similarly exhausted when I saw them at breakfast the next morning. It was oatmeal for everyone, stingy on the brown sugar. The success of getting the generators running had lifted everyone's mood, but there were few people who didn't look as though they were asleep on their feet. It was grueling, physical work, and they had only made a tiny dent. We had air and exhaust and the bare necessities, but we were still completely surrounded in tons of snow that would need to be moved if anyone was ever going to get in or out again. I didn't even know where they would start.

"Have they started digging us out yet?" I asked Vaughn, who was sitting beside me spooning oatmeal into his mouth.

He shook his head.

"We're supposed to start today"

"How are they going to do it? Do you know?"

"From what I understand the process is kind of like mining... you dig for a while, build some supports to prevent cave-ins and dig some more."

"Sounds dangerous."

"It is, but not getting out is more dangerous."

I nodded. We had clean air now, and minimal electricity from the generators, but the massive solar panels on the roof needed to be cleared and possibly fixed before we would be able to run at proper capacity. That was, of course, assuming that they weren't completely destroyed or swept away entirely. The generators couldn't run forever, and while there was a large fuel reserve for emergencies, it wouldn't last long if it was our only energy source.

Until we were able to dig ourselves out, we would be eating

freeze-dried military rations and oatmeal, and spending our days in almost complete darkness.

"I don't think I can handle the dark much longer," I said, more to myself than anyone else.

I had spent many years surviving on oatmeal and canned food that this wasn't a hardship to me, but being unable to see the sun, to know day from night, had already started to eat at me.

Vaughn said nothing, but slid his hand across the table to grip mine for a moment before he needed it to shovel some more oatmeal into his mouth. His hand was rough and calloused, scattered with scabs and scars in different stages of healing.

I didn't see the boys much, since their young, strong, expendable backs were needed for all the heavy lifting. Whatever time I wasn't spending in the clinic patching up minor injuries or strained muscles, I spent with the girls. My only understanding of the passage of time was their healing and changing bodies. I didn't like going there. It was eerie to stand among them in their silent, blue sarcophaguses, but it didn't feel right to leave them alone.

Vaughn and Harris finished up their oatmeal and grunted a goodbye as they rose from the table. I could see the toll their hard work had taken on their bodies. They moved with a stiff awkwardness that told the tale of their aching muscles and stiff joints. I knew they weren't getting enough food to compensate for the added work they were putting in, but there was nothing that could be done. They were strong, they had always been strong, and if there was anyone I would trust to dig us out of here, it would be my boys. The ones I had left.

As I stood from the breakfast table, I heard the one sound that no one in the building wanted to hear again. The shrill peal of the emergency system rang through the room, and everyone leapt to their feet. Screams echoed through the estate as we were plunged into darkness again.

THIRTY-THREE

Delta – Six years earlier

EVERYTHING WAS HARRIED AND buzzing. You could almost taste the levels of fear and excitement in the estate. It was a natural disaster like no other and we, the chosen few, were safe. Everyone was moving, organizing, directing, exploring. The newness of our situation kept us from remembering the others who were not as lucky as we were. We could focus on finding our way in this new place rather than looking back into the swirling snow and letting the devastation of it all sink us. I didn't want to look out there. I didn't want to see all that snow or feel the bite of the wind on my skin. I didn't want to remember that I didn't know where all my boys were.

Simeon was with me—or rather, I was with him, for without his connections it was unlikely I would have had a place to go—but Elias, and Amos and Rayne were unaccounted for. Simeon tried to assure me that they were likely safe, wherever they were, but I didn't listen. He didn't know any better than I did, so what good were his empty words?

"Marine One is landing," shouted one of the military personnel who had been the most vocal coordinating the evacuation.

It was a relief. Meredith had insisted that she be the last to leave, the metaphorical captain, poised to go down with the ship rather than see anyone left behind. The stories of her bravery had already started to circulate within the estate as more and more of her staff arrived. She had saved a young girl, no one knew who she was, but they had lifted her off the helicopter about an hour earlier. She was conscious, but barely, and Dr. Murray was now doing her best to stabilize her. Meredith had put her on the helicopter herself, if the stories were to be believed.

I had travelled here with the five young men in my care, who were all now put to work unloading gear and baggage and helping people find their assigned rooms.

The sound of beating helicopter wings was increasingly evident over the sound of the wind. The steady and consistent whirr overpowered the erratic howls that had pounded the walls of the estate since we arrived.

"Is she here?"

I heard Jude's voice over the jibber-jabber of the others who had assembled in the main hallway.

"She just landed," I said.

He nodded and waited silently beside me, as if he too knew how important it was for me to see her. Perhaps he felt the same.

Meredith Kroeker was the kind of president you felt could do anything, the one you wanted to stand behind. The fact that she was the only person standing in the way of her half-sister Nadia made her job even more important.

"Clear the hallway!" shouted someone, the voice sharp,

cutting through the sounds.

It struck me as odd, considering how much Meredith appreciated her staff and constituents. I had pictured her stepping off the helicopter into the ready embrace of her people.

I wasn't ready to see the stretcher.

I caught the flash of red hair as Dr.Murray ran past me. I followed her through the crowd, hearing the worried murmurs, but no information of substance.

"What happened?" asked Dr. Murray with a crisp businesslike voice that belied the anguish on her face.

"She fell."

There was something about Nadia that made her words difficult to believe. It was almost as if she was slightly miffed they needed to bring Meredith with them at all—no concern, no compassion.

"This looks like one heck of a fall," said Dr.Murray, scanning over the unconscious body of her president. "With the amount of contusions, we're probably looking at vast internal bleeding."

Nadia nodded.

"Most likely."

Dr.Murray stopped short. "I'm not a surgeon."

Nadia patted her shoulders as she walked past, parting the crowds.

"Just do your best, dear," she shouted back to us.

"Take her to the clinic," Dr.Murray shouted to the men carrying the stretcher. "And hurry."

She turned to follow them, which was when she noticed me standing beside her.

"Delta," she said, her eyes searching mine. "I need some extra hands."

"Of course."

She knew I wasn't trained in anything more than basic first aid, but I think we both knew that something was wrong. She could trust me, and I her, and Meredith could trust us both.

DR.MURRAY AND I were up to our elbows in blood when I saw them go past the clinic door. All my boys were together and dressed for going outside. I pulled off the gloves and trauma gown I had donned to help in the clinic, and tossed them in the garbage can by the door before pushing against the window.

"What's going on?"

They stopped in the hallway and I noted the sheepish look on their faces. They hadn't planned on telling me.

Jude spoke up while the others glanced at each other.

"The last helicopter went down."

"That's terrible," I said, "but what does that have to do with you?"

"They need people to go check for survivors," said Jude, his defiance uneasy and bolstered by the support of his brothers.

"And you thought that would be you?"

"We'll be fine. The GPS tracked it; it's not too far from here."

"Have you looked outside?"

"Of course, Delta," said Finn, his characteristic impish grin peeking out from under his raised helmet visor. "We had a good teacher. She always told us to look outside before doing something crazy."

"So you admit that it's crazy?"

"Of course," said Jude. I could tell he was decided. "There are people out there, and if any of them survived, we can't just let them die."

He knew exactly the words to say to me.

"It's not them I worry about." I said the words, though I wasn't sure I meant them. I did worry about anyone stuck out there; I just worried about my boys more.

"You taught us how to be the people we are," said Vaughn, his voice stronger and more determined than I had ever heard it. "And the people we are can't just sit here and let someone die if we can do something."

My heart surged with pride even as a tear tickled at my nose.

"Yeah!" shouted Finn, in a mock call-to-arms. "And they said that the helicopter is full of girls, and that doesn't hurt either."

The others cheered with him, and even I couldn't resist a chuckle.

"Don't be stupid," I said, herding them off down the hall. "Take care of each other."

Jude wrapped an arm around my shoulders as his

brothers started off down the hall.

"We'll all come back, Delta. I promise," he said, as he kissed my cheek.

I nodded and pushed him off to join the others. I watched him don his helmet aa the five of them turned a corner and disappeared from sight.

It was the first time I had ever let them go, and every moment they were gone I waited for them to return.

"YOU CAN GO IF you need to," said Dr.Murray. "I think we have things under control here."

She could tell my mind was elsewhere.

"The other girl?" I asked.

She shrugged. "I doubt she'll walk again, but she's stable."

"Do we know who she is?"

Dr.Murray shook her head. "She was pretty out of it, when she came in. They had to sedate her on the helicopter because she was screaming about someone named Aaron. That's all I heard out of her too, but I'm sure we'll find out in time, once she's had a chance to rest."

I nodded. I was exhausted.

"Go, Delta," She said. "We're fine here. Go see about your boys."

I didn't object. I discarded my gown and gloves again and made a quick stop at my room for a heavy wool sweater. It would be cold by the garages, but that's where I would wait for them.

THEY CAME IN WITH the air of heroes, the ice fog and errant gusts of icy snowflakes trailing after them as one by one I saw them return—each helping at least one girl into the hallways of the estate. There were seven of the red-coated girls with them— short of the eight I had been told to expect—but I didn't care.

My boys made it home.

Jude was the last one through the door. In his arms was one of the girls. I hurried to him.

"Is she ok?" I asked.

"Take off my helmet," he said.

I reached up and pulled it off his head, taking the ski cap he wore with it. His hair was sweaty and curled up around his ears. He was breathing hard.

"I think she broke something. She can't move her arm."

I offered to take her to the clinic but he refused, insisting he take her there himself. I followed him through the halls, his heavy boots clunking with a deadened thud. When we reached the clinic I held the door for them as Dr. Anderson directed him to the bed. I would have preferred to have Dr. Murray look at her, but she was busy with Meredith and the other girl. Dr. Anderson had a lot of seniority, but he had an odd, awkward persona that typically put me off. Jude laid her down as gently as if she were a sleeping child.

"What'cha got Jude?" Dr. Anderson asked.

"I'm not sure," said Jude. "She's one of the helicopter crash survivors. She screamed when I pulled her arm, the right one."

With Dr. Anderson directing, we got her into a sitting position, and began to slowly peel the layers off her. I watched her eyes as we worked; they were the most beautiful color I had ever seen. At first I thought they were a bluish-grey, but as I looked closer, I realized they were a clear, vivid violet color. I looked up to see Jude watching her as well.

I wanted to scream at him, push him away from this girl, from a future that would bring him nothing but pain, but I knew by the look on his face that I was already too late.

Jude left his heart in the hands of a girl who could not decide her own fate, and there was nothing I could do to stop him.

THIRTY-FOUR

Jude

"HANG ON," I shouted to no one in particular. There was no way Meredith would be able to hear me through the helmets and over the roar of the snowmobile. She was doing her best; though I could tell her grip was weakening. We would need to stop and rest soon—just right after we busted through this snow bank.

The light snow burst around us like one hundred years of dust from a beaten rug, rendering me blind until the clear blue sky materialized again. I eased off the throttle and dropped my speed. It would be getting dark soon, and we were going to need a shelter.

A quick tap on my shoulder made me turn my head to see Meredith's arm pointing to our left. Looking in the direction she indicated, I knew she was thinking the same thing I was. A steep cliff towered over us and set into it was a small cleft in the rock wall. It wasn't huge, but it was enough for both of us to fit into as comfortably as anyone could fit into a hole in solid rock. I turned the snowmobile toward it and slid to a stop. It was nice to stand up and stretch my legs. I never sat this much, and there was a dull ache in my shoulders from wrangling the heavy snowmobile through the drifts. The snow was deep and I sunk to my knees as soon as I got off the sled. Meredith stayed where she was, taking the opportunity to stretch her legs out in front of her on my vacated seat. She didn't pull her helmet from her head like I did. I was tired of looking out through the partially frosted visor. It would be colder, I knew, but I needed the fresh air. I wore a heavy ski cap and a thick fleece neck warmer that was meant to keep my face warm, though I still stiffened when I sucked in a breath of the icy air. It was almost hard to breathe—my lungs protested at the sudden change of temperature.

I struggled through the snow, leaving Meredith on the sled. She would wait there until I had checked everything out. She knew better than to waste what little energy she had coming with me. I pushed my boot forward, leaning on it until I was sure the snow would hold me and then shifted my weight. It held for a second and then I dropped farther as the snow gave way again. It was a tedious and jarring way to walk, never sure of my footing. I reached the cleft. I would need to lift Meredith into it, since the base of the opening was nearly at chest level from where I stood. Turning, I headed back to the snowmobile.

"It's bigger than it looks," I said. "There is easily room for both of us and we can make a fire in the opening."

The fire would serve a few purposes. The most obvious were that it would warm the space and allow us to heat some food, but as we travelled I had seen evidence of wildlife. Not a mile back a patch of the pristine white snow had been stained with blood and the remains of what I assumed to be a deer. There were animals here—hunters, and I wasn't about to be their prey. A fire would keep them back and let us sleep.

Meredith nodded and flipped up the visor of her helmet.

"Do you figure this is a safe place?"

I watched her as she scanned the top of the ridge. I knew what she was wondering though neither of us would say the word out loud. It was as if we both refused to believe what we had seen only hours before.

I shrugged. "Who knows? I don't think we'll really be safe until we get off this mountain."

She nodded slowly.

"Come on," I said, "Let's get you up there, and then I'll go find some firewood."

I reached down to lift her weakened body from the seat and she wrapped her arms around my neck. She wasn't terribly heavy, but by the time I made it back through the deep snow again I was panting. I lifted her as high as I could at the lip of the cave and she reached up to find a handhold. Pushing from behind I helped her scramble up unto the ledge. It was easier going back to the snowmobile, now relieved of my burden and able to step into my own footprints. I had packed down the snow there, so it was less likely to give way beneath me. I slung my pack over my shoulder. It had much of what we'd need in the cave: blankets, some food, matches. I left the saddlebags where they were, and slid the key to the sled into one of the pockets on my parka, zipping it tight.

Heaving the heavy pack onto the ledge I called to Meredith, who had ventured a little ways into the cave.

"I'll be back in a sec; I'm going to see if I can find any dry wood for a fire."

"Okay."

Thankfully I didn't need to go far. The snow was even deeper the farther into the trees I went.

"This should do us for the night," I said as I returned, heaving an armload of dry branches onto the ledge. Meredith pulled it away from the edge to give me room to crawl up.

My legs trembled from the exertion once I was finally up into the cave. I was accustomed to physical labor, but I always had stable ground to rely on. Trudging through the snow added a whole other element my body wasn't used to. I sat for a minute to let myself rest while Meredith snapped small twigs from the branches to start a pile of kindling.

"Are you hungry?"

I nodded. "Ravenous." I hadn't realized it until she asked.

"Do you know what we have in here?"

"Not really," I said. "Finn packed it."

She unclipped the bag and rummaged through it.

"We have enough in here for maybe two weeks... more if we're smart about it."

I assumed as much. Finn was smart.

Meredith started to laugh.

"Freeze dried ice cream?"

Finn was smart. He was also hilarious. It had zero nutritional value, but did everything for my spirits.

I snorted and shook my head.

"Give me one of those," I said, holding out my hand.

She passed one to me and pulled out a second one for herself. It was difficult to get the package open with the heavy mittens we wore, but I wasn't about to take them off until we had a roaring fire. The ice cream would be enough to hold me over until I could get a fire going, and then we could cook some proper food.

It was sweet and light on my tongue, dissolving quickly and filling my mouth with the sugary, minty chocolate flavor. I'd have to commend Finn on his choice. Mint Chocolate Chip was my favorite. It wasn't the same as real ice cream, but it did the trick.

Suddenly the sweet substance tasted bitter in my mouth and I felt something like a punch to the stomach when I remembered.

I'd never get to commend Finn.

Rhea.

Her name sprung into my mind unbidden from wherever I had been hiding it. I swallowed hard, trying to push it back to wherever it came from. I couldn't deal with that now. Not here. Not until I got off this freaking mountain.

The irony was thick. I left to save her, I ran out into the madness the world had become and here I was, alive, with nothing left to save. A few minutes stood between my life and death, and yet those same minutes changed it forever.

"Jude?"

I shoved my emotions into whatever compartment I could find for them. They would eat me up from there, I knew, but for now I had no other option.

"Are you ok?"

I nodded, not trusting my voice yet.

"Do you want stew or spaghetti?"

"Stew." I sounded strange. Coarse and gruff.

Meredith said nothing, just quietly pulled out the packages of food, some utensils and a small metal pot to heat the water.

I busied myself making a fire and it wasn't until after we had prepared our food and were sitting in its warmth and light that she spoke again.

"I'm sorry Jude," she said, her voice barely perceptible above the crackling of the fire. "I'm not going to pretend I know what you're going through, but I want you to know if there's anything I can do to help, anything at all, I will."

It was a big promise coming from the President of the United States, but I couldn't answer. I nodded and stuffed another spoonful of stew into my mouth in a hasty attempt to quell the rising emotions.

"You saved my life. I'm never going to forget that. Even though we couldn't save the others, that avalanche stopped Nadia, and that fact alone will save so many others."

I continued to eat in silence until I felt I could control myself if I spoke.

"What was she doing?" I asked.

"Nadia?"

I nodded.

"Why did she take the girls?"

Meredith pursed her lips and furrowed her brow, as if

searching for the right answer to the question.

"From what Delta and I could surmise, was planning on establishing a new social order."

I raised an eyebrow and let her continue.

"She told me once that she believed children were a necessary evil. You needed them to keep society alive, but they were leeches on a productive society, on women especially."

"Leeches?"

Meredith smiled. "I didn't agree with her, as you can probably imagine."

"You have the mark."

She frowned. "I know."

"Why did you do it?"

"I'm a politician, I had no other choice. No one would put me in an office only to have me turn around and have babies and abandon all the work I had done."

"So you sterilized yourself?"

"Without this mark on my face, I wouldn't be the President," she said, her voice stern and thick. "It wasn't something I chose lightly; I hope you can understand that. I just truly felt that I could do more good for more people where I stand now."

"How did that work out for you?" I asked.

She burst out laughing. "Apparently not well. It was a nice thought though."

I snickered.

"But seriously, I've been living in a man-made prison for

the last few years, to be honest it boggles my mind how long I have been there. Years. It's hard to even say that."

"But you're out now, and Nadia is gone."

It was easier to think about Nadia buried in a tomb of snow if I forgot how many people I loved were with her.

Meredith nodded. "She has a lot of friends, and a lot of supporters. But without her at the helm, I doubt her plan will see the light."

"How was she planning on doing it?"

Meredith shrugged. "She didn't let me in on much of her ideas. You might think the President should know everything, but she had many of my personal advisors on her payroll. I didn't really start to put the pieces together until I met Isis, and when I spoke with Delta this morning everything kind of fell into place."

I tried to separate Isis from Finn's wife Rebekkah to make the name easier to hear, but it proved impossible so I said nothing.

"When I heard what Delta had learned in the last weeks, I understood. Nadia would create a lower social class completely dedicated to creating and raising children, leaving people like her 'free' to work, climb the social and political ladders. To her, it was the best of both worlds. The children would be raised, educated and introduced into society once they were old enough to be productive and useful. The upper classes would gladly pay more taxes to be relieved of the burden, and the lowest classes would have no choice in the matter."

"She would take away their choice?"

"Did the girls she took have a choice?"

Point taken.

With enough money and power, you can take away free will, especially if you can convince yourself it's for a greater good.

"Who is she to determine the greater good?" I asked, my thoughts tumbling out of my mouth unbidden.

Meredith didn't answer.

"Wait a minute," I said, a sudden thought coming to me. "Are you saying she would have had whole factories of people like Rhea and Willow and Kenzie? Stuck in some kind of coma?"

Meredith nodded.

"I can only assume so. She must have been planning for that all along. She wouldn't have had the technological capabilities to make those machines at the estate."

The thought was horrifying to me. Human incubators, row upon row of pods emitting a soft blue glow. It couldn't be possible.

"Surely the public would revolt to such a thing," I said.

I knew I would.

"I doubted she planned to tell the public, at least not at first."

"They wouldn't notice?"

Meredith frowned. "There are so many marginalized areas of our society. Would you notice a few dozen poor women, maybe prostitutes, disappearing?"

I liked to think I was one of the marginalized, having been abandoned by my parents, but the truth was no. I wouldn't notice. I lived in comfort and stability, at least I did until very recently.

"You move slowly, a few dozen here, a few dozen there, not

to mention, after a while you can start growing your own women that no one ever knew about."

"Girls raised into a world where reproduction was their only duty," I mumbled. It seemed so impossible, yet so easy at the same time.

"Population growth was almost at a standstill in the years before... this," Meredith said, waving her hand at the snow around us. "Women weren't having babies, far from enough to keep society running properly. How would my generation, or even yours, think of retiring with no one to take our place? To Nadia it was the only logical conclusion."

"To just force someone to do it for her?"

"Sounds about right for Nadia."

"And you didn't agree?"

"No, and had I been awake for the last few years, it's very likely she would have killed me for disagreeing with her by now."

I couldn't argue with that. I had doubts Meredith would have stayed in her coma if she didn't fear for her life.

"I couldn't stay under much longer, the medications were already wreaking havoc on my organs, and Delta and I agreed, we needed to get me out of there so I could find people to oppose Nadia."

"You would have needed an army."

It was strange to refer to a mission—that only this morning had been a very real possibility—in the past tense.

"I know," she said. "I had a plan, but that's all changed. I'm not exactly sure what to do now."

She pulled her knees to her chest and looked very much like a scared child.

I had never seen Meredith like this. Before coming to the estate she had always been very confident, impossible to shake, the perfect President. It seemed very odd to me that she was indeed a person. When the lights and cameras turned off, and the advisors and security left her alone, she wasn't the President, she was Meredith.

I shrugged, "You have a lot of time to figure it out."

"I know," she said. "It's impossible to say how much of my country is left out there, much less what to do with it."

I knew I should offer some words of comfort, some platitude that would give her a boost in morale, but I had nothing. The past twenty-four hours had taken any hope from me. I too was lost and alone, so I said nothing.

THE FIRE HAD BURNED down to embers when I woke up. The rising sun was almost blinding on the white snow. It hadn't been comfortable to sleep on the rocks, but the heavy snowsuits we wore had enough padding that we were actually able to drift off. I stretched my arms over my head and yawned. Meredith was already awake, sitting with her legs hanging over the side of the ledge. I wondered how long she had been there.

"I didn't stoke the fire," she said. "I figured there was enough heat to boil some water on the embers so we could eat before we left."

The pot was sitting on the coals, snow already melting inside it.

I made my way out of the cave. It wasn't tall enough for me to stand upright, but if I hunched it was easy enough. Reaching down to the pack, I pulled out some meal portions.

"I assume we should eat breakfast food? I see oatmeal, and scrambled eggs with bacon."

"Bacon," said Meredith. "Always bacon."

I had to agree. I dug through the packages until I found a second one, and crouched by the fire watching the pot, as if that would speed up the melting.

"How are you feeling?" I asked.

"Physically? Still not back to myself yet, but I'll be ok."

I didn't bother to ask about her mental state, I knew what she was feeling well enough to not need her to verbalize it again. I trusted she felt the same way about me.

The eggs were bland, and while I was sure Finn would have thrown in some salt and maybe even a bottle of Tabasco sauce, I didn't feel like looking for them. We could take a better inventory of our supplies another time. For now, the warmth and nutrition trumped any concerns about flavor.

"So, is our plan still the same?" I asked. "Find this Rayne guy? Delta's son?"

Meredith nodded. "I guess. If he is safe like Delta believed he would be, at the very least he could provide a place for me to regroup, figure out the next step."

It made sense. We weren't supplied well enough to last very

long on our own.

"I probably have enough fuel in the snowmobile for another day of driving." I said. "I don't know if that will get us to him, but it should get us out of the mountains."

"Let's hope so."

Thirty-five

WE MADE IT TO the foothills easily and still had enough fuel to continue. The most difficult part was navigating with everything covered in snow. It was impossible to tell if a long narrow pathway through the trees had once been a highway or a stream. We had a basic compass in the saddlebags, but without knowing exactly where the estate was, it was difficult to know which direction we needed to go. Generally we needed to travel east—away from the mountain range—to get to the city, but whether we were north or south of it now, I had no idea. It was entirely possible we could travel in one direction only to realize we had wasted a lot of fuel going the wrong way.

We stopped for lunch and to stretch our legs. We didn't bother to make a fire, but opted instead for some of the cold food we had; granola bars, beef jerky and dried fruit. Meredith had been steadily getting stronger, finding she was able to stand and walk a bit on her own. It was a relief to me that she was feeling better so quickly. Soon, I wouldn't need to help her. We didn't talk much as we ate. Neither of us was in a particularly chatty frame of mind, and I was thankful that we seemed to have the same mindset.

"Did you hear that?" Meredith asked in a whisper.

I shook my head and listened more carefully. I heard nothing but the creaks and pops of the trees shifting in the wind.

She furrowed her brow and closed her eyes.

"I know I heard something," she said.

We sat in silence, concentrating on the sounds around us until I heard it too. It was faint, barely louder than the wind, but it was a cry.

"It doesn't sound like an animal," I said.

Meredith shook her head and whispered in a tiny voice, "It sounds like a child."

As soon as the words were out of her mouth, it made complete sense to me. It was a sound I had definitely heard before but here, in the woods, out of context it didn't make sense. I didn't want to believe a child was alone out here in this cold, so the only reasonable explanation I could come up with was that there was a group of other people somewhere nearby.

"Pull up your neck warmer over your face, and tuck your hair into your cap," I said to Meredith. Without knowing if these people supported her or not, it would be foolish to march into an unknown camp with the President of the United States.

She obeyed without a word, obviously aware of her personal standing. It would be strange to be her—for years she had been surrounded by security, but out here, she was completely exposed.

We walked slowly in the direction we heard the cries, scanning the woods for signs of people. We saw none, though every so often, as if carried to us in the wind, we heard the cries. They got louder as we moved, reinforcing our belief that we were moving in the right direction, but still we saw no one. I breathed as quietly as I could, straining to hear—trying to pinpoint the location of the sound. Meredith was doing the same.

"There." Her voice was little more than a breath.

I looked in the direction she was pointing and saw what she was looking at. There was a small basket—not much bigger than a bushel basket—strung up by ropes from a tree.

"What is that?" I asked.

"I don't know, but the cries are coming from there."

She was right.

"Keep your eyes open," I said.

"Wasn't planning on closing them," she whispered back to me.

Nothing about being here was sitting well with me. People had to be nearby, and something seemed very sinister about the potential of a child in a basket hanging from a tree.

We trudged through the snow, slowly closing the gap between us and the basket. I could hear Meredith slowing behind me, still not up to the strain of navigating the deep snow. I pressed on, trying to balance my desire to get to the basket, with the duty to protect her from potential threat.

"Jude, I'm fine here," she said. I looked back to see her leaning on a tree, obviously exhausted. "I'll watch the woods, go find out what's in that basket."

I made my way forward, stopping now and then to scour

my surroundings. Meredith was still where I had left her, using the tree to keep her on her feet. I inched closer. There were blankets in the basket, and as I neared it, I could see them move slightly. I couldn't even comprehend what was happening here. This couldn't possibly be real, it seemed almost like one of those strange dreams you'd have after eating pizza too close to bedtime. Nothing made sense.

I reached out to the basket, my fingertips resting on the woven twigs, and took one step closer.

One step too much.

The pain was blinding, and it surged through me before my brain even registered the loud snapping noise. I screamed louder than I imagined possible, shattering the relative silence of the woods. Logically I knew I needed to stay quiet, but I didn't know how.

I crumpled to the ground, unable to reconcile the pain in my leg.

"Jude!" said Meredith in something between a shout and a whisper, she was coming to me, I could see through the tears that blurred my vision.

"What happened?" I asked, unwilling and unable to look down at my leg, even as the throbbing pain radiated through my body.

"It's a trap, Jude," she said, dropping to her knees beside me. "A bear trap."

"Get it off!" I shouted, still unable to modulate the volume of my voice.

"I'm trying," she said, her voice cracking with the stress of it. "I don't know how these things work."

"There's probably some kind of release," I said, gritting my teeth.

I could feel her tiny movements as she searched for a release, they seemed amplified.

"Hurry up!" I shouted.

"I'm sorry Jude, I can't figure it out!"

Without another word, she was on her feet.

"Meredith!" I said, trying to force her to concentrate. "Meredith!"

"Jude," her voice was eerily strained. "We're not alone."

I strained to turn my head without moving the rest of my body, but even that small motion seemed to send fresh waves of pain up my leg. Clenching my jaw I rolled slightly to find the reason she was acting so strange. Through my hazy vision I could see the figure of a man, his arrow notched and ready, his bowstring pulled.

"Who are you?" he asked.

"Nobody important," I said, wincing.

"We mean you no harm," said Meredith, "We're just passing through."

He snickered.

"Not as quickly as you'd like to I'd assume."

I didn't find his attempt at humor amusing.

He let the bow drop and slid the arrow back into the quiver on his back. He was dressed in tanned leather and fur, and wore snowshoes on his feet.

"That's gotta hurt, dude."

"Please stop."

"Could you help him?" asked Meredith. "I couldn't figure out how to spring the release."

The man crouched down beside me, and with expert hands, he pressed whatever lever he needed to and the trap loosened.

"You've likely got a broken leg here... not to mention the wound itself. You're not going to be walking for a while."

I cursed under my breath as he lifted the trap to where I could see it. The heavy rusted iron teeth were covered in my blood. I dropped my head back to the ground and swore loudly.

"I guarantee that you're not going to want to stick around. I can help you splint it, and then if you can manage, you'll need to get out of here."

"Get out of here? You can't be serious," said Meredith, "I demand that you take us to wherever you live until this boy heals."

He laughed. It wasn't an amused laugh, or a lighthearted laugh, but one that sounded like he almost pitied us.

"You don't want to go where I live."

"I'm going to need some sticks, thicker than your thumb and as straight as you can get them."

He gave the order easily, and Meredith obeyed—the sound of my moaning extra incentive for her to forget her personal exhaustion. The man crouched beside my leg with his back to me and slid his buckskin jacket from his shoulders. Layer by layer he peeled off his clothing, until he got down to a worn cotton t-shirt. He slid it over his head and despite my light-headedness I could see the deep pink scars crisscrossing his back. They were unlike any I had seen before.

"What happened to your back?"

"I told you, coming where I live is a bad idea."

He didn't elaborate, though I was suddenly and completely decided against going home with him.

He pulled his shirts and sweaters back on, layering them under the buckskin jacket. It had a heavy fur hood that framed his face, and with his scarf over his mouth and cap pulled low, I could no longer see more than his eyes. Taking a stout knife from a sheath strapped to his thigh, he sliced through the hem and began to tear strips from the material.

Meredith returned with a handful of sticks, and the man chose a few of the straightest ones. He sliced off the smaller twigs, and measuring them to my leg, he cut them to length.

"My wife would do a better job of this, I'm sure, but I'm all you've got."

"Can you go get her?" asked Meredith.

"Easier said than done."

He seemed to prefer being vague, and I wasn't about to press him. I was more than happy to flee the area after seeing the marks on his back.

"Do you have some bandages? Or something I could use to stop the bleeding?"

Meredith nodded and headed back to the snowmobile. Neither of us had mentioned it, and it was probably a prudent decision. The last thing we needed was for this man to decide he wanted it and leave us stuck here with no hope of escape.

She returned in a few minutes with the first aid kid from the saddlebags, opening it on the ground beside me.She pulled out a few packages of gauze and some rolls of bandages.

The man handed me a short stick.

"You're going to want to bite on this."

My eyes widened, but I did as he said.

The pain was fresh and hot as they packed the gauze around the wound and tied the bandages as tightly as possible to stop the blood.

I could hear them talking, him giving Meredith instructions, but none of their words made sense to me beyond the searing pain. I did my best not to whimper, but I couldn't control many more of the sounds that came out of me.

They splinted my leg as quickly as they could over the thick ski pants.

"It likely won't move much, but you'll obviously need to stay off of it," said the man before cursing. Meredith seemed taken aback by his language, until he stood, pulled out his bow, deftly notched an arrow and fired a single shot directly into the eye of a small, grey bear. It fell to the ground in a heap and he dropped next to me to help me into a sitting position.

"Are you kidding me?" I said. "A bear? What's next?"

"Were you expecting a unicorn? We trap bears around

here. They have lots of meat and warm fur."

Meredith gasped.

"You were baiting bears with a baby?" She scrambled to her feet, only now remembering the purpose of our quest. Standing under the basket, she reached inside and pulled the child out.

"It's freezing..."

"He," offered the man.

"He's freezing! Any longer and he would have been dead. You could have killed him."

"Not me. I didn't put him there."

"You left him there, knowingly!" Meredith was fuming as she unzipped her down jacket and slid the cold child inside to make use of her body heat. She zipped it back up partially, making a simple carrier.

"What exactly was I supposed to do with him? Carry him around in my shirt and feed him venison?"

"He's a child!"

"A child I could be killed for protecting. A child you could be killed for protecting. You should be glad I was the one who found you here."

"Right," I said, "Because we wouldn't want to go where you live, right?"

He glared at me, but didn't answer.

"Take him if you want, but I can't help you anymore."

"I think we'd prefer it that way," said Meredith, her words clipped and terse.

"Suit yourself."

I heard the horses at the same time everyone else did, but neither Meredith nor I seemed as irritated about it as the man did.

"You guys need to hide. Now. And keep that flipping child quiet."

"Who are they?" asked Meredith.

"No one you want to know."

He slipped his hands under my arms and pulled me toward a few thick trees that stood together. There were some dead evergreen boughs in a pile at the base, enough that both Meredith and I fit behind them. The man dropped me there with a final glare, reminding us to stay hidden, and then he ran off, dragged the bear to where I was only seconds before and slit its throat, spilling its blood to hide mine.

"Dax, what a pleasant surprise," said a man who didn't seem surprised at all.

"Elias, what are you doing here?"

"I doubt I need to tell you."

"She's not going with you."

The man on horseback, Elias, snorted. I could see there were six or seven men with him, each riding a massive steed. They were well bundled, wearing mainly high-tech winter gear, mixed with some fur pieces that were obviously handmade. He got down from his horse and strolled toward Dax.

"Have you given her the option?" Elias asked.

"You think I kidnapped my own wife?"

"I've met your sister, I wouldn't put it past you."

Dax spit in his face.

"We could kill you now."

"I'd love to see you try. Come find me without a herd of goons and we'll see who makes it out on top."

Elias chuckled. He was smaller than Dax, though his apparent lack of muscles did little to tone down his bravado.

"If you ever want to see your daughter again, you might want to consider letting me talk to her."

Dax leaned in closer so they were almost nose to nose. "You and I both know I have no say in that, but I will tell you, if you harm a hair on her head, I will find you, and I will kill you."

"Big words for such a small man."

"Here are a few more:" said Dax. "If I ever see your face here, or anywhere close to Nova, I will kill you. That's a promise."

They stared each other down for what seemed like a minute, but Elias broke the stare.

"Let's go," he said, climbing back onto his horse.

"I'm not going to forget it, Elias. So you'd do best not to forget either."

Dax stood where he was until the horses were gone, and then stalked over to the bushes where we hid.

"Now you guys really need to go. I've been gone too long, someone is going to come looking for me soon," he said. "Can you two manage? At least to get far enough away that they couldn't see you from here?"

I nodded. There was no place I wanted to be more than on the snowmobile, getting out of here.

"Which way is the city?" I asked.

He shook his head. "Just get out of this area, don't worry about going that far."

"Which way?"

He pointed north.

"I need to go. Good luck," he said.

He ran over to another stand of trees and retrieved a sled he must have had with him, loaded the bear onto it and headed off through the trees, pulling it with him.

"Let's get out of here," said Meredith.

I agreed wholeheartedly.

I managed to get to my feet and wrapped my arm over her shoulders. The pain had started to numb, or perhaps my body was going into shock, but somehow we managed to hobble and limp and hop all the way back to the sled.

"Are you ok to drive?"

I nodded, gritting my teeth. "I don't need my legs to drive. Are you ok to hold on with the baby?"

"I think so, just don't do anything crazy."

"Not a problem," I said. "I've had enough crazy for one day."

I stuck the key into the ignition and the snowmobile roared to life. Meredith slid the first aid kit into the saddlebag and swung my backpack onto her back so there would be more room in front of her for the child.

I needed to focus. We needed to get going. We couldn't stay

out here longer than absolutely necessary. I pointed the sled north and we were on our way.

THIRTY-SIX

THE SUN HAD JUST set when we reached the city. I hadn't been here since the snow started, so seeing the deserted streets came as a shock to me. Part of me had expected more people to survive, and perhaps they had, though no one was out at this hour. Maybe there were pockets of survivors hidden in the dark buildings, like the ones we were looking for.

Some of the landmarks I remembered were still standing, though everything looked different in the dark, and under a deep layer of snow.

"I think it's on the west side of town," said Meredith.

I didn't answer, but I agreed. I was starting to feel dizzy, but I tightened my grip on the handlebars and travelled as quickly as I dared. We had to be low on fuel by now, and neither Meredith nor I were capable of walking more than a few steps at this point. We needed to get there soon.

There were no lights visible as we pulled up to the building we were looking for.

"You've got to be kidding me," said Meredith.

I couldn't have said it better myself.

Delta told us it was an abandoned hospital, but I had

pictured something more modern. This place must have been abandoned for decades, maybe even a century. Dead vines snaked their way up the crumbling brick walls, and broken windows stared at us like empty eye sockets.

"Do we have to go in there?" Meredith asked.

"Do we have a choice?" I asked. "Rayne is the only person we know of that might be able to help us, and Delta said we would find him here."

"If he's alive." Meredith added.

She made a good point. We had been at the estate for years. Anything could have happened to Rayne in that time, if he even survived the very beginning of it.

"I think we need to check, at the very least."

"Brave words from the man who can't walk."

"I'm not going to send you in there alone," I said. "I just need to figure this out."

"I don't think you need to figure anything out," said a voice from behind us as Meredith shrieked.

"He's got a gun to my back," she hissed in my ear.

"Start talking," said another voice. "Give us one good reason why we shouldn't shoot you here and be done with it."

"We're looking for Rayne."

They whispered to each other before speaking again.

"Lots of people by that name."

"Really?" I asked. "Lots of 'Raynes' in the world? I didn't ask about a 'John'."

"Don't be smart."

"Sorry," I said, trying to remind myself that they had a gun. "Rayne Parsons. Delta sent us."

They whispered again.

"Enough you two."

A new voice had joined them, deeper and more authoritative.

"Who are you and how do you know Delta?"

"She's, um, my mother? As close to a mother as someone gets without giving birth to you, that is."

A light shone directly into my face.

"Show your face."

I reached up and pulled my helmet and cap from my head and pushed my neck warmer below my chin.

I heard the man gasp.

"What?"

"You look just like..."

"Simeon?"

Silence. I knew in a heartbeat that I had found the person I was looking for. The strong, sure voice was that of the man who could be considered both my brother and my uncle... Rayne.

"He was my father, apparently."

"Who's your friend?" he asked.

"I'll tell you when you get us inside and get me some painkillers. I might pass out before then if you keep talking."

I watched as the light panned from my face down my body, looking for obvious wounds. I heard him whistle as the light came to rest on the splint on my leg, which was, by now, probably very bloody.

"Bring them inside."

The sudden commotion was a bit hard to handle. It seemed as though we were surrounded by dozens of people, all talking at once. I breathed a sigh of relief when I saw a stretcher. Someone had helped Meredith off the sled and she was halfway up the steps when they loaded me onto the canvas and hoisted me up. The ride was rough and uncomfortable, but I was pleased I didn't need to walk. With the crowd of people, bearing lanterns and flashlights it seemed less intimidating to enter the hospital, though I did my best not to look around much.

The air was still cold until they opened a solid door that led to the basement. Only then did the warmth begin to sting at my face and seep through the layers of my clothing. I held on tight as they carried me down the wide staircase. There were lights down here, dim ones, but more than enough to see, so all the lanterns and flashlights were quickly extinguished.

Everywhere we went there were more and more people, and I couldn't figure out why they all talked so much until I realized many of them were children. Boys. So very many boys of all different ages.

"Take them to the infirmary and find Angela," said Rayne, and the boys that weren't carrying the stretcher scattered like mice through the hallways.

"These are boys," said Meredith once it was bit quieter. "You let boys threaten people with guns?"

Rayne laughed. "I let boys threaten people with sticks."

Meredith gasped, and then began to laugh. Rayne had looped an arm around her and was helping her down the hall.

"Careful," she said, raising her hand to her zipper and slowly lowering it so he could see the child inside.

"Good grief, you two," said Rayne. "Any more surprises for me? Someone find Phoebe too."

"Do you have any more women locked up around here?"

"Locked up?" Rayne hooted. "They're gonna love that. We've only got the two at the moment, and trust me, without them I'd be lost. Angela is my wife, and Phoebe is her sister. Phoebe is still nursing her new daughter, so I thought this baby might want to hang out with her for a bit."

Meredith sighed audibly.

"Where'd you find him?"

"South of here, in the woods."

"Basket hanging from a tree?"

"How did you know?" asked Meredith.

"You're not from around here, huh? Everyone knows about them. We've pulled a few little boys out of that basket over the years."

"And why haven't you done anything about it?"

"Me, a few women and a bunch of boys with sticks versus a highly trained band of Amazon warriors? Who knows, just lazy I guess."

Meredith didn't answer.

"But seriously, we haven't figured out how to stop them yet. Once we do, I assure you we will try. It grates at me that they're still out there."

We reached the infirmary and Angela was already there waiting for us, at least I assumed she was Angela because she reached up to give Rayne a kiss before looking us over.

"Did they get Phoebe?"

"She was sleeping," said Angela, "Mila has been a bear. She's on her way. What happened to these two?"

"Based on the baby she's carrying, I'd say he stepped in a bear trap."

It irritated me that Rayne found this funny enough to hoot out a loud laugh at his own, very shrewd observation.

"Very astute," I mumbled as Angela gasped.

"What did you do that for?"

"Trust me, it wasn't intentional."

I moaned.

"Put him on the bed."

For a group of teenage boys, they put me down with remarkable care.

They must have had practice.

The thought was grim, but realistic based on the encounters we'd had today.

Angela sat on a stool with wheels and slid across the floor to me.

"Is she ok?" she asked Rayne.

"I'm fine, long story," said Meredith. "Just find me someplace to sit."

"And some soup, Rayne," Angela ordered, presuming her

husband would take charge of the seating too.

"This looks nasty," she said to me.

"It doesn't feel great either."

"I'll give you some painkillers, but if the bone is broken and I need to set it, they're not going to help much."

I nodded, feeling suddenly ill.

She wheeled her chair over to a cabinet stocked with medical supplies, and pushed through the jars of pills until she found the one she needed. There was a pitcher of water on the counter and she poured a glass.

"It's probably stale, the boys don't get me fresh stuff all that often," she said as she handed me the glass and a few pills. "But it's clean and it'll get the pills down."

She placed a hand under my neck and helped me up far enough to swallow the pills. The water was stale, but I couldn't remember the last time I'd had something to drink.

"Ok, lay back for a few minutes and I'll let those kick in before I get started."

I was relived to be able to do nothing but lie there. The pills were strong and fast-acting. Before too long I was feeling warm and numb all over.

She began working, humming as her fingers moved. She snipped away the strips of t-shirt that held the splint together and began unwrapping the bandages.

I heard the sound of her sucking air through her teeth.

"That good, huh?" I asked, my voice thick and slightly garbled.

She didn't answer, which seemed a bit ominous to me, even in my drugged state.

I laid my head back on the pillow and did my best to ignore that all her 'tsks' and sighs were as a result of my leg.

"Is he going to be ok?" asked Meredith.

I would need to remember to thank her for asking. I wasn't sure I would have been able to get the words out without breaking down. The shock and adrenaline were wearing off and I was starting to feel myself losing it.

"I think so," said Angela. "It's not going to be easy on him, the next bit for sure, but as long as we can keep his wounds from getting infected, he should e ok."

I glanced around at the far-from-sanitary conditions of the room where we sat and pushed back a lump that was gathering in my throat. I wasn't going to be able to control it much longer. It was all too much.

Rayne returned with a bowl of soup and a glass jar full of water for Meredith, who looked at it and smiled. The smell made my stomach churn and roll.

"I'm going to need to set the bone. I'm sorry..." she paused, "I don't know your name."

"Jude," I said.

"I'm going to need to set the bones Jude. It's not going to be pretty, I can guarantee that, but I'll try to be as quick as I can."

I nodded.

"Rayne, could you hold him?"

Rayne came around behind me, and braced his arm across

my chest.

"Just scream, it'll make you feel better," he whispered into my ear just before I felt Angela's hands give a sharp tug.

I didn't need to scream. I must have done something very good to deserve some mercy, because as the pain hit, I fainted dead away.

THIRTY-SEVEN

IT WAS STILL DARK when I woke up again. My mind was slow and unresponsive, and it took me a while to remember where I was. The dull throbbing pain in my leg brought it all back piece by piece until they tumbled into my heart like the avalanche that took so much from me. I gasped for breath, unable to put words to the crushing weight of the buried emotion.

"Are you ok?"

I heard Angela's voice, barely there but piercing through the haze.

"No."

Her hand was cool and soft on my forehead, stroking my hair. I wanted to cry, to curl up on the bed and sob like a child, but the tears wouldn't come.

"I need to check the wounds, ok?" she said. "It shouldn't hurt, the hard part is done."

I didn't answer. I didn't think she actually expected me to.

I could feel her hands gently untie the tight bandages.

"It was lucky you passed out," she said, "Setting the bones was trickier than I hoped. But you stayed out and I was able to stitch you up much more easily than if you'd been awake."

Hooray for small mercies.

"It looks like it's healing alright. How is the pain?"

"Manageable." I said, the hoarse and raspy voice strange in my mouth.

I answered only about my leg. The pain everywhere else was slipping from my grasp and threatening to overtake me. I could feel my muscles quivering, though I wasn't cold.

"Drink some water and then sleep some more, ok? You've been through a lot, and you need your rest."

She brought a jar of water to my lips. It was fresh this time, and icy cold, as if it had only recently been melted from the snow. I had never tasted better water, and for a moment I reveled in it, until guilt crushed me. Rhea would never drink again, nor would Delta, or Finn... I nearly gagged on the water spilling down my throat. Angela pulled it away, whispering encouragements while I sputtered and coughed.

I should have died with them, because living without them was no life at all.

I DON'T KNOW HOW long I avoided life, because that's what I did. When I wasn't asleep I stared at the ceiling in a catatonic state. I knew the exact number of cracks in the plaster ceiling, and could trace them in my mind from memory. Meredith came to sit with me regularly, but rarely spoke because I never answered. They spooned broths and watered-down oatmeal into my mouth when I grew tired of their pleas and opened my mouth.

The pain in my leg was the only thing that reminded me that I wasn't dead. Dead people don't hurt. I wasn't alive though, that much I knew.

"OK PRINCESS, WE'VE GIVEN you long enough. It's time to get dressed for the ball."

I knew Rayne's voice, though it felt like I had only ever heard it in a dream. I rolled my head to the side and focused on where they stood. Meredith was there, still hiding under the thick wool cap. Angela wore a look of concern while Rayne mainly looked irritated.

"It's time to get back on the horse and bite the bullet."

"Rayne, I don't think your manly mixed metaphors are going to help," said Angela.

"Why not? He's been in this bed for weeks and it's high time he makes himself useful."

Angela rolled her eyes. I noticed Rayne was leaning on the handles of a wheelchair.

"Jude, we came to give you a tour of the place," she said. "I assume you're going to be with us for a while, so you might as well know your way around."

I shrugged. I didn't presume I'd have any choice in the matter.

Rayne came over to the bed and pulled me up to a sitting position, while Angela and Meredith helped me swing my legs over the edge. I closed my eyes and let the room spin for a minute I hadn't been upright much in the last... was Rayne right? Was it weeks?

It didn't seem like weeks, though at the same time it felt like I had been in this room forever. My leg was still splinted with some flat, wide boards and wrapped in clean bandages. It still hurt to move around, but I could tell it was much better than it had been.

Once I was sitting, Rayne leaned into me and hefted me up, his arms wrapped around my chest under my arms. He grunted with my weight, but was able to single-handedly heave me into the wheelchair. He looked nothing like my father, though I didn't expect him to since they weren't actually brothers. Where Simeon was fair, Rayne was dark. His dark brown skin was rough and calloused from years of hard work and his thick waves black as a shadow. He was broad and strong, whereas Simeon had grown accustomed to an easier life, his belly growing spongy in the process.

Once I was securely seated in the wheelchair, Rayne moved behind me to push. I didn't remember much more than the hallways from when they brought me into this place, and even then I could only remember the ceiling tiles that went by as we passed beneath them. Meredith and Angela moved ahead of us, and I could tell Meredith had grown familiar with the place.

She wasn't dead like me.

Rayne swung the wheelchair into a large open room that seemed louder than necessary. There were boys everywhere, some as young as nine or ten, and others that would be close to my own age. It appeared to be some kind of bunk room, but the openings to the beds were small and square, going deep, unlike most bunk beds. It wasn't until one of the older boys pulled one of them out that I realized what room we were in.

"It's the morgue," said Rayne, reading my mind.

"Creepy," I muttered.

"It made sense at the time. Where else were we going to stick all these kids? Here we can stack 'em up four-high and no one falls out of bed."

I sincerely hoped I wouldn't be given a bed here, however appropriate it may have seemed.

"Let's go see Renny," suggested Meredith. "Seeing him would do Jude some good."

I was not given any opportunity to interject my own opinion as to where we should go, my chair just followed Meredith and Angela from the room and down the hall.

This room was much smaller, originally an office perhaps, with a few mattresses piled on the floor in a corner. Sitting on the mattresses was a girl, close to my age, perhaps a bit younger. She sat cross-legged and in front of her on the mattress were two small bundles, wrapped tightly in flannel. One was much bigger than the other. When she saw us coming, her face lit up with a smile.

"Renny," she said to the little bundle, "you have visitors."

She reached forward and scooped the bundle from the bed, passing it into Meredith's welcoming hands.

"Renny?" I asked.

"It means, 'small, but strong'," offered Angela. "It sounded right for him."

Meredith brought the child to me, assuming I would take him, but I shook my head. I didn't know how to hold a child properly. Meredith didn't press the issue, rather holding him securely where I could see him.

"He's grown a lot," she said. "He doesn't fit in my parka anymore."

He still seemed tiny to me, impossibly small. How miniscule had he been when we pulled him from that basket?

"He seems completely healthy," said Phoebe, "If I let him he'd take all of Mila's milk too."

"Mila?"

"My daughter." Phoebe smiled as she looked down at the larger bundle on the bed, her pale hair falling in her face. "She's almost ten months now."

"Congratulations," I said, not really knowing what else to say.

"Phoebe here lucked into being the nursemaid for all the little ones," said Angela. "I didn't have the time because with the number of boys in this place, I'm kept hopping just bandaging them up."

"There are three more little boys here," said Meredith in a soft voice, "All from the same basket we found Renny in. They might be brothers."

I didn't answer.

Renny began to squawk and fuss.

"He's going to need to eat right away," said Phoebe.

"We'll leave you to that, little sister," said Angela, shooing the men from the room as Meredith handed the child back to Phoebe.

As we left Renny began to scream louder. I could hear Phoebe singing softly as his shouts suddenly stopped.

A tiny little piece of me felt alive again. It was deep and it was hidden, but it was there.

THEY SHOWED ME THE rest of the compound, the dining area with long tables crudely hammered together with rough and splintered pieces of wood and a small kitchen. There was an area they used for a school. Angela said it was very important for the kids to learn to read and write properly so that they could get jobs when the weather went back to normal. I didn't ask how normal she thought the world would be when the snow melted.

Eventually we ended up back at the infirmary, where Rayne helped me to a standing position on one leg, and helped me turn myself out of the wheelchair and back onto the bed. It seemed somewhat more dignified than just letting him carry me around. Meredith settled into the old office chair at Angela's desk while Angela sat on the opposite bed.

"Alright," he said once I was seated, with my back against the wall, and my broken leg on a pillow. "It's time for you to talk."

"What do you want to know?"

"Everything," he said. "Where you were living. How you got there. How you got here."

I wasn't quite sure where to begin.

"You said Simeon was your father? I believe it, since you're a dead ringer for him at that age."

"Only in the most literal sense of the word," I said. "I didn't know we shared any DNA until just before I left. I was raised by Delta."

Rayne nodded. "Makes sense, that senator wife of his wouldn't have been all that happy about you. I remember when he found out he had a son."

It would have been easier if Rayne would tell me what he knew first, since so far I didn't seem to be telling him anything he didn't already know.

I described the estate—leaving out the part about Rhea and the other girls—told him about Delta and my brothers, how she sent me to find Rayne, and then about our experiences in the woods.

"You're leaving a lot out," said Rayne when I finished.

I stared at him trying to understand what he meant. Of course I was leaving a lot out, but what did he know that I was missing?

"I'm sorry Ms. Kroeker. We know who you are, as hard as you've been trying to hide it. Angela recognized you right away, though most of the boys here are too young to know your face."

Rayne stood and began to pace the small room.

"We were trying to wait until you told us, figuring there must be some kind of reason the President was on a snowmobile with no one but Jude here, but the pieces aren't fitting together."

Meredith frowned.

"My sister Nadia is a woman without scruples," she said, finally finding the right words. "I was in fear for my life, and Jude rescued me."

"Are they going to come after you here?" asked Rayne. "I have a lot of boys to protect here, many of them children and I can't have the military swooping down on us."

Meredith shook her head. I could see the anguish on her face.

"I don't think any of them survived," she said.

I looked up at the corner where the wall met the ceiling and bit the inside of my cheek to keep the tears from coming.

Rayne didn't say anything else, apparently satisfied with her answer.

"You two can stay here as long as you need to," said Angela. "Once you're better we'll find some jobs for you to do, Jude. Meredith has already been assigned hers, but you can wait until you're a bit stronger. Everyone needs to pull their weight."

"SO, WHAT HAPPENED TO Mila's father?" I asked Meredith one evening. They had assigned her to the school for the time being. She had been working hard to figure out what levels everyone was at and come up with a teaching plan for them. I, in turn had still been stuck in the infirmary, though Angela said I was almost well enough to try to put weight on my leg.

Meredith frowned. "She never had one, Phoebe was raped."

I had assumed Mila's father had gone missing, or was killed, or maybe was just out there somewhere, and would come back soon. I couldn't reconcile Phoebe's happy demeanor with someone who had been dealt such a lousy hand.

"From what I understand, there was a group of men passing through a while ago, and while Rayne didn't really want them staying here, it was hard to say no when you had no one but children to back you up," said Meredith. Her brows were furrowed and she spoke slowly. "One of them got into her room that night."

"That's terrible." My words felt insignificant and empty in my mouth.

She nodded.

"Angela said Rayne had a lot of trouble with it. It's the main reason he was so wary when we arrived. You just never know."

So senseless. So sad, and yet, to look at Phoebe one would never know she had gone through that. She was a pretty girl, happy and serene. There was none of the anger or bitterness I would expect to see after hearing her story.

"She and Angela don't look anything alike." Phoebe was so fair and lithe, while Angela had darker hair, and a sturdiness of both body and character that reminded me so much of Delta, but how could she not? Anyone who could envelop so many young boys under her wings needed to be sturdy and selfless and strong, all the qualities I admired so much about Delta.

Meredith laughed. "That's because they were adopted."

"Right."

I couldn't believe I hadn't thought of that. With so many unconventional families around me, including my own, and knowing the connection I'd had to those I called my brothers, even now, when they were all gone.

I felt a strange kinship to Phoebe. She came to visit with Renny somewhat regularly, and I had grown to look forward to their visits. She often came with Mila strapped to her back in some kind of sling, and Renny in her arms, sometimes with a brood of other toddlers trailing behind. Their visits were like a breath of clean air in a stale basement. Every day, after they left I would start looking forward to the next day when they might come back again. They gave me a purpose.

"LOOK AT YOU!" SAID Phoebe with a giant smile.

I was on my feet, though I wasn't sure I would be for much longer.

"Angela said I could try to go for a walk. She gave me a cane," I said, leaning on the door frame. Perhaps getting all the way to Phoebe's room on my first try was a little overambitious, but the look on her face made up for the sweat pouring down my back and the shortness of breath. I had to stop three times just in this short hallway, but I made it.

"I need to sit down."

Phoebe laughed and hurried over to help me into the chair. It was an old office chair that should have had casters, so it was very low. I half sat—half fell into the cracked leather upholstery.

Two little boys, Ricker and Landon if I remembered correctly, were sitting in the corner of the room, poking sticks into the concrete walls and making growling noises.

"I asked them to fix the walls," Phoebe said, winking.

Mila was sitting on the mattress poking Renny on the nose and laughing.

"Mila! Leave him be, you big bully," said Phoebe, scooping Renny into her arms.

I enjoyed spending time with Phoebe. The older boys were so loud and energetic, constantly shouting over each other in an attempt to be heard. Phoebe often said very little. She had an ease about her that I didn't see anywhere else. Rayne and Angela were constantly fixated on the stresses of keeping so many young people fed, and clothed, and warm. They had a massive undertaking here, and there seemed to be no better pair for the job. Phoebe though, she was charged only with these little lives, at least until they could fend for themselves. The air around her seemed calmer than everywhere else, and if there was anything I needed right now, it was calm.

She never asked about my past, nor was I eager to tell her. I didn't ask about hers. It was bad enough to know that someone had taken advantage of her without asking her to relive it to satisfy my curiosity.

"You want him?" she asked, holding Renny out to me. "I need to change Mila and she's been really squirmy about it lately."

She didn't give me the opportunity to answer before plopping Renny into my arms. I had held him before, but I was still uncomfortable sometimes. He seemed a lot less breakable these days, but infants were still a bit alien to me. I held him with stiff arms, doing my best to provide the gentle, natural cradle everyone else seemed to offer. Even Rayne handled the children easily, making me wonder out loud once why he and Angela had never had any of their own. He laughed with a giant hoot.

"Have our own?" he had said, tears streaming down his face. "We can barely keep track of the ones we have already!"

There were twenty nine boys in this place, ranging in age from infancy to twenty-one, adding in the rest of us made for a grand total of thirty-seven souls, every last one of them depending on the others for basic survival.

"We have a treat for dinner tonight," Phoebe said, her eyes twinkling with excitement. "You're never going to guess."

I didn't try. I was pretty sure I didn't need to. I was right.

"Strawberries!" she said.

"Where did they find strawberries?" I asked, watching as she fastened a clean cloth diaper around Mila's chubby legs.

"Rayne has friends out there, and they help us out with the food situation sometimes. I guess they have a bigger space, and are set up better than we are here."

"Then why didn't you guys go there?"

Phoebe shrugged. "I don't know, I always assumed there just wasn't enough room for us. We're a lot of extra mouths to feed and not terribly useful yet."

"But if they're feeding you anyway..."

"We feed ourselves," she said, "well, mostly. The things

we get from them are traded for usually. The boys are great at scrounging up materials and useful items from all the buildings nearby."

"Do you know where they are?"

She shook her head. "Maybe Rayne does, but I don't. I've only seen them once myself but you can't miss them. They always ride these giant horses."

That sounded familiar.

"Is one of them named Elias?"

She thought for a moment and shrugged. "The name doesn't sound familiar to me, but that doesn't mean there isn't someone by that name. Why?"

"I think we might have met them in the woods. Well, we saw them. They didn't see us."

"They give me the willies," said Phoebe. "Probably because I can never see their faces—maybe they're nice people under there."

I doubted it.

"They brought strawberries," Phoebe continued. "Why would bad people bring us strawberries? They were frozen by the time they got here, but they'll still taste good. Angela said she was going to make something with them."

I didn't have much to say about strawberries.

"I should go back to my room," I said.

"Do you need help? I can go get the wheelchair."

I shook my head. "I need to move. I'm tired of being carted around."

"Suit yourself," she said. "If you get into trouble, just call and I'll come rescue you."

I smiled. I'd never had anyone volunteer to rescue me before.

"Don't hold your breath," I said, smiling. I wasn't sure that I wasn't going to need help, but I had a pretty deep stubborn streak which usually resulted in taking on more challenge than I should.

I let Phoebe take Renny from me and hoisted myself to my feet, fumbling for the cane. It wasn't much more than a whittled stick, but it did the trick. Rayne had very thoughtfully carved the bark off the branch that stuck out sideways to form the handle. It wasn't comfortable, but I wasn't planning on using it for very long.

I made my way into the hallway, one hand on the walls for balance and the other on the cane to spread out my weight. I was nearly back to the infirmary when I heard a commotion coming down the halls. Shouting was far from abnormal here, but this one seemed more heated than the constant boyish arguments.

"I told you not to go near there!" said Rayne

"I was tracking a deer, and I almost had it too."

"And look what it got you. You're lucky they shot you in the leg. Those women are rarely so merciful."

The voices rounded the corner and I could see Rayne and another one of the older boys carrying the stretcher. Another boy lay on the stretcher, a feathered arrow protruding from his leg.

"They probably wanted to kidnap you and have their way with you," said the other boy carrying the stretcher. "Look at that face of yours. How could they resist?"

The other boys hooted with laughter at his joke. The boy in the stretcher pouted and grumbled.

"Sometimes that doesn't seem like such a bad idea."

They turned into the infirmary while I leaned on the doorway to let them pass. They set the stretcher down on the bed opposite my own and Rayne promptly cuffed the boy on the back of the head.

"If I hear you talk like that again, I'll drop you off at their camp. If you think they'll take care of you like we do, they can have you."

The boy glared at Rayne, but remained silent.

"Now, everyone else, back to whatever the hell it was you were doing," Rayne stormed out of the room, leaving only Angela, and the two older boys.

"Seriously, Dutch? Do you have to push his buttons?"

"I got shot by an arrow, for Pete's sake, I didn't need a lecture," said Dutch, pouting.

"You're going to get another one from me if you don't quit frowning at me. And remember, I can take that arrow out as gently as I deem necessary."

"Sorry Angela. You should have seen that deer."

"It would have been better if you boys came home with an arrow in a deer, I'll admit, but you know as well as I do that hunting in Amazon territory is a risk that isn't worth taking, even for a big deer."

"I told him," said the other boy. "It was a freaking big deer though."

"Shut up Olly," said Dutch.

I made my way into the room and limped to my bed, moaning as I sunk down into it.

"Long walk," Angela commented.

I nodded.

"At least we know better than to step in their traps," muttered Dutch.

He yelped in pain as Angela apparently reminded him of his situation.

"You know better Dutch. When you know better, you do better. I doubt Jude will make that mistake again."

"Unlikely," I said, stretching my leg out onto the bed.

Dutch and Olly seemed close to my age, and listening to their banter reminded me of my time at the estate. How often had Delta chided us for stupid behavior?

"Hey Olly, go get Shi, He's gonna love my deer story."

"He'd love it better with a bowl of venison stew in his belly."

"Shut up and go get him."

"Shi?" I asked.

Angela rolled her eyes. "You put this many boys in one place and everyone ends up with a weird name. 'Shi' is short for 'Shiner', for the first few years that boy had more shiners than anyone I had ever met. It's like he had a black eye every week."

She jerked suddenly and the arrow was out of Dutch's leg. He shrieked in pain and then clamped his mouth shut, glaring at me as if I was about to go run and tell everyone how unmanly he was.

"Olly is just short for Oliver, and Dutch here was named after a candy bar after he found a few cases of them in the city. It's a miracle we all didn't rot our teeth."

"Then we could call you 'Toothless Ang'," said Dutch.

"You're a brave boy, making fun of me before I clean out your wound."

His eyes widened and he glanced at me for a hint as to what he could expect.

"No clue, I passed out by then."

Angela started laughing.

"He's not lying," she said. "I'm really good at my job. Take a deep breath, you're going to need it."

THIRTY-EIGHT

Two years later

"You know we can't go any farther, Dutch."

"I know," he said. "I can get the shot from here."

He had a clean shot. With luck he would drop the deer where it stood.

"You planning on going in there to drag it out?" asked Olly.

"I'll shoot it, one of you can go get it," whispered Dutch.

His leg had healed eventually, though not without a nasty infection and nearly two months in the infirmary. Miraculously Angela didn't need to take his leg, but he was regularly reminded of it by the awful, jagged scar.

"It still hurts sometimes," he added.

"I'll go," I said. I could be quick about it. In and out.

My leg was as strong as it ever was, and since recovering I did my best to keep it in tip top condition. Angela was pleased by my progress. They had started me with the hunting teams shortly after I was well enough to work. I wasn't overly familiar with archery, but bullets were hard to come by, and even if you could find some, were not quickly wasted on hunting. An arrow could usually be retrieved, and if not, they weren't too difficult to make. I had become an expert in arrow-making in the two years I had been here. The younger boys brought me the straightest sticks they found and with the few rudimentary tools and a hot furnace, I was able to fashion some passable arrowheads from old coins. It was a pity I couldn't shoot them.

"Careful," I said, as Dutch pulled back the bowstring and took a slow deep breath.

Just as he was about to release, the deer fell.

"Nice job, Dutch!" shouted Olly, not noticing he had yet to let his arrow fly.

Dutch grabbed him by the shoulder and all of us dropped to the ground.

"That wasn't me," he hissed.

Olly's eyes widened.

"Are the Amazons out there?"

"I'm not planning on hanging around to find out," said Dutch, starting to slither backwards toward the nearest tree.

I peeked over the snow bank.

"It's not them," I said. "It's a man."

"It could be that dude they have with them," said Olly.

"No, he's not dressed like them," I said, "He looks more like one of the scouts. He has a horse like them too, a big one." Dutch scrambled forward, and he and Olly peered over the bank together.

"I know him, well, I don't know what his name is, but I've seen him before."

He was young—maybe Olly's age, seventeen or eighteen—but he was big. He towered over the doe, straddling it and bending down to pull the arrow from its chest.

"Hey!" I shouted. "Psssst."

The man assumed a defensive crouch before scanning the trees, pulling an arrow from his quiver and readying it on his bow. I lifted my hands above my head to show him I meant him no harm. Olly and Dutch did the same.

The man stood, watching us, but not speaking.

"This isn't a smart place to hunt," I said.

"You were hunting here," he said.

"Nobody said we were smart," said Olly glaring at Dutch with a pointed expression.

I rolled my eyes.

"The Amazons... the women... they hunt here. They don't like it when you take their deer..." I started.

"And they have no problems shooting you over it," said Dutch. "Trust me."

"I was planning on bringing them the deer."

We all stared at him like he had suddenly sprouted a few extra arms and a third eye.

"You don't think they'd like it?" he asked, amused by our expressions.

Olly coughed.

"We've just never heard of anyone going there willingly."

"Well, there's a first time for everything."

"Can I ask why?" I said.

"You can, but I won't answer."

"It's foolish you know." Dutch said, dragging out the word

'foolish' into more syllables than necessary. It didn't seem like a word he would say, but I'd heard Angela say it to enough boys to know where it came from.

"A lot of things are foolish," he said. "Doesn't make them wrong."

He stooped down, picked up the deer by the legs and swung the limp carcass across the shoulders of the horse and climbed up into the saddle.

"Are you sure about this?" Olly called. "You can come with us if you have nowhere else to go."

"I have somewhere to go, and I'm going there. They're the only people who would understand."

With that, he turned and rode away from us, deeper into the woods. We stood and watched him until he disappeared between the trees.

"Let's get out of here," said Dutch.

Neither Olly nor I disagreed.

"HE WAS GOING TO the Amazons? You're sure?"

"He said so," said Dutch, "We're not the smartest people in the world, but when someone says he's going someplace, I assume he's going there."

Rayne ran his fingers through his hair.

"Why would he do that?"

"I'm not sure why you're asking us," I said. "You just wanted to know why we didn't get a deer, we told you."

Rayne's eyes bore into mine. I could tell he was looking for a snappy comeback but nothing was coming.

"I guess if he wanted to go, there's nothing you could have done to stop him."

"That's what I figured."

"Stay away from that area, though," said Rayne. "If they're collecting men now, it's only going to make them more dangerous."

He didn't need to tell me twice.

IT WASN'T LONG BEFORE we found out exactly how much more dangerous they would become.

There was scarcely a night that went by where I didn't relive the sounds of the avalanche—the rumbles and roars, the trees snapping in its wake—the sounds had never left me, and I doubted they ever would.

The pain never left.

That day I added another sound to haunt my dreams.

It was a wail.

It started in the middle of the night as a scream of horror.

It was Angela, I could tell, even through the thick cinderblock walls. I tumbled out of my bed to the sound of dozens of bare feet slapping against the concrete floor. No one spoke, and the hushed silence was even more horrifying than the wail itself.

She was standing outside Phoebe's room, I pushed my way to the front of the crowd that had gathered in the hallway. Angela's screams didn't stop, but the blood rushing through my ears deadened them as I surveyed the scene. Phoebe was gone, and so was Mila. I breathed a sigh when I saw Renny in Meredith's arms, half asleep on her shoulder. He must have climbed into bed in her room as he did sometimes. Phoebe's mattresses were scattered across the floor and I couldn't figure out how someone could have come in here without anyone noticing or hearing anything.

There was blood on the floor, not much, not enough to make me fear for her life. It was smeared by boots and bare feet. My knees felt weak, but I forced my fear and pain to morph into the same anger I saw in the eyes of the men around me. The bloody footprints tracked out of the room and down the hall until they disappeared.

"The Amazons," whispered Dutch beside me.

It didn't make sense. What could they possibly want to Phoebe? They could have the deer, they could have their land, they could even have that freaking lumbering idiot who thought they would welcome him with open arms—but why Phoebe?

"We need to go after her," I said. "We can't leave her."

"They have us outnumbered four to one, easily," said Rayne, muttering as he held Angela through her sobs, "and that's even if we count our children."

"We can't leave her," I repeated, looking from person to person to find anyone who was willing. They avoided my eyes.

"We can't afford to go," said Rayne, his voice cracking. Angela sobbed into his shoulder. "It's just not possible."

"It has to be possible!" I roared. "We can make it possible!"

I saw the others begin to move away, silently down the

halls. Some of the younger ones were sobbing, the older ones taking them by the hands and guiding them back to bed. I saw Meredith hand Renny to Olly and walk to me.

"Jude, let's go to your room."

I didn't object, I didn't fight her—the numbness that I had worked so hard to bury was back.

"I can't let them take her." I muttered. "I can't let them have Rhea."

Meredith led me to the bed.

"They don't have Rhea," she said.

No, an avalanche took Rhea. These people took Phoebe. I wasn't able to stop either of them. As surely as the avalanche would have mowed me down where I stood in opposition, the Amazons too would annihilate me. There was truly nothing I could do.

"Nightly watch starts tonight," said Rayne, calling down the hallway to the boys who had begun to filter back to their beds. "Everyone over seventeen—on a rotation. This is never going to happen again!" His voice got louder with each word until the final ones rattled the walls and echoed through our heads.

THIRTY-NINE

Ten years later

It was perfect, probably the best arrow I had made, definitely the straightest. The point was sharp enough to draw blood with the slightest pressure, and the fletching was perfect. With a sturdy longbow, this arrow would be deadly.

Unfortunately in my hands it was more likely to be driven straight into a tree, if it managed to hit anything at all.

It wasn't as if I hadn't tried. Dutch had done his very best to make a marksmen out of me, but for some reason my eyes, hands and brain didn't work well together. I could make arrows, lethal instruments in the hands of others, but I had yet to use one to its fullest potential, and had doubts I ever would. This one would be for Rayne.

Rayne never missed.

"Happy birthday, Jude."

I heard the voice from the doorway of my workshop. It had used to be my bedroom, but I had taken to sleeping in the bunks with the others. It was less lonely there, the constant whispers of boys, mostly men now, kept the demons from coming. It wasn't as loud now, the shouts of boyhood had grown and developed into the laughter of men. The only boys left were the toddlers that had grown up with Renny, and he was almost thirteen already. As eerie as it was to push my bed into the dark hole like a drawer, it was less terrifying than being alone, where my ghosts would find me.

"How do you even know what day it is, Meredith?" I asked. She laughed.

"I don't," she said. "I figured it was probably close enough."

"Busted."

She probably was close, I had to admit. My birthday had always fallen during the late spring. The weather had started to warm, and the sun was beginning to melt the frost from the windows. Only a year ago we had experienced the first hint that the weather was going back to normal, and we all hoped silently that we would soon see summer again. It had been a year since the snow melted for the first time. It had been heartening to see green again, to forage for weeds and greens with Angela and feel the sun on our backs. We had eaten our fill of dandelion salads and sautéed nettles. The boys had resisted at first but it didn't take long for them to realize the effects green food had on their bodies. It was the happiest I had seen everyone. We were able to peel off the layers we wore and expose our skin to the sun, feeling the clean pure warmth that didn't come from burning something. One day Angela had built a fire in the courtyard of the hospital and dragged out her heavy laundry cauldron. We spent the day washing everything and hanging it to dry on makeshift clotheslines. Once the laundry was done, she had started on us.

It was a sight to see.

The air wasn't quite warm enough, but the courtyard was full of naked boys and men scrubbing themselves with rags and Angela's homemade soap and pouring the cold water over our goose-pimpled flesh. We didn't bother to heat the water much, and it didn't take long before the whole thing degraded into a water fight of epic proportions. Even Rayne had gotten in on the fun, his dark, muscled body chasing the younger boys and dunking them into the laundry cauldron that had been refilled with frigid water.

I hadn't laughed that hard in a long time.

It hadn't lasted long though, and before we knew it the snow began to fall again, erasing any hope we may have let ourselves feel.

But perhaps it wasn't the last we would see of the green.

"How old are you now?" Meredith asked.

I had tried to stop keeping track—every year that passed was another one that Rhea would never experience—but it had been impossible.

"Thirty-five," I said quietly. It was a monumental age. I had been almost seventeen when the frozen days began, so now I had spent more than half of my life in this icy prison. What made me the saddest was that I could barely remember the time before. I held on in glimpses and heartbeats and dreams to the time before the ice came, but every day that passed made those memories slip further away.

Renny was getting taller by the day, his auburn hair falling in his eyes as he raced through the hallways. Meredith had done a brilliant job teaching him and the other children. He was as smart as a tack, and learning to tie snares and chop wood. We hadn't gone to the woods where we found him since. Just the thought that other boys may have been left there to die—bait for wild animals—was too hard to take. I had wanted to go, and a few times I had found myself getting ready for the hike, but every time I found a reason to stay here. As much as I wanted to rescue them, as much as I knew no one else would, I couldn't risk seeing death again. As it was, I held on with a tenuous grip. Having lost everyone I had held dear in one rumbling cascade of snow, I had little left of my heart to put out on the line, even now. Even so many years after.

"How is it that you're catching up on me?" asked Meredith. She had found herself a place behind me and squeezed my shoulders. "I swear I'm only in my forties, still."

I chuckled. She had aged a lot in the past years. Her hair— that had once been black as night—was mostly grey, and the lines that had formed on her face got deeper as the years went by.

I often forgot, in my own narcissistic agony, that she too had lost much, and weighing most heavily on her shoulders was the duty she had to her country. She was the Commander in Chief, the President—or at least she had been once. No one knew what world would await us when the weather finally settled into a proper rhythm, if indeed it ever did. Pockets of people had likely survived, but without the technology we had grown so accustomed to in the days before, I had no idea how we could find each other again.

"I'm sure you're younger than me by now," I said, forcing a

laugh to keep her from worrying.

It was unlikely that she didn't see through my light-hearted façade, but she didn't mention it.

"Rayne sent me to get you. A scout party is coming, and he wants you to come with him to meet them."

I nodded but said nothing. We traded with the scouts and had a generally amicable relationship, but they were an intimidating bunch. It was unlikely we would have survived without their help, and I had always wanted to ask Rayne why our trades never really seemed fair. We had venison sometimes, if the hunting had been good, and Angela's soap, and occasionally some of my arrows and spears were traded, but they always brought us a veritable bounty in return. Goat cheeses, eggs, fresh vegetables, sacks of beans and grains. They even brought medicines for Angela sometimes, bandages and clothing.

I stood up from my work table and placed the perfect arrow in the quiver that hung from a hook on the wall where I had collected a number of fine specimens. I tended to collect them until the others ran out. There was no sense filling their quivers with extra arrows until they had lost or broken the last batch. Too many arrows encouraged waste, less care with the ones they had.

"He's in the courtyard," said Meredith, answering the question I had yet to ask.

"I'll be out in a minute."

IT WAS A LONG hike to our meeting spot, and I carried a basket slung over my back with a large package of soap and some metal pots someone had scavenged from the nearby buildings. They were next to useless, honestly, and part of me was ashamed to bring them, but we had very little to trade. Rayne didn't seem terribly concerned by it when I had voiced my opinion, so I just shut my mouth and carried my share. Dutch and Olly were with us, as well as Fernie and Gibs, who were probably in their early twenties. I wondered if they remembered anything about the years before the world froze. Based on how much I could remember, I doubted it.

Fernie was as tall as Finn was, though his long blonde hair and pale eyes reminded me little of my friend. Gibs was shorter, stout, with dark curls and a muscled build from hard labor. We were all lean and hardened, it was impossible to grow soft when you had minimal food and nothing but work to do. It was a fine balance to stay healthy.

"You don't work, you don't eat—you don't eat, you don't work."

It was Angela's favorite saying, usually to remind the younger boys to stop complaining about the endless drudgery of flavorless beans and oats. I didn't even taste anything anymore.

The five of us hiked in silence. As we neared the meeting spot, the sounds of horses' feet stomping on the packed snow and the clinking of bridles as they shook their heads alerted us to the fact that the scouts were already there.

There were seven of them—as there always were—each of

them seated on a large horse. They wore goggles over their eyes and scarves to cover their mouths, so it was impossible to see their faces. One of them slid from his saddle onto the ground as we approached, and signaled a few of the others to do the same. Three men remained on their horses, watching, as the others untied the saddlebags.

"Good afternoon gentlemen," said Rayne.

"Rayne." The man who spoke was one of the ones who remained on horseback.

"Good to see you Archer," said Rayne. "It's been a while."

"I've been busy."

Rayne didn't respond, just swung his pack to the ground. He carried some venison, some dried nettle tea, some wild herbs we had foraged, and a rolled up piece of buckskin he had tanned.

"Seems like it's warming up again," he said, making conversation.

"Seems so," said Archer.

We continued our trading in silence. My basket was notably heavier than it was for the trip here, but we would wait until we got back to open and exclaim over the contents. Angela always liked to be part of that.

We all tied up the packs and baskets we carried, securing our loads. As Rayne thanked them and we turned to leave, Archer spoke again.

"Have you seen anyone in the woods recently?"

Rayne shrugged, "Not recently. You guys looking for someone?"

Archer nodded, pulling the goggles off his face for the first time so I could see the crinkles around his eyes and the fringe of grey eyebrows.

"One of our girls ran away. I assume she's dead, but she's smart, and skilled, so I thought there was a chance she might have made it to you."

Rayne frowned.

"Sorry, we haven't seen her," he said, then turning to us, "Have any of you?"

We shook our heads.

"If you see her, or hear anything about her, she's seventeen. Her name is Leona."

"Leona?" said Rayne, obviously shocked. "Elias' girl?"

"One and the same."

Rayne swore under his breath.

"Is there a chance..." he started.

"That's what we're thinking," said Archer, finishing his thought, "Heaven help her if that's the case."

Rayne said nothing, but just shook his head.

They didn't need to elaborate. I could still hear Angela's screams from when we realized Phoebe had been taken. If Leona had been found by the Amazons, there was little hope for her.

"We'll keep an eye out," said Rayne, but the tone in his voice spoke volumes about whether he expected to see her.

"I'd appreciate that."

We left in silence, listening as the sounds of horses mingled and disappeared into the sounds of the wind in the trees.

FORTY

"SERIOUSLY JUDE, DO YOU have your eyes open at all when you shoot?" said Dutch, frustrated. "I've all but given up on you."

I shrugged. I was beyond the point of feeling embarrassed about my marksmanship, though Dutch still took me out into the woods now and then to practice. I think it was just to fend off boredom and routine, but I didn't care. Fresh air did me good too.

I slung my longbow over my shoulder and headed out to retrieve my arrows. The problem with being a terrible shot was finding the arrows afterward. Dutch came with me, for which I was grateful. Two eyes were better than one, and apparently his were much better than mine.

I found one arrow wedged into the base of a tree, and as I tugged gently and wiggled it to release it from the bark, I felt Dutch grab me from behind and pull me to the ground.

"What are you...?"

"Shut up," he said in a sharp whisper. "Listen."

It took me a minute to hear what he did. Apparently all of his senses were better than mine.

It came in on a breeze, still far away, but the sound was

distinct, and I knew instantly what is was.

"A snowmobile," I whispered.

Dutch nodded.

My own snowmobile had been hiding under a tarp inside the ambulance bay of the hospital. It was empty of fuel—Rayne had said it was a miracle we made it to them at all, since they couldn't even start it again to bring it inside. We kept it hidden just in case we managed to find some fuel someday.

I hadn't heard another snowmobile since.

We scanned the trees, watching as the sound became louder. It was coming toward us. Dutch looked at me with wide eyes, and I had nothing comforting to tell him.

We waited.

It wasn't long before we could see the sled bouncing over the drifts between the trees. It was coming directly toward us. We weren't far from home, and we knew someone would need to run back, but there was no way to warn the others without being spotted. From where I sat I could see two riders, each decked out in black snowsuits and helmets.

Dutch pulled an arrow from his quiver. I recognized it as my perfect one. Notching it in the string of his bow he stood and pulled back.

"Wait!" I whispered. "A child."

As the snowmobile came closer, I could see that seated between the larger riders was a much smaller one, who couldn't be much bigger than Renny.

"Who would come find us with a child?" Dutch asked,

dropping back to his knees.

"I don't know. But would they pose a danger to us with a kid on there?"

Dutch shrugged.

I had no idea either.

On an impulse, I stood, held up my hands and walked from behind the trees into the path of the sled.

I could hear Dutch swearing behind me, but he followed, hands in the air, though I noted he still carried his bow.

The snowmobile whined to a stop, and as the driver stood, I could sense Dutch readying another arrow. The child and the second rider remained on the sled, and made no move toward us.

The driver began to walk toward us, slowly, as if reading the situation. I wished I could see his face as he could see ours, but I set my jaw to look as intimidating as possible.

"Where are you headed?" I asked.

"Where are you from?" he answered, his voice muffled, but obviously male. "I think I might want to go there."

"I'd advise against it. We mean you no harm, but it would be best for you to pass quietly."

The helmet cocked for a minute, and I heard a chuckle, which infuriated me. Dutch was poised to shoot, offered any provocation.

"Tell your goon to drop his weapon," the man said.

"Give me one good reason," said Dutch, though he lowered the tip of his arrow enough to give the rider a second's head start.

"Because I want to do this."

He lurched forward and in a second was on top of me, dragging me to the ground. Dutch aimed again, but couldn't get a clear shot.

I fought against the man until I realized he wasn't fighting, just holding on. Not to mention, he was laughing.

"Jude, honestly, quit kicking me!"

The voice shot through me like a knife in the heart. I stopped moving. He was still laughing as he sat up, pulling me with him.

"Don't mind that I use you as a shield until you tell Robin Hood over there not to kill me."

"Don't shoot, Dutch. They aren't a threat."

I barely got the words out, before a sob caught in my throat. I could feel my eyes filling with tears.

It was impossible. I stood and turned toward him, watching as he too stood to face me.

I couldn't close my mouth, for I feared I would faint for lack of air. I struggled for breath and stared at him, my mouth agape.

He pulled off his helmet in an instant and I saw him, a ghost I had never thought I would see again, and emotions ran through me. I dropped to my knees and began to cry.

"Jude, man, I know it's been a long time, but you don't need to cry," said Finn, his eyes flashing with amusement.

"Finn." It was all I could get out.

"In the flesh. I didn't think I'd find you again. We all thought you died in the avalanche."

"We?" I squeaked.

"Well of course..." Finn started. "Wait, you thought we died?"

I nodded.

"We're all still kicking, Jude. That's 'Bekkah and Jonah on that sled with me. Delta told us I needed to take 'Bekkah out and find some Rayne guy... It wasn't safe for her anymore."

"Delta?"

"Oh man, Jude. I was so happy to see you. Let me start again."

He dropped his helmet into the snow, fell to his knees beside me and pulled me toward him, enveloping me in his long arms.

"Delta is alive, and so are Vaughn and Harris.."

I had no words to say. It had been years since I left the estate, believing everyone dead. I had been grieving for more than twelve years. My body shook and I started to laugh. Tears flowed down my face and I laughed and cried at the same time.

"Rhea?"

"She's alive, like you left her, but she's alive."

I hadn't expected to feel much of anything again, but here I was, on my knees in the snow, feeling everything at once. Fear, pain, joy, hope, and excitement coursed through me simultaneously. I couldn't stop myself from shaking.

"Dutch," I said. "Run ahead and tell Rayne to make some room. We have guests."

Dutch nodded and ran off through the trees.

"I feel like I should be surprised that you were with Rayne," said Finn. "But I'm not."

I shook my head at him, still drinking in the sight of his smiling face.

"C'mon man," he said. "Grab onto the back of the sled, and I'll drag you home."

He stood beside me and offered me his hand. I took it gratefully and let him help me to my feet.

"It's nice to see you again, Jude," said Rebekkah as I made my way on wobbling legs to the sled.

"You have no idea," I said, still shaking my head in disbelief.

"Jonah, take careful note," said Finn. "This is what we used to call 'bumpershining' and I never want you to try it."

Finn winked at me as he slid his helmet back on.

I grasped hold of the bar behind Rebekkah's seat and spread my legs so my feet were clear of the track on both sides.

"Ready?" shouted Finn as the engine roared to life.

"GO!" I shouted and bent my knees, letting my feet slide on the surface of the snow.

The sled started slowly and I laughed as Finn sped off in the direction Dutch had disappeared to.

When we pulled into the courtyard, there was a crowd assembled to meet us. Finn slowed down and I let go of the bar, every muscle in my body twitching and aching.

I slid a bit before tumbling to the ground in a heap.

Still lying on my back I shouted to Rayne, who was standing with his arms crossed in front of a large group of curious young men and boys, an amused Angela, and a shocked Meredith.

"Rayne, I'd like you to meet my brother, Finn."

I laughed until my sides ached.

I DIDN'T LAUGH VERY long.

Once Finn told us what had been happening at the estate, my laughter turned to dread, though I was glad to have it. It meant there was someone there to be fearful for, and even that was better than the emptiness of loss I had felt before. Everyone was still alive, but with Meredith gone, Nadia had declared her dead and taken complete control. Other maids and cooks had joined Rhea and the Sisters, though most of them hadn't needed to be sedated, Nadia's threats had been enough for them to comply.

"There are at least thirty of them now," said Finn, his brow furrowed. "When Delta heard they were coming to get 'Bekkah too, we had to leave."

Rebekkah smiled at him from where she sat on a chair in the corner, her arms wrapped around Jonah who looked like a carbon copy of Kenzie, right down to the pale eyes and dark curls.

"We didn't think she'd come for Rebekkah, her condition and all, but..."

"Now that I'm expecting..." finished Rebekkah.

Finn winked at her, and a smile broke out on my face. It felt like everything was a surprise and then at the same time, like nothing was at all.

"We didn't know it could happen," said Finn, laughing. "Apparently it can." He whispered the last part to me with a meaningful grin, while Rebekkah blushed.

"Congratulations," I said, folding him into another of the many hugs I had given him. I felt that if I went too long without touching him, that I would lose him again, or at the very least find out this was all some kind of dream.

Meredith sat beside Rebekkah, her hand spending much of its time on Rebekkah's knee or shoulder. Tears trailed down her face as she listened to Finn recount their tale. Rayne hadn't said much, but had listened silently as he sat backwards on a chair, his arms folded across the backrest. Meredith and I had told him about Nadia and her plans over the years, but that had always been under the assumption that her plans had died with her and everyone else at the estate. Knowing they were alive changed everything.

It had taken them almost a full year to dig themselves out, and then that long again to get everything back to normal, fix the electrical and ventilation systems. Even now, ten years later, they were still looking for some of the solar panels that had been ripped from the roof. The snow never fully melted in the mountains last summer, but they were able to find and dig out most of them.

"It hasn't been so much fun since you left, Jude, I'll tell you that."

He said it as a joke, but he couldn't hide the sad tone in his voice as well as he had probably hoped. It had been a long time, and we had all aged, but the lighthearted Finn I knew was all but gone. I could see glimpses of it in his laugh and his jokes, but there was a dark side to him now that I didn't like. Though, there was probably a dark side to me too.

"What are we supposed to do?" I asked, not sure who would answer, if anyone.

We sat in silence, each looking at each other as if searching for answers in our distressed faces.

"Well, I know one thing," said Rayne. "I don't like this Nadia chick."

"You and me both, brother," said Finn.

Rayne looked at Angela, and she nodded. Whatever words they exchanged were silent to the rest of us.

"I think," said Rayne, his voice slow and deliberate. "I think it's time to go talk to my brothers."

Simeon was dead, I knew that, and Rayne only had two other brothers.

"Elias and Amos?" I asked. Remembering the names Delta had told me.

Rayne nodded.

"But do me a favor and get used to calling Amos 'The Shepherd'," he said. "He prefers it that way."

EPILOGUE

I could feel the baby kicking in my belly. I had felt it before, but hadn't wanted to mention it for fear the feeling would stop and never return. It had, many times, each time stronger than the last.

It's strong. It would be a boy, I thought, laughing to myself, or perhaps a girl.

I was strong too.

I could feel him lying next to me, breathing deeply in his sleep. I hadn't even told him about the child yet, though I was surprised he hadn't noticed already. My lean, hard body was softening and I could see the small roundness in my belly, and the new fullness of my breasts.

He saw me naked on a daily basis, but if he had noticed, he hadn't said anything to me.

We didn't say much to each other as it was, not actual talking. He shouted my name a lot in the heat of the moment, but when we weren't in our bed, I didn't see much of him. I could count the number of conversations we'd had on one hand, even though we'd been married for months.

I swallowed hard and focused on the child inside of me, the

flutters and kicks beneath my hand. I didn't know if we would ever truly love each other, he and I. I wanted him, I yearned for him, the sight of him was pleasing to me, but we skimmed the surface, enjoying each other like the deer in the woods.

At first it didn't bother me. I didn't want depth any more than I sensed he did. I enjoyed the carefree lovemaking and simplicity of our relationship. He was a handsome man, his body as tight and strong as my own.

We had fun—a lot of fun.

But somehow, with this child inside me, the amusement I felt to have this boy drooling over me—panting after me like a dog—had faded.

It was still fun, but it was obvious to me that there was something missing, and I had no idea how to change that.

Would he be happy about the child?

Most men were, but was he the same as most men?

I didn't even know.

What could I possibly know about men?

The hut around me suddenly seemed too hot. Stifling. The fire was barely more than embers, the smoke rising up through the hole in the center of the roof. I wished I could follow it, out into the cold fresh air, into the stars.

I could feel him stir beside me, reaching for me, his hands fumbling through the furs to find me.

"Torren," I said in a whisper.

"Athena," he mumbled, barely awake, if he was at all.

I felt his hand find my breast, fondling it through the thin shirt I wore.

"I need to tell you something."

COMING IN 2015

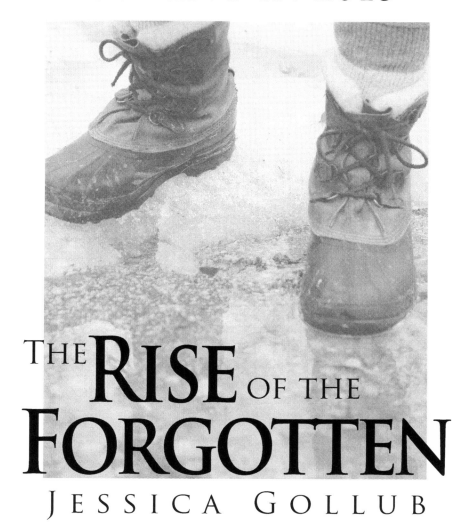

THE RISE OF THE FORGOTTEN

JESSICA GOLLUB

Find out more:
www.jessicagollub.com
On Twitter: **@GollubJessica**
On Facebook: **www.facebook.com/Jessica.Gollub.Author**

ACKNOWLEDGEMENTS

Sometimes, when you publish books yourself you assume you have only yourself to thank, but there are so many people that deserve my deepest gratitude for being part of my dreams.

John, I know I drive you crazy sometimes, but thank you for being the concrete wall I can brace myself against. You stand by me, encourage me and you push me to be the best person/mother/ writer I can be.

To Mom, thank you for giving me the gift of writing days and encouraging me every step of the way. Thanks for believing that I could and should, and never letting me doubt it.

Heidi Gollub, Sarah Hood, Marissa Knight, Jen Kroeker, Anna McCarthy, Shayna Murray, Laura Pauls, Nancy Paschke, Audrey Plew, Bonnie Reimer, Karen Scott, Jordan Treder, and Ashlea Zirk: You guys are fantastic! Thank you for being my readers and helping make my books as good as they can be. Special props to Marissa for making sure I only use the word "ethereal" once. And also to Brian Klassen for donning your "neurotic-hat" and making sure I get as close to typo-free as possible.

Audrey, thank you for once again modelling for my cover and also for all answering all my random pleas for help when I just couldn't get my spreads and kerning the way I wanted it. I promise I will figure it out eventually!

To my social media gurus: Shayna Murray (@mommyoutside) and Sarah DeDiego (@zoojourneys). You two know more about the internet and self-promotion than anyone I know, and I thank you for engaging, for all the retweets, likes, favourites, blog posts and tweets that help me spread the word. You two are the best!

To Catherine (@alwaysaredhead), Amanda (@_astav) and Jen (@ OramJen), Thank you for your tweets and support! They are invaluable to me! Sometimes on social media it feels like you stand alone, shouting into a void, and it's always nice to know someone is listening.

Finally, thank you to every single person who asked me when this book was coming out. Your excitement and lack of patience mean the world to me, and with all of you chomping at my heels, I have no doubt I will make it to the end of this series. I just couldn't possibly let you down!

82557974R00200

Made in the USA
Columbia, SC
18 December 2017